OMEGA CITY

OMEGA CITY

Diana
Peterfreund

An Imprint of HarperCollins*Publishers*

Balzer + Bray is an imprint of HarperCollins Publishers.

Omega City
 For information address HarperCollins Children's Books, a division of HarperCollins Publishers, 195 Broadway, New York, NY 10007.
www.harpercollinschildrens.com

Library of Congress Control Number: 2014952614
ISBN 978-0-06-231085-9 (trade bdg.)

Typography by Carla Weise
15 16 17 18 19 CG/RRDH 10 9 8 7 6 5 4 3 2 1
❖
First Edition

For Luke and Brian,

my brothers and fellow adventurers

CONTENTS

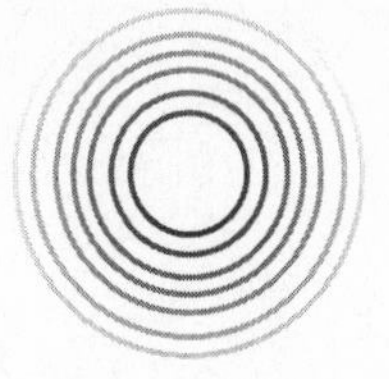

Some secrets are small—the size of a battery, or a button, or a scrap of paper. Other secrets are so big they can bury a man alive, or tear apart a family . . . or even destroy the world.

Omega City was both.

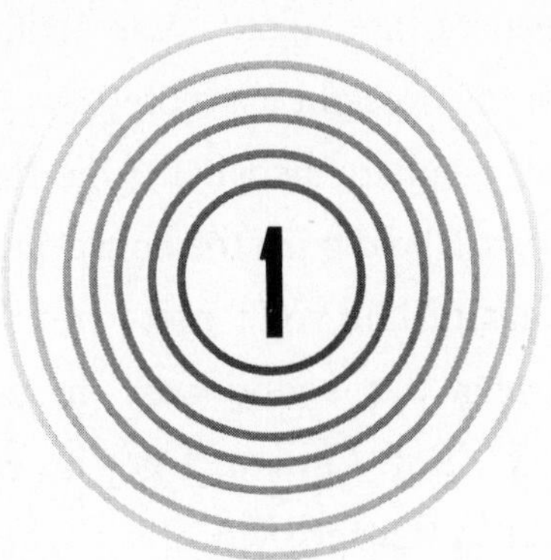

POST-NUCLEAR FAMILY

IT STARTED WITH A FIRE. WHEN ERIC AND I WALKED THROUGH THE FRONT door, we were met by a wall of gray haze filling the rooms of the cottage, hot and thick and smelling very strongly of charred meat.

My brother gave me a look. "Third time this month."

"You get the oven," I suggested, coughing. "I'll make sure Dad's still conscious." I headed down the narrow, smoky hall to his office.

Dad was bent over his desk, reading a file, his glasses inches from the page. "Dad!" I shouted as I rushed to the window, released the locks, and shoved them open. "Didn't you see the smoke?"

He blinked at the murky room, stacked wall to wall with books, papers, and Cold War artifacts. "What a relief. I thought my eyesight was going."

I shook my head in disbelief. One day he'd get so wrapped up in work he'd burn the house down. "Were you trying to cook again? Did you forget to set the timer?"

"So that's what that sound was," he said sheepishly, then brightened. "But, Gillian, I got an email from the diner owner over in Reistertown."

For a moment, I forgot about the fire. "Really?" My historian father had been trying to track down that guy for over a month. He usually interviewed actual scientists or politicians for his books, but ever since the scandal, most of his sources wouldn't return his calls.

"He says there were definitely two men at the table with President Reagan that night, not one like it says in the official record."

I clapped my hands and leaned over to check out his screen. "And he thinks one of them might have been Dr. Underberg? Are you going to call him back?" If Dad could get verification from one source, even if it was just the guy pouring coffee at a diner thirty years ago, it would help to verify the claims he made in his book. One fact down, nine thousand, nine hundred and ninety-nine to go.

Eric appeared at the door, wearing oven mitts and holding a smoldering pan. "Space rocks for dinner again, Dad?"

"Oh dear," said Dad as we dragged our attention away from his discovery. "That was supposed to be a roast."

"Well, it's definitely roasted."

Dad took the charred hunk of meat off my brother's hands, frowning down at it like it was just another mystery to be solved.

Paper Clip, our yellow cat, had emerged from whatever spot she'd taken shelter in when the smoke started, and now had her whiskered nose working overtime.

"Out of here, cat," Dad said. "I wouldn't give this mess to my worst enemy, and you're only my tenth worst."

She rubbed her cheek against Dad's pant leg in response. Paper Clip's named after a secret post–World War Two operation to smuggle former Nazi scientists into America to help win the Cold War, despite what an obviously huge no-no that should have been. Dad chose the name because Eric and I sneaked her in one night despite the strict house policy against pets, and she was here for a week before Dad wondered why we were all suddenly eating so much tuna.

"Maybe I could throw together some pasta?" Dad wondered aloud, and wandered off to the kitchen.

"Uh-oh. I'll get the fire extinguisher," Eric whispered to me.

"Come on," I said, "he can't wreck pasta."

"Depends on your definition of 'wreck.'" Eric headed

into the hall. He was right. I'd never forget Dad's invention of peanut-butter-and-jelly spaghetti.

I fanned the rest of the smoke out the window with the map of Area 51 Dad used for his "Roswell Secrets" lectures. When the air cleared, I closed everything up and made sure the locks and the anti-tampering devices were back in place. Dad was militant about security. You would be, too, if you knew the stuff he knew.

When Dad was still a professor at the university, his classes were all about the Cold War—the time in the twentieth century when everyone was pretty sure that any second, Russia and the USA were going to nuke the whole world. My parents were still in high school when the Cold War ended, and Dad says that when he was our age, they used to do nuclear bomb drills at school the way we have fire drills. Not that it would have done much good—everyone knows you can't survive a nuclear blast just by hiding under your desk.

Dad's specialty is Cold War conspiracies, classified intelligence stuff, atomic age secrets, things like that. You used to be able to find his books everywhere, and he was even on TV a couple of times. His latest book, *World Power,* was about Aloysius Underberg, a really brilliant Cold War engineer. He worked for the government, but not on nuclear bombs—no one was more afraid of the bomb than Dr. Underberg. So he invented things for people to use for *after* humans destroyed the world, like air purifiers and food that never spoiled and special basements where people could protect themselves from nuclear radiation. He also worked for NASA on space stations and suits and other technology that helped people survive on missions. Astronaut ice cream? That was his idea. His greatest invention was a battery that would supposedly last a hundred years. But unlike astronaut ice cream, the battery went missing years ago. And so did Dr. Underberg.

Dad's book tells the whole story. You can't buy it anymore, though. You may have heard about the scandal on the news last year. The one about the history professor who lost his job and his reputation after he published a book full of "faulty and fraudulent research."

Yes, that's the exact quote. It's easy to memorize after the tenth newspaper article calling your father names.

It's not true, of course. Dad's good at his job. And that's why getting this diner owner to confirm that President Reagan took that meeting with Underberg was such a big deal, the first step toward proving that the stuff Dad wrote in his book was true all along.

I went out to the living room to find Eric already stationed at his usual spot in front of the TV, video game controller in hand, even though I knew he hadn't done his homework yet.

"Better not let Dad see you with that."

"Mail's here" was his only reply. He swiped a hand across his eyes and kicked the paper-strewn coffee table, leaving a new scuff on its battered top. There were a few bills, some with a telltale "Past Due" stamp on the envelope, and a couple of very thin letters from universities I'd never even heard of. More rejections, probably. No one wanted a history professor with Dad's reputation. Finally, I saw the source of my brother's bad mood: an envelope nearly plastered over with stamps was already torn open and tossed aside. *Mom.*

I gave my brother a look. "What did she say?"

He shrugged and killed something on-screen. "What do you think?"

I took a deep breath and pulled out her letter.

Dear Gillian and Eric,

Hi, kids! How is school? I bet it's getting cold out there at the cottage. Did you join any sports teams this fall? I put some extra money in the account last month for whatever fees or uniforms you have to buy. I know your father needs all the help he can get.

Guangzhou has been fantastic. I'm almost done with the new manuscript, and my publisher has all kinds of great plans for the release next year. I know I told you I'd be home by Christmas, but I just got an invitation to a conference in Kyoto for New Year's, and it would be silly to fly halfway across the world just to turn around and go back to Asia. But we'll definitely make plans for spring break.

Give my best to your father. Did he ever hear back from the community college about his application?

Love,

Mom

Yeah, Mom. It would be totally silly to fly to America and see your kids for Christmas. Just like it was silly to take us with you on your research trip to China when Dad was at home, "doing nothing" except teaching a weekly evening lecture at the VA Hall.

I plopped down on the couch next to Eric and laid my head on his shoulder. Most people think of us as the Seagret twins, since we're in the same grade, but don't be fooled by his tough act. Eric's my kid brother by eleven whole months.

"At least she'll be home in the spring," I tried, though I don't think I sounded very convincing.

"Yeah," he lied back to me.

"And her book seems to be going well." Or at least, better than Dad's was.

"You think she put enough money in the account to get

my boat back?" Eric asked. His shoulder jerked beneath me as he worked the video game controller.

"I think she meant more like bathing suits and goggles for the swim team." Even if we could still afford Eric's little racing dinghy, we didn't live by the water anymore. The sailboat, the house near the university—that was our old life. All we had left was this little cottage in the middle of nowhere.

"Oh." The tiny figure on the screen lowered his weapon and got pummeled by the bad guys. Eric watched its gruesome and prolonged death, then jabbed a button on his controller and loaded up another life.

Dad may burn all our food, and he only works on Thursday evenings, but at least he knows whether or not we're on any sports teams. Eric hasn't joined a thing since the divorce.

Eric shrugged me off his arm. "Swim team's boring. Call me when there's a scuba team."

Eric had wanted to get certified the second he turned ten, and Dad had signed the whole family up for scuba classes. The training came in handy back when Dad was researching missing submarines, two books back. But I don't even think they have scuba diving teams in the cities, let alone in little hick towns like ours.

This used to be just our summer house. We'd live here during vacation or whenever our parents were taking what the university would call "sabbaticals" so they could finish their books. This is where Dad wrote *World Power,* just a half-hour drive from Dr. Underberg's childhood home. And sometime between turning in the manuscript and everything going to pieces, a pipe burst here and destroyed his computer and pretty much all of his notes, so Dad could never prove he did the research everyone said was fake.

I actually did see his notes—I spent a whole summer keeping towering piles of them from burying Dad alive in his office—but no one was going to believe Sam Seagret's twelve-year-old daughter. And once all the accusations started coming out, even his primary sources began to claim they'd never spoken to him.

Which, ironically, is exactly the sort of thing Dad's book was about.

Dad appeared at the door. "So," he said sheepishly, "we're out of pasta."

Eric rolled his eyes and whispered, "I think we should be relieved."

But I wasn't relieved. I was hungry. And worried. Eric was going to spend the rest of the day moping over Mom's letter, and who knows what sort of food-shaped object Dad might try to serve us while he was busy thinking about that diner owner.

Wait. "Hey, Dad, that diner where Underberg ate . . . is it still open?"

Dad's face broke into a smile. "Why? You want to go on a field trip?"

"Like the old days?" I sat up straight and gave Eric a hopeful grin. He didn't look convinced.

"Yep." Dad leaned over and ruffled my brother's dark hair, looking just a bit like he used to whenever he got excited about our adventures. "Come on, Eric."

I turned to him, silently pleading. It wasn't scuba diving on a submarine wreck, but at least we could get a decent dinner out of it. At least we could get *something*.

"We can stop for frozen yogurt at that fancy place that lets you put on your own toppings," Dad coaxed.

Eric sighed and paused the game. "Okay," he said. "I'll go. But only for the fro-yo."

"Awesome!" I said, hugging him. "We have lift-off."

I had no idea how right I was.

ATTACK OF THE PAPER CLIP

ON THE DRIVE TO REISTERTOWN, DAD FILLED US IN ON THE DETAILS OF his research and Eric stared out the window at the passing countryside like he was looking for escape routes.

"In the official record, Dr. Underberg had already been fired from the State Department in 1984," Dad was saying. "So the question is, why would the President of the United States be having dinner with him and the Speaker of the House?"

"No," Eric mumbled under his breath, "the question is why Dad thinks the memory of some old waiter is going to change people's minds."

Dad says Eric's going through a mainstream phase

right now. I just call it sulking.

"Why was he fired?" I asked Dad.

Eric made a sound like a cuckoo clock.

"The official explanation was unauthorized use of funds," Dad said. "But just because they didn't like what his research produced, that doesn't mean he was wrong to make it. Think of all the things the Underberg battery could have done for us. Prevented wars over oil, stopped the spread of global warming—"

"Made sure my video game didn't run out of juice so I could have taken it with us," Eric grumbled.

"Exactly," Dad said cheerily. "Meanwhile, it's not our fault you forgot to plug in the charger."

"Why wouldn't people want something like that?" I asked Dad.

"That's the important question, isn't it, kiddo? The sad truth is, sometimes it's easier for people to stick with the problems they know than try to imagine a new way of life."

That didn't make a whole lot of sense to me. "But if the new way would work better, then wouldn't people at least try it? I didn't like it when you took the training wheels off my bike, but I practiced until I could ride it faster than before."

"Well, you're smarter than most people, Gillian," said Dad.

"That's what she's always telling me," added Eric from the backseat.

"And what if you made training wheels for a living?" Dad asked. "Then you wouldn't want people to learn how to ride a real bike, or you'd be out of a job."

I'd never thought of it like that.

The phone on the console buzzed and I saw the name *Fiona* flash on-screen. Dad instantly forgot what he was saying and picked up.

"Hi! Are you there yet? Yes, we're on our way." There was a pause. "Me and the kids."

Dad invited Fiona?

Fiona and Dad met a month ago, when she showed up at his "Roswell Secrets" lecture at the Learning Annex one Thursday night. She came the following week to "The Myth of the Moon Landing." The week after that, they went out to dinner, and last Saturday he took her to the movies. Guess Dad's reentered the dating pool.

Sure enough, when we pulled in to the parking lot of the diner five minutes later, I saw Fiona waiting for us outside.

I'll tell you right now, Fiona Smythe was not the kind of person who usually attended Dad's conspiracy theory lectures. Most of his students either wore tinfoil hats to protect themselves from what they believed were the government's mind-control rays, or they were bored retirees with nothing better to do than go to beginner slide shows with titles like "JFK: The Facts Don't Add Up." Fiona had sleek, bouncy shampoo-commercial hair, four-inch patent-leather heels, and diamond earrings the size of gumdrops.

And I had to remind Dad to change his underwear last week. They aren't exactly an obvious couple. Still, she was on Dad's side, and that's hard to come by these days. My best friend, Savannah, thinks Fiona will be good for Dad, like maybe convince him to get his salt-and-pepper hair trimmed before his sideburns meet at his chin. Or actually fix the fraying elbows of his blazers.

"The nerdy professor look is cool," she once told me. "But your dad is getting a little too close to hobo."

I took a look at my father as he parked. Pants: clean. Shirt: wrinkled, but serviceable. His glasses weren't crooked, and it looked like he'd trimmed his beard. Could be worse.

And Fiona looked happy to see him. She air-kissed his cheeks when we got out of the car and gave us an awkward wave. "Hello, Eric and . . ."

"Gillian," I prompted.

She faced Dad and gave a little pout. "The diner looks closed."

"That's weird." Dad peered through the windows. "I just called an hour ago."

I looked inside, too. The diner obviously hadn't been updated since before I was born. Old beige booths with cracks spiderwebbing the vinyl lined up on one side, while a white laminate lunch counter sat on the other. Behind it, I saw a shadow move in the doorway to the kitchen. "Dad! There's someone inside."

"No," said Fiona. "I'm sure there's—"

I pointed as the shadow shifted. "Look!"

Dad banged on the door for probably ten seconds until a squat man came out from the kitchen. His dingy apron was streaked with grease and his eyes were wide and suspicious. He ran his hand through what little white hair remained on his broad scalp.

"Maurice?" Dad asked through the window. "Maurice Pappas? I'm Sam Seagret. We spoke on the phone."

The man shook his head through the window. "Sorry. I think you've got the wrong guy."

"We just talked!" Dad insisted. "I wanted to ask you a few more questions about that dinner you witnessed in June of '84."

Maurice Pappas examined me and Eric, and then finally Fiona. "Who are they?"

Dad gave him an open smile. "Oh, these are my kids and this is my research assistant, Fiona."

"Fiona *Smythe,*" she added, giving the man on the other side of the glass a smooth, even look. "Like *smite,* but with an aitch."

That was weird. I glanced at Eric, who made a face. *Research assistant?* I mouthed to him. He shrugged.

The restaurant manager stared at us for a long moment. "I'm sorry," he said at last, "I don't think I remember anything after all."

"But you just said—"

"I'm sorry," he repeated firmly, meeting Dad's and Fiona's eyes. "I think you're mistaken."

"But—"

"Look, I've got a family, too, man," he said, and pulled the shade on the door.

Dad's face fell. Fiona patted his shoulder in sympathy.

"I can't believe it," Dad said. He banged on the door again, but we all knew Maurice wasn't coming back. Dad had been down this road before. None of his sources would help him these days. "It's only been an hour since we spoke and someone got to him already."

"Yes." Fiona nodded. "It was rather speedy of them, wasn't it?"

"I'm so sorry, Dad," I said. We stood there for a minute, not saying anything.

After a moment, Eric cleared his throat. "You know what might help right now? Fro-yo."

I glared at him.

"What?" my brother whispered. "It's true."

I HATE TO say it, but fro-yo did seem to make Dad feel marginally better. Well, fro-yo and the fact that we ate it in Solar Park.

Solar Park is big and round and in the middle of the Reistertown town center. It was donated to the city by Aloysius Underberg, who was born and raised here. When Dad was working on the book, we spent a lot of time in this park, climbing on the jungle gyms in the playground and Rollerblading over the walkways while Dad sat on a park bench and typed, soaking up all the good Underberg vibes. Though Dr. Underberg might not be getting any love at the Air and Space Museum in Washington, DC, or on TV specials about the moon landing, he was still a presence in his hometown.

Well, as long as you brushed the fall leaves off the dedication plaque. Which was what Dad and Fiona were doing now, while Eric licked sprinkles out of the inside of his cup and I tried to make sure every bite of my frozen yogurt had the same proportion of kiwi fruit.

"See," Dad was explaining to Fiona, pointing at the plaque, which was set into a big block of granite on the side of the walkway, "he had the town motto engraved right here: *Where history meets tomorrow.*"

"Fascinating," said Fiona. She circled the sign, rapping

lightly on the granite with her knuckles. "This is the only place in the park with his name on it, is that right?"

Dad nodded, smiling down at the bronze plaque. I joined him. It was your basic dedication plaque. Dates, a snippet of the speech, a cool, scientific-looking engraving of nine concentric circles like an atom or something.

Fiona circled the plaque again, running her fingers up and down the seams of the granite.

"*Today, my dream for a better future has become a reality*," Dad read. "Isn't it funny, Gillian, that a guy who dedicated his life to preparing for the very worst was always so hopeful that it was never going to come to pass?"

I slipped my hand into his. "But he was right. We're here and we're fine." Dad might be having career trouble, but it wasn't *actually* the end of the world.

I looked up and caught Fiona frowning at the plaque. "This isn't working," she muttered.

"Pardon me?" I asked.

"This whole evening. It's been a bust from the research angle." She turned to Dad. "I can't believe Mr. Pappas wouldn't talk to you, Sam."

Dad shrugged. "Let's not dwell on it. It's a nice night."

"It's getting dark," Fiona said. "Why don't we all go back to your place? You promised to show me some of those pages from your new book."

I nearly dropped my yogurt cup. What? No, he most

definitely had not. Dad never showed his works in progress to anyone. That was one of the ways they nailed him on the Underberg thing. He didn't have any colleagues who'd read his research and could back up his claims. He never even showed things to Mom, and she was both a fellow history professor and his wife.

But Dad's eyes lit up like they do whenever he gets going on one of his projects, and he said the impossible: "Right. I did." He gestured to Eric and me. "Come on, kids. Let's head home. We can pick up burgers from a drive-through on the way."

Eric was practically skipping. Fro-yo and fast food. I trudged behind. Fiona, Dad's new girlfriend, was one thing. And I guess I could even accept Fiona, Dad's new research assistant. But Fiona, Dad's trusted confidante? Who *was* this lady?

FIONA FOLLOWED US in her car as we stopped at the last fast-food place on the highway, and then down the unlit, country roads that led to the cottage. Inside, the stench of smoke still lingered in the air, but Fiona was polite enough not to mention it.

"I'll get some coffee started," Dad suggested, and headed off to the kitchen.

"Be afraid," Eric said to Fiona. "Be very afraid."

Fiona's eyes widened and she gave Dad a weak smile.

"Actually, do you have tea?"

Eric shook his head. "Like that'll be better?"

"So, Fiona," I asked her as we headed for the living room. "What do you do when you aren't going to Dad's lectures?" What made her good enough to get a peek at Dad's stuff?

"Nothing too interesting," she replied, running a hand through her dark hair. "Resource management for a small development firm."

"Oh," I replied. I knew what each of those words meant on their own, but I had no idea what they added up to. And what in the world would her firm develop out here in the sticks, anyway? Farm equipment?

Dad returned with the tea, and as she held out her hand to take the mug, I noticed a mark on the inside of her wrist. A bit like a scar, maybe, but too regular and precise. Did they make flesh-colored tattoos? It looked like the outline of a letter J, but with a tiny little tail on the end of it.

"What does the J stand for?" I asked, pointing at her arm. "Do you have a kid? An ex-husband?"

"No," she said, and tugged her sleeve down. "I've never been married. Never found the right guy, I guess." She made googly eyes at Dad. Gross.

Dad, unfortunately, was making googly eyes back. Come on, Dad. Just because Mom dumped you doesn't mean you have to get all serious with Miss Smite-with-an-Aitch.

"How did you do in Dad's Roswell class anyway?" I couldn't help but ask.

"She aced it." My father raised his teacup in acknowledgment.

So what? I'd had that lecture memorized since first grade. You didn't see me getting to be Dad's research assistant. "What's the name of the secret government project they claim resulted in the incident?"

"Project Mogul, involving spy microphones mounted to high-altitude balloons."

Spitballs. "And what was the name of the man who initially found the crash debris?"

"William Brazel, a manager at the Foster farm." She took a sip of tea.

"Gillian," Dad warned me. "This is not quiz night. Fiona's interested in more high-level info."

I frowned. That's what I was afraid of. It had been a while since we'd been hounded by reporters, but that didn't mean we could let our guard down.

"Your father is one of the most accomplished scholars of his generation, children," Fiona cooed.

I hate it when grown-ups say "children" like that, probably because it's usually substitute teachers trying to silence a classroom or shopkeepers kicking us out of their store. Mom used it once, too. "Children, your father and I are taking some time apart."

Children! Mom of all people should remember our names. She gave them to us.

"So, Sam," Fiona prompted. "You were showing me your notes?"

"Right!" Dad said. And just like that, they were gone. Eric flipped on the TV. I crossed my arms and slumped in my seat.

"What's with the face, Gills?" Eric asked, powering up his video game.

I softened. Eric's the only one who can get away with calling me that, ever since he stood up for me in third grade when the teacher told the whole class my name should *properly* be spelled with a J. It might have been the last time I appreciated having my kid brother in the same grade.

"Don't you think it's weird that Dad is showing his research to some lady from his beginner classes?" I asked him now.

"Some lady? You mean his *girlfriend*?" Eric corrected.

"Whatever. We barely know her. What if she's another one of those reporters, looking to do a story on crazy Dr. Seagret and his conspiracy theories?"

Eric looked up from the screen. "She'd better not be. I'm not going off the grid again. It took me three months to get my rankings back on this game after last time."

When the book scandal first broke and Dad was put on leave, we were hounded by journalists, got mysterious hang-up phone calls in the middle of the night, and some other scary stuff Dad wouldn't even tell us about. So he packed tents and supplies in the car and drove us out to the wilderness until, as he put it, "things cooled down."

A month later, Mom walked off our campsite and filed for divorce. We came home all right, but it's never been the same. Dad said it was Dr. Underberg's enemies, out to ruin him, too. And if that's true, then it worked. Because here we were, totally ruined.

"On the plus side," he added, "she keeps paying for his classes."

"I don't like her."

"Why? Afraid she's going to be competition for president of Dad's fan club?" Eric put down his controller. "You're the one always saying people should believe Dad. You should be glad someone finally does."

"Fiona isn't the someone I meant."

He just returned to his game. I knew that pose: mainstream phase activated, conversation over. Eric was not going to be any help. *Again.* Biting back a sigh, I headed into the kitchen. Time for Paper Clip's dinner. I grabbed a can of cat food, then rooted around in the drawer for a can opener.

Some resource manager—whatever that meant—Dad met in a beginner class at the Learning Annex was in no position to help him. Nobody could, except maybe if Aloysius Underberg himself rose from the grave and proved all Dad's theories were true.

The way things were going, that would probably be Dad's next talk. "The Government's Secret Zombie Program for Dead Geniuses: From Einstein to Steve Jobs."

I popped open the can, but weirdly enough, Paper Clip didn't appear. She usually had a sixth sense about food. I wondered where she'd gone.

Dad and Fiona were holed up in the study, and knowing how Dad felt about Paper Clip, I doubted I'd find her in there. In the living room, Eric was engrossed in his game. I headed for the mudroom. The second I opened the door, a yellow furball darted past me and into the house, like she already knew she was in trouble. As soon as I flipped on the light, I saw why.

"Paper Clip," I groaned. "What did you *do*?"

Paper Clip is generally a pretty good cat. She has just one tiny vice: she loves mint. Like, *loves*. It's insane. Dad says if she ruins anything else trying to get to her favorite treat she's out on her furry little ear. So Eric and I know enough not to keep gum or candy anywhere Paper Clip can get at it. She'd tear through pockets and chew open backpacks and scratch apart pantry doors. But I guess Dad never informed Fiona about the mint thief in the house. From the tiny green speckles all over the floor of the mudroom, I guessed Tic Tacs, a Paper Clip delicacy.

The black zippered laptop case still hung on its peg, gaping wide open. Paper Clip is oddly skilled at zippers. She just hooks a little claw in the hole and lets her body weight do the rest. Papers were strewn all over the floor, along with file folders, a whole mess of business cards, an assortment of chargers and, worst of all, a laptop.

Yet another reason Fiona was trouble. Now Dad would make us get rid of the cat because she killed his stupid new girlfriend's laptop. That was, unless I could fix it. As quickly as possible, I gathered up Fiona's stuff. She probably wouldn't miss the mints. The big issue was going to be the computer. If it was broken, we were done for. Holding my breath, I booted it up.

It made exactly the kind of grinding sound you'd expect an expensive laptop to make after being violently attacked by a mint-crazed cat. But then I heard fans start to whir. The screen flickered to life, and all kinds of windows popped up with "(Recovered)" in the file name. Maybe Fiona would think she'd just bumped it a little and forced a restart?

As long as it worked, right?

I was about to close the cover and slip it back in the bag when one of the files caught my eye. It was a scan of a diary page of some sort, and the file name read "Omega-AU-pg126 (Recovered)." You could see the edges of the book and the shadow of the spine from where it had been pressed against the scanner plate. Most of the page seemed to be a doodle of concentric circles, like a bull's-eye. But there was a single line of handwriting on the bottom of the page.

"X marks the spot" has been done. I far prefer IX.

I knew that handwriting. I'd seen it a lot in the months and months I'd spent helping Dad in his office.

It was Aloysius Underberg's.

A SCAN, A PLAN, A PIZZA MAN

"EXACTLY HOW MANY FILES DID YOU STEAL OFF YOUR DAD'S GIRLfriend's computer?" Savannah asked me, her blue eyes looking even bigger and rounder than usual.

"Would you all please stop calling her that?" I said, exasperated.

Eric smirked and knocked off three or four zombies with his grenade launcher on the TV screen. "Could be worse, Gills," he said, his fingers moving fast over the game controller. "Could be 'stepmom.'"

"That doesn't sound half bad," Savannah said, sweeping her blond hair behind her shoulders. "You say she's really pretty and knows how to dress."

"You're missing the point, Sav," I said.

"Right." She nodded. "Stolen files."

Savannah always comes to dinner on Thursdays, because Dad teaches his night class and leaves money for Eric and me to buy pizza. She loves ordering pizza, especially on Thursdays.

Savannah's been my best friend since we were both six years old. Well, kind of. Until recently, we were only summer best friends. She lived in one of the mobile homes in the park on the other side of the creek, and we'd spent every summer for as long as I could remember splashing back and forth across the water, splitting Popsicles and trading books. In the winters, when I lived in the city, we sent emails. I told her about all the cool city stuff—like first-run movies and music festivals and ice-skating rinks in the park. She told me about how she was the most popular girl at school. Sav was the only one happy we were moving into the summer cottage for good, and even I had to admit that I liked the idea of starting at my new school with a ready-made best friend.

And it has been great. Mostly. Savannah's different in the fall. Like how she spends more energy deciding where to sit at lunch than she does on the average quiz, and last week, she pretended not to know the answer to a problem in math class, even though she was the one who showed me how to solve it when we were doing our homework the night before. School Savannah introduced me to all the cool kids and made sure we were in the same homeroom, despite the fact that her last name starts with an F and mine starts with an S. But I still miss summer Savannah.

I spread out my evidence on the coffee table: four printouts and my pink jelly USB bracelet, the one I'd used to copy Fiona's files off her laptop before I'd stuffed it back in her bag, zipped it up, and pushed it far out of Paper Clip's reach. "They're stolen files all right. Only I don't think I was the first person to steal them."

Eric snorted from in front of his video game. "You think Fiona stole the stuff you found on her computer?"

I waved one of the scanned diary pages in the air. "Yep. From Dad."

Aside from the sheet marked "pg126," there were two others that also looked like they were from the same diary and then one that made even less sense to me, since it was just a spreadsheet of really big numbers with words like "steel" and "pipe" and "lead sheeting" next to every row. I only took that one because it was also marked "Omega" in the file name.

Only problem was, I wasn't sure what "Omega" meant.

"AU," however, I felt much more confident about. "All these diary pages were saved under the heading 'Omega-AU.' I think that last part—'AU'—stands for Aloysius Underberg."

"Or maybe gold," said Savannah. "'Au' is the chemical symbol for gold."

I shot her a look. This was exactly the kind of thing she acted like she didn't know at school.

"And astronomical unit," Eric prompted without looking up from the screen. "And alternate universe."

"Dude, get off the internet," said Savannah.

"*Dude,* get out of the jewelry aisle," he replied as he made his character duck and cover behind an overturned car. Savannah thought Eric was a huge dork. Eric thought Savannah was a huge airhead. It had been this way for as long as I could remember.

"It's Aloysius Underberg," I insisted. "It's his handwriting. I think it's his diary."

Now Eric paused his game and turned to me. "What are you talking about, Gillian? Dr. Underberg's diary was destroyed when that pipe burst. Remember? The Reistertown Historical Society banned Dad for life."

"Exactly!" I said. Eric and I had shoveled soggy pulp out of the office for two days. "And yet, here are pages from the diary. What does that say to you?"

"That someone was smarter than Dad and scanned it a long time ago, before it was destroyed?"

"Nope." I tapped the page. "The scan is date-stamped. Date-stamped *last month.* Which means that this diary wasn't destroyed in the flood. Maybe none of Dad's notes were. Maybe that pipe in the wall didn't even burst."

"Don't joke about that," said Eric. "I lost my comic book collection and my PlayStation in that flood."

"Just hear me out," I argued. "Someone out there didn't want Dad to publish that book about Dr. Underberg. That part we know."

"*You* know."

"What if the flood wasn't an accident?" I pushed on, ignoring Eric's crack. "What if it was all part of the plan? They broke into the house and staged it to look like the flood ruined Dad's stuff, but really *they* broke the pipe and stole his files, hoping that if his research was gone, he'd have to stop writing the book."

"Ha," Eric interrupted. "They've clearly never met Dad."

I ignored him. "And when he published the book despite everything, they knew the only thing to do was ruin *him*." Ruin us.

"*They?*" Savannah asked, wrinkling her eyebrows. "Who is *they?*"

Eric snorted. "With Dad and Gillian, there's always a *they*. *They* covered up the Roswell experiments. *They* know who killed JFK. *They* destroyed Dr. Underberg and now *they* are out to get *me*—"

"Well, if there is a *they*," I said, cutting off my brother, "then Fiona is one of *them*. Because she has pages from

Dad's Underberg diary, which supposedly doesn't even exist anymore."

"If she's part of the conspiracy, she must be getting a real laugh from the nuts in Dad's beginner classes," Eric said.

Savannah looked more contemplative. "What do you think she's trying to do, Gillian? I mean, your dad can't do anything to expose"—she made air quotes—"*them* anymore. After everything that's happened, well . . . people just sort of think he's crazy."

"You can say that again." Eric unpaused his game and went back to killing zombies like the conversation was over. Fine. He could waste his time chasing video game monsters. I was going after real ones.

"I don't think she's trying to do anything to my dad," I said to Savannah. "I think she's trying to get something *from* him."

"Like what?"

"She said last night that Dad was the greatest scholar of his generation. If anyone can figure out what happened to Dr. Underberg, it's him."

"I thought you said Dr. Underberg was dead."

"Right, but there's still a lot we don't know about how he died. Or where. Or what happened to his stuff." Soon after the government fired him over the Underberg battery, he stopped filing patents, sold his house . . . and then one day, he disappeared. Like he got bumped off by the CIA or the KGB or some other organization with a couple of letters and a lot of spies. The prototype for the hundred-year battery disappeared, too. Official sources say the battery never worked. But Dad's book says different.

"Look." I pointed at the first page. "The things Underberg is writing in these pages, it's all really weird, like he's talking in code."

"*Underberg?*" Eric mocked as he battled the undead. "*Weird?* You don't say."

Savannah read the top page. "'X marks the spot has been done. I far prefer IX.' Yeah, that makes no sense." She picked up the next one, which Fiona had given the file name of "Omega-AU-pg125." "'My last and lasting gift to mankind . . .' blah blah blah '. . . we are not ready for the stars, though there are those who would Shepherd us there against our wills. While the Earth remains, so shall I.'" She glanced at me over the top of the page. "Your dad read this whole diary?"

"And it all sounded just as nuts," said Eric. He tossed the controller to the couch. "I can't listen to this anymore. I'm going to be in my room. Come get me when the pizza's here." He leaped over Savannah and stomped off.

Savannah nodded at the other papers. "So what do the rest say?"

I handed over the spreadsheet with a shrug. "There's

this one, which is just a bunch of numbers to me. And then this one, which I can't even figure out why she bothered scanning." I passed Savannah the last scan, which simply showed the edge of a torn-off sheet. The only writing visible was a few pen marks on the edge of the ragged page.

Savannah looked at them all, then tapped the edges against the coffee table until they were in a nice, neat stack and laid them down carefully. "Gillian," she said slowly. "Let's say Fiona *did* break into this house two years ago and stole your dad's files and caused a flood and then ruined his life. If all that's true, then she's already got whatever information he has about Underberg. So why is she dating him now? Why is she going to all his conspiracy theory lectures and stuff?"

"You're siding with Eric?" Some friend!

"No." She held up her hands in defense. "I'm just saying . . . it's a big leap. Maybe she's not one of . . . *them* or whatever. Maybe Fiona doesn't have the diary because she stole it from your dad. Maybe she bought it off eBay or something, not realizing it was stolen. You said she met your dad in one of his classes. What if she's just interested in this stuff, same as him? Maybe your dad even knows about the scans."

I narrowed my eyes. "If my dad knew that diary was still around, he would have mentioned it to me." He'd complained often enough about it being gone. Fiona was fishy. Why didn't anyone believe me?

The doorbell rang. Savannah perked up. "He's here! How do I look?"

"Great," I said. Sav always looked great.

This was the thing about Thursdays.

"Girls," came the voice on the other side of the door. "Can we not do this today? I've got, like, ten deliveries to make."

Savannah, already crawling toward the windows near the door, covered her mouth with her hand and squealed. She twisted around and beckoned to me, eyes glittering with excitement. I sighed and crawled after her. Paper Clip followed, yellow tail flicking in the air. When we reached the window, Savannah lifted the curtain a fraction of an inch, peeked out, then slammed her body to the floor.

"He's there! Gillian!"

"Of course he's there," I whispered. "We ordered pizza from him."

"Girls?" came his voice again. "Please? I'll give you a free order of egg-roll calzones."

Savannah crouched beneath the windowsill and lifted the curtain again. I caught a glimpse of his truck, a beat-up red pickup with a magnetic General Tso's Pizza sign affixed to the side. Our town's too small to have more than one delivery place, so General Tso's does pizza and Chinese food—and to be honest, they're kind of bad at both. The only decent thing they have going for them is this delivery guy, who Savannah, in keeping with the military theme, has christened Private Pizza.

Private Pizza is really, really cute. He's very tall, very tan, has very dark hair and very beautiful green eyes and as far as we can tell, he only works on Tuesdays and Thursdays.

Savannah was now putting on lip gloss and arranging her long, stick-straight blond hair over her shoulders. She handed me the lip gloss but I shook my head. Banana-flavored. Yuck. I did, however, tighten my ponytail.

She stood up, smoothed her top down over the waist of her jeans, and took a deep breath. "Okay. I'm going in."

I gave her a thumbs-up.

She yanked the door open. "Hi," she cooed.

Private Pizza stood under the porch light, pizza in his hands. He wore his red General Tso's T-shirt with its ironed-on military fringe and Mandarin collar under an unzipped blue hoodie. "Hi."

"Is this our pizza? Tomato, cheese, and sesame chicken?"

"Should be."

Savannah cocked her head to the side. "I don't think that's what you're supposed to say."

Private Pizza rolled his eyes. "Come on, kid."

"I think," Savannah went on coyly, "that if you don't say it, we get it free."

He sighed, straightened, and clicked his heels together. "I present to you, lovely maiden, this golden disk of the seven heavens, baked by the flame of four noble dragons." He bowed his head over the pizza box and held it out.

Savannah giggled, took the box, and handed him the money Dad left for us. "Awesome."

Private Pizza stepped back. "Yeah, no free egg-roll calzones for you," he said, and jogged off the porch.

Savannah closed the door, but watched him as he got back in the car and peeled off down the driveway, gravel spinning out from under his wheels. "He's so hot."

"Hotter than the pizza," I said, grabbing the box. "Since you make him stand out there for five minutes first."

"He's my future husband!" Savannah insisted, following me back to the dining room table. "I want to spend as much time with him as possible."

"Your future husband?" I asked skeptically. "You don't even know his name." I opened the box. Nestled into the corners around the pizza were four wrapped fortune cookies. I yelled for Eric.

"That'll come later," Sav declared, and snagged a slice.

"I'm just saying, we could have had calzones if you'd

just answered the door and didn't make him do the whole routine."

"Egg-roll calzones?" Eric asked, materializing by my side.

"Forget it." Savannah peeled the cheese off her pizza. "They're fattening anyway."

"So how's the Fiona conspiracy coming along?" Eric asked as we all sat down with our pizza. "Have you figured out her evil plot of evil against Dad yet? Just tell me if Paper Clip is in on it. And to think of all the catnip I've given that traitor."

"Paper Clip is on our side," I said as the cat rubbed against my legs and whined for her dinner.

"That's what she wants you to think." He turned to Savannah. "See, it's not enough for conspiracy theorists that there's a *they*. There also has to be an evil plot, and it usually involves taking over the world."

"I don't think Fiona is trying to take over the world."

"No," said Eric, with his mouth full. "Just Dad."

That was it. I'd had enough of the doubters. I pushed back from the table and stood. "Okay. I'll get proof."

"This ought to be good," Eric said. I ignored him and stalked into Dad's office. His inner sanctum.

After the flood and the scandal, Dad became much more careful about his records. He even invented a filing system—of sorts. As he'd pointed out to me, if the system was too straightforward, it would be easy for *them* to get in. So, for instance, Eric's and my medical and school records aren't filed under our names. They are filed under K for "kids." You have to be one of us to figure out the secret codes and find anything.

On top of that, the whole cabinet is housed in a fire-proof safe, every file is enclosed in a waterproof plastic bag, and—because it's Dad we're talking about here—he's even made sure to include some tamper-proof elements, just in case *they* come around. Every single plastic bag is sealed with a minuscule hair trapped precisely one inch from the left side of the bag. That way, if someone came and opened it without Dad's knowledge, the hair would fall out of place and he'd know.

It's truly brilliant, and not paranoid or whatever Mom called it on her last visit.

"If Fiona really *was* into the whole conspiracy theory thing," I said loudly, storming over to the safe, "then she would have had at least basic password protection on her laptop files. I wouldn't have been able to copy them." I dialed in the combination to the safe, then yanked open the cabinet marked P–Z. "And if Fiona really *was* into my dad, and had gone out of her way to get copies of the Underberg diary for him, then she would have given them to him."

S-section for scientist, A-folder for Aloysius. I flipped to the appropriate waterproof bag. "And he would have put them away . . . right here."

I looked down at the seal.

No hair.

LOST AND LAST

I LOOKED UP AT ERIC, MY MOUTH OPEN IN SHOCK. "ERIC, THERE'S NO hair."

"What?" Savannah asked, her eyebrows knitting.

"My dad always seals these files with a hair. That way he knows if someone comes along and tampers with it. There's no hair on the seal of this file."

Savannah blinked at me several times, then turned to my brother. "Okay, Eric, I'm officially on your side. This is ridiculous."

But the color had drained from my brother's face. "No, Gillian is right. Dad's nuts about his system. I mean, he might forget to turn off the iron, but he never, ever forgets the hair seal on his files." I was sure he was already envisioning Dad breaking out the tent and mapping a secret campsite. Eric would go into video game withdrawal. "If he'd shown this to Fiona, the hair would still be there."

"Eww, really?" Savannah asked. "Whose hair does he use?"

"His," Eric said, pushing past Savannah to join me at the cabinet. "He almost went bald after the flood when he first set this up." Eric turned to me. "Is there any way to tell if something's missing?"

I glanced at the file, the pages and CDs of info contained within. "I don't know. But I do think I know Fiona's plan. Savannah said maybe Fiona had somehow bought Dr. Underberg's diary for my dad, like maybe she thought he'd like some extra information on him."

"So?" Savannah asked.

"Well, what if it's exactly the opposite? What if *she* needs some extra information about Underberg—something that's not in the diary—and she thinks my dad still has it?"

"And she's dating him to sweet-talk him into giving it to her?" Eric had definitely dropped the sarcasm.

"Or to get close enough to him so she could get into his office and see what he had left."

My brother nodded slowly. "That would explain what she sees in him, at least."

"All her files were named Omega," I said. "Whatever she's looking for, it's called Omega."

"You could look under O?" Savannah suggested.

Eric snorted. "Dad's system doesn't work like that. We'd need to know what Omega means to Dad."

"Or what it meant to Underberg." I closed up the filing cabinet and grabbed a copy of Dad's Underberg book off the shelf. We have loads of copies lying around, ever since the publisher stopped selling them. I turned to the index, looking for any mention of "Omega."

"Nothing in the book," I said. "What does Omega even mean?"

"I think it's a Greek letter," said Savannah. "My cousin is a Chi Omega at college. Sororities all have Greek-letter names."

"So maybe Underberg was in a fraternity called Omega?" I asked.

"It also means 'last,'" Eric pointed out. "Like *The Omega Man* is a zombie movie about the last human on Earth. And a lot of final bosses in video games are Omega this or Omega that."

Savannah was already paging through Dad's dictionary to O. "We're both right. It's the last letter in the Greek alphabet, so sometimes people use it to mean 'last' or 'end.'"

"G for Greek?" Eric asked me, turning back to the filing cabinet. "F for foreign languages?"

I smiled at him. Finally, he'd seen the light. I pulled open a drawer. "Let's try L for Last." But there was no file marked "Last" in the drawer. Just one marked "Loose Pages." I lifted it out and opened the waterproof bag, making sure to press my finger over the hair seal to keep it from slipping out.

The file was pretty thick, with all kinds of paper scraps—what looked like everything from old grocery lists to a few notes scrawled on the backs of receipts. A small, yellowed page of lined paper caught my eye and I yanked it out of the stack.

The size and shape matched the scans from Fiona's computer. The edge was ragged, as if it had been torn from a notebook. The handwriting was Aloysius Underberg's.

I clutched the page to my chest and ran back to the living room with Paper Clip—who knew quite well never to enter Dad's office—hot on my heels from the second I hit the hall. The printouts of Fiona's files were still sitting on the coffee table and I lined the loose page up against the torn edges on the final printout, the one marked "Omega-AU-pg127."

It was a perfect match.

I heard Savannah and Eric behind me.

"This is what she's looking for," I whispered, holding up the matching pages. "It's the missing last page of Underberg's diary. It must have fallen out and gotten lost with Dad's stuff before the rest of the diary was stolen." I dropped back on the couch.

"So Omega means the last page of Dr. Underberg's diary?" Savannah asked.

"I guess."

"Wait, no," said Eric. "That doesn't make sense. All Fiona's files are named Omega, not just the one for this page."

"True." So if she wasn't looking for this one piece of paper, what was she looking for? Paper Clip leaped up beside me and scratched her cheek against the edge of the page. "But then what is it?"

"Well," prompted Eric, plucking the page out of my hand. "What does the magical page say?"

I tried to grab it back, but he held it out of my reach, vaulting over the back of the couch.

"A whole lot of gibberish," he said with a shrug. "Typical Underberg stuff."

I lunged for the page and snatched it back. And, though I hated to admit it, Eric was right. Because this is what it said:

I find I cannot be so cruel as to destroy my greatest creation, despite the cruelty of those I trusted. Very well. For those who trust me it shall not be difficult to reach safety, for you know my heart:

You know who I am, and the heavenly body that heralded my arrival. IX marks the spot.

You know where I'm from, and the gifts I have left there. And even if the sun sets on this Earth, you can use it to start your journey.

Follow the path I've laid for you, in the direction marked by the birth of ice.

When you find my twin, you will find my treasure.

Underneath that, in a different shade of pen, like it was written later, was what looked like a phone number:

x=5906376272

And then a line, with more numbers underneath:

0.05=1391000

"Are either of you planning on telling me what it says?" Savannah asked. She was still holding the dictionary open to O for omega.

"Eric's right." I sighed. "More gibberish."

Savannah leaned over my shoulder to read. "What's all that stuff about heavenly bodies? Hey, you said Dr. Underberg was a NASA scientist, right?"

"Yeah?"

"Well, that other sheet said something about the stars, and this one is all about 'heavenly bodies' and the sun and the Earth. Maybe Omega is some sort of space thing. A . . . moon or an asteroid or something."

"You know who might be able to tell us?" Eric said. "That kid at school. The one who's obsessed with NASA?"

"Eww," said Savannah. "Howard Noland? He's such a dweeb. Nobody talks to him on purpose."

Eric nodded. "But he knows everything there is to know about space. We have PE together and it's the only thing he'll talk about."

"Exactly," said Savannah. "*Literally* the only thing. He's our age, but he's only in fifth. They held him back in first grade, you know, because he was such a freak." She twirled her finger around her ears.

Like people didn't say that every day about my dad.

"And we're just as crazy if we actually encourage him on his whole space obsession. He'll talk your ear off."

"If he can help me figure out what Fiona is up to, I'll risk both my ears. I don't know what's going on, but someone was willing to ruin Dad's life over this Underberg thing last year, and Fiona is definitely involved now. I can't let anyone hurt Dad like that again."

Eric was staring at me. "So you don't think we should tell Dad what we found?"

“We can try,” I said, “but if he gets paranoid, you know what that means.”

Eric shuddered.

“What does it mean?” Savannah asked.

“Best-case scenario?” my brother said. “We’re all eating packaged foods and drinking bottled water for a week. Worst-case? He takes us off the grid until things calm down.”

“Off the grid?”

“Camping,” I explained. “No phone, no TV, no internet, no footprints if he’s feeling especially cautious.”

I’d never forget what Mom told Dad the morning she left the campsite. We’d done a full month of it when the scandal had first hit, and lost our mom in the deal. What would we lose if Dad started down that road again? Paper Clip? The house?

“Okay. Let’s keep it a secret until we know if we’re dealing with anything at all. Who knows?” I forced a smile. “Maybe Eric’s right and this is all in my head.”

But I don’t think even Eric believed that anymore.

SPACE CASE

THE NEXT DAY, BEFORE SCHOOL STARTED, ERIC AND I MET SAVANNAH IN front of the doors. "So where's Howard?"

Eric pointed at a kid sitting on the stoop, his face buried in a book even thicker than most of the ones in Dad's office. Our school wasn't that big, but I don't think I'd ever talked to this kid before—or even seen him. I guess he didn't rate among Savannah's lunchtime companions. Howard Noland had unruly black hair and wore a faded green T-shirt with frayed edges. As I watched, he sneezed, then rubbed the back of his hand across his nose.

Savannah pursed her lips. "This is a terrible idea."

"You have a better one?" Eric asked her.

"No, but let's do it quick, before anyone catches us talking to him."

I was already striding toward Howard, the printouts clutched firmly in my hands.

Savannah and Eric trotted along behind me, still arguing.

"You might have had PE with Howard for a few months," Savannah was saying, "but I've known him for years. And I'm telling you, this is not going to go well."

"What makes you think that?" he shot back.

I reached him. "Hi," I said, but he didn't look up from his book. "Are you Howard? I'm Gillian Seagret—"

"I know who you are," he said, eyes still on the book. "You're the one who doesn't believe in the moon landing."

Savannah turned to Eric, her eyes flashing in triumph. "See?"

"Point taken," said Eric.

"No," I corrected Howard. Dad and I might like conspiracies, but we weren't *crackpots*. "I think Apollo 11 landed on the moon. I just don't think NASA did a live broadcast of it." What, did this kid keep tabs of every time NASA was mentioned at school? I'd made one comment at lunch one day. . . . "They claimed there were problems with the cameras that kept Buzz Aldrin and Neil Armstrong in the lander for a full hour after—"

Now Howard looked up from his book, but his gaze

traveled no farther than my knees. "Actually, the truth is that NASA wanted them to take a five-hour sleep period but they were too excited and wanted to go down right away—"

"Which also doesn't make sense if they were planning a live broadcast for prime time!" I argued. "That would have put the broadcast at four a.m. Remember, this is the America that accidentally caught Lee Harvey Oswald, the man who killed President Kennedy, getting shot on *live* TV earlier in the decade. Do you really think NASA wanted to risk the world watching Neil Armstrong get eaten by green moon monsters, too?"

"Wait. There aren't green moon monsters," said Savannah. "Are there?"

"They delayed the broadcast," I stated firmly. "It's the only rational explanation."

"Rational!" Howard blurted. "Do you even know the definition of that word?"

Eric cleared his throat and stepped between us. "Anyway," he said, glaring at me. "We were wondering, Howard, if you could help us out with a little puzzle. Gillian?" he prompted.

I thrust the papers at Howard.

"What is this?" he asked, drawing back from them like they might bite. "More NASA conspiracy theories?"

"Maybe," Eric admitted.

"It's a riddle," said Savannah. "Something to do with space—stars, planets, stuff like that. Anyway, it was written by a NASA scientist and we thought if anyone in this town could figure it out, it would be you." She batted her eyelashes at him.

He didn't seem to notice, probably because he still wouldn't look any of us in the face. "Well, that's the only *rational* statement you've made so far. Who is the NASA scientist?"

I hesitated. If Howard was already suspicious of me because of my totally understandable concerns about the inconsistencies in the official moon landing report—which, by the way, Dad taught a whole class about if Howard ever wanted to hear the *real* story—what would he think if we told him that we wanted his help interpreting the diaries of a scientist NASA had fired for being crazy?

"Aloysius Underberg," Savannah said before I could stop her. She shot me a look and moved her hand in a *hurry-up* gesture.

"Really?" Howard straightened. "It's so hard to find stuff about him. He may have ended up disgraced, but before he started going bad, he contributed a lot to the program. It's a shame they scrubbed the record. I heard someone was writing a biography about him, but I haven't been able to find it."

"Our dad wrote it," my brother offered.

"Eric!" I warned. But Howard had focused in on him like no one else existed.

"How much is about the space program?"

"Seven chapters," I said, since it was clear this was our only option. And that gave me an idea. "And you can have it . . . if you help us." Why not? We had dozens of copies at home.

Howard popped up off the curb and stuck out his hand—not the one he'd used to wipe his nose, thank goodness. "Deal."

Instead of shaking his hand, I gave him the papers.

MUCH TO SAVANNAH'S embarrassment, Howard came to see us at lunch and told us he had a few ideas, but he needed to check some books he had at home before "presenting his findings." I thought Sav's eyes might roll out of her head. At first he wanted us to come home with him, but Savannah put her foot down.

"I have things to do after school," she'd argued.

"What things?" I asked, and she elbowed me. "Oh. Actually, Howard, we're going to have to go to my house to get the book first."

"I can come with you," he said. Savannah shook her head vehemently.

"No, it's okay," I said. "We'll meet you at your place. It'll save time."

So after school, Eric, Savannah, and I stopped off at home to pick up Dad's book, then biked over to the address Howard had given us.

"Are you sure doing this won't hurt your reputation?" Eric asked Savannah.

"No more than being seen at school with you does," she said with a smirk.

The Nolands lived closer to the center of town than we did, so all the streets and driveways were paved, though to judge from the antlers affixed to the grill of what I assumed was Howard's dad's pickup truck taking up the entire driveway, that didn't necessarily make them city folks.

We parked our bikes in the driveway and headed up the walk. We rang the bell out front, and a few seconds later, the door opened.

There, on the threshold, stood Private Pizza.

Savannah dug her nails into my arm and squealed in the back of her throat.

"Hi," said Eric as Private Pizza gaped at us. "Is Howard home?"

He wasn't dressed in his uniform, of course, just a black T-shirt and track pants. "Is this some kind of joke?"

"Um," I said, somehow finding my voice through the shock of seeing him and the pain Savannah was inflicting on my arm. "We're looking for Howard Noland. Does he live here?"

"He's my brother," said the guy Sav and I had tormented on our front porch once a week since Dad's classes had started.

Savannah seemed to be having trouble breathing. "You're . . . Howard's . . . omigod."

Private Pizza shook his head and whistled through his teeth. "The Creek Terrace Terrible Twosome, here for Howard. Does he have any idea what you two are like?"

Eric turned to look at us. "What are you two like?"

"You don't want to know," I told him under my breath. I didn't need Eric getting any more ammunition to use against Savannah.

Private Pizza called into the interior of the house. "Howard! You have, uh, *visitors*."

Eric entered and I stumbled after him, pulling a hyperventilating Savannah along.

"Gillian!" she whispered to me as we headed down the hall. "He has a *name* for us."

I grunted as we passed a large recliner upholstered in camouflage print. "Not a good one." The living room had three deer heads and a whole flock of ducks on the wall. I wondered if any were Howard's. Or Private Pizza's.

We reached Howard's room and knocked.

"You may enter," came the reply from inside.

Savannah snickered behind her hands. I elbowed her.

In comparison to the rest of the house, Howard's bedroom looked like Tomorrowland had exploded inside. The walls were painted midnight blue and dotted with glow-in-the-dark star stickers, each carefully labeled with the name of the constellation they depicted. Models of rockets and other spacecraft lined the shelf above the bed—I recognized Sputnik, Mercury, Saturn, the lunar landing module from the Apollo missions, and the space shuttle. There was a map of the moon with all its landmarks labeled behind the desk, which was piled high with books on astronomy and NASA, and a signed photograph of Buzz Aldrin held pride of place in a frame on the nightstand. Howard was seated at the desk, the papers spread out in front of him.

"Hi," I said brightly. "Thanks for having us ov—"

"Did you bring the book?" he asked, his tone brusque.

I reached into my backpack. "Do you have answers for us?"

"Book first. I've been tricked into doing work for people like you before." He gestured in Savannah's general direction.

"*People like us?*" Savannah said. "What's *that* supposed to mean?" She turned to me. "Don't give it to him, Gillian. He doesn't know anything."

I looked at Howard, who was sitting there with a bland expression on his face. Savannah could play stupid all she wanted, but I knew what he was getting at. If Sav and I didn't have six years of best friendship between us, I might even have agreed with him.

I shrugged and handed over the Underberg book. "Whatever. We have other copies."

Howard took it, spun around and carefully slid it on a shelf, then turned immediately back to the pages on his desk. "All right. So, these pages. I probably should have guessed, given the questionable reputation of Dr. Underberg at NASA, but he's not actually talking about stars or spaceships or anything like that."

"His questionable reputation?" I echoed angrily. "What are you talking about?"

"Please, Gills. You know exactly what he means," Eric said. "Underberg was cuckoo. Even Dad thought he was a little bit nutty toward the end."

"And this must have been the *very* end," said Savannah. "It's the last page from his diary before he disappeared."

They had a point, but still, I didn't want to work with Howard if he was going to insult Dr. Underberg at every turn. How could I trust anything he said?

On the other hand, whatever information the page contained, Fiona clearly thought it was important. Which meant I wanted to understand it. "Then what is he talking about?"

Howard held up the mysterious last page. "This right here? It's not a riddle."

"No?"

"It's a treasure map."

PLUTO IS A PLANET

WE ALL STOOD IN SILENCE.

"A treasure map?" Howard repeated, gesturing wildly with his arms. "A drawing or list of instructions, usually coded, that are directions to some sort of valuable object or objects hidden by the maker of the map?"

"Well, yeah," I said, crossing my arms over my chest. "But I don't think you earned the book if that's all you have to say about it. We aren't idiots. Of course it's a treasure map: it says 'find my treasure' and 'X marks the spot.'"

But what *was* the treasure? Why was it so secret that *they* had had Dr. Underberg killed? Why was it so valuable that Fiona was dating my dad just to find a map to it?

"It doesn't say that," Howard pointed out. "Not exactly. It says he prefers IX."

"So what?" I snapped. "You were supposed to tell us what Omega means. That was your job."

"That's a dumb job," he said. "I'm not an encyclopedia."

"We did try a dictionary," Savannah pointed out.

Howard was silent for a second. "Omega means a lot of things in space. There's the Omega Nebula, which is also called the Horseshoe Nebula. I have a picture of it. . . ." He shuffled around a few papers and pulled out a picture of what looked like a colorful outer-space cloud. "Because horseshoes and the Greek letter omega sort of look the same."

Except the cloud didn't really look like a horseshoe or the letter omega. At least, not to me. "So you think he's talking about this nebula?"

"No. There are also a lot of stars called Omega."

"A *lot* of stars?" Savannah groaned. "Oh boy."

"It's to make star identification easier. See, constellations are made up of many stars—well, stars and other bright objects. Like clusters and nebulas and—"

Savannah looked at me as if to say, *See?* Okay, she had a point about Howard. This was way more than I needed to know about astronomy. It sounded like he was ready to go on all day about everything in the sky remotely connected to the word omega. Now he was talking about something called the Bayer designation.

"—and each star in a designation is given a Greek letter, usually from brightest to dullest, though not always—"

"Like Alpha Centauri?" Eric asked, probably more to stop Howard's flow than anything.

"Yeah."

"Is there an Omega Centauri?" I cut in. Let's get to the point.

"Yes. It's a globular cluster. But that's not what the guy in those pages you gave me is writing about."

I bit my lip and took a deep breath. Maybe Savannah was right. Asking Howard to talk about space was like trying to get a spoonful of water out of a hose. This wasn't getting me anywhere, and who knew what else Fiona knew that we didn't? Maybe she had already figured out another way to get the information on this last diary page. "So what is he talking about?"

"Nothing in space."

Savannah groaned. I wanted to join her.

"I don't know *what* it is," Howard admitted. "But I think I know how to find it."

Okay. That was something at least. Maybe we'd recognize . . . whatever it was when we saw it. Or we could take it to Dad and he could figure it out.

He pointed at the concentric circles on the first diary

page, where it read *I prefer IX*. "Look at the drawing. Nine circles around this central dot—just like the solar system. I think that by IX, he means Pluto. 'IX' is often a symbol for Pluto in astronomy textbooks. Look—" He stood to grab one of the big, dusty textbooks from the shelf over his desk and opened it up. Sure enough, the illustration showed a solar system model where every planet was marked with a Roman numeral: I for Mercury, II for Venus, III for Earth, and so on. "Pluto is the ninth planet, so it gets an IX."

"Pluto's not a planet, though," said Eric.

"It was for most of the twentieth century," said Howard. "It was only in the past few years that they demoted it to dwarf planet status."

"Dr. Underberg died ten years before we were even born," I said.

"So whenever he wrote this, Pluto was still a planet."

"Wait. Just because he wrote IX, that means Pluto?" Savannah asked. "I think that's kind of a stretch."

"Not really," I said. Howard seemed like he was on the right track at last. "Underberg was obsessed with Pluto, all his life. It was discovered on his birthday: February 18, 1930. He'd had murals of it painted on the wall of his office, used it as his code word when working on secret stuff for the State Department . . ."

"His exact birthday?" Howard asked. "Like it's his twin?"

I thought of the last line of the riddle: *When you find my twin, you will find my treasure.* "Maybe. But who leaves a treasure on Pluto? No one's been to Pluto, right?"

"Maybe the green moon monsters," said Savannah.

"There aren't any green moon—" Howard stopped. "Oh. That was a joke."

She snickered. I glared at her. *Don't distract him.* He was finally giving us useful info.

He turned to me. "And that's not all. See this number?" He pointed at the long number at the bottom of the last diary page. "That's the average distance from the sun to Pluto: 5,906,376,272 kilometers."

"Okay," I conceded. "So you *are* saying there's some kind of treasure on Pluto?"

"Not exactly." He pointed at the other group of numbers. "This number here: 1,391,000? That's the diameter of the sun."

"Do you have all those memorized or something?" Savannah asked, rolling her eyes.

"Just the planets," Howard replied. "I'm still working on the moons. Anyway, he says here to '*use the sun to start your journey.*' That made me think. In fourth grade, we made a scale model of the solar system. Do you remember?" he asked her.

Savannah shrugged. "Not really. It was two years ago for me."

"Sav," I hissed. She totally remembered that project. I know because she wrote me an email about it, back when I still lived in the city and she wasn't afraid to let people know she could do long division in her head.

But Howard didn't seem to hear her anyway. "Well, one of the things we had to do was figure out the relative size and distance of the planets. There was a worksheet with the measurements on them, and we had to translate them all to smaller sizes. The sun is really one point three-nine million kilometers across, but what if it was the size of an orange? How big would the planets be, how far away? All those calculations. And we made a solar system on the soccer field. Well, mostly on the soccer field. It didn't all fit, because if the sun was the size of an orange, then the relative distance to Pluto would be—"

"You think the treasure map is a scale model of the solar system?" I asked before he gave me the entire run-down.

Howard blinked at the interruption. Then he nodded. "Yes. And IX—Pluto—marks the spot."

I looked at the page with Underberg's riddle. *You know where I'm from, and the gifts I have left there. And even if the sun sets on this Earth, you can use it to start your journey.* Howard was right—it did sound like he was trying to make the sun the start of a trail to the treasure.

"So all we'd have to do to find this treasure is figure

out the relative distance of the planets, like on the worksheet!" I exclaimed.

Eric tapped the page, where it said *0.05=1,391,000*. "But in this case, instead of the sun being an orange, it's 0.05 . . . something."

"That's probably kilometers, too," said Savannah. "0.05 kilometers is fifty meters." I gave her a look but she didn't seem to notice.

"That's as far as I got." Howard sat back down at the desk chair. "But I don't know what this fifty-meter thing was that Dr. Underberg was using for the sun."

"Well, that's going to be impossible to find out," said Eric. "It's been decades since he wrote this riddle. Whatever it was has been moved or destroyed long ago."

I looked down at the diary page, and the concentric circles drawn there. When I'd first seen it, I'd thought it was a target. But now I knew it was supposed to be the solar system.

I also knew where I'd seen it before.

"No," I said softly. "It hasn't been destroyed. We were just there."

Eric's eyes got really wide. "Solar Park?"

"*Solar*," I said. "Like the sun. And he says 'you know where I'm from, and the gifts I have left there.' He has to be talking about the park. It's in his hometown. There's even an engraving of the solar system on the dedication plaque that looks just like this one." How funny. I always thought that was just because it was called Solar Park. I'd never even wondered why they'd called it that.

And then I remembered something else. Fiona, knocking on the granite block where the plaque was set. Did she think that was where Underberg's treasure was hidden?

"The park is fifty meters across?"

"It must be close," said Eric. "Like half a football field?"

"It has to be precise," Howard said. "Any variation could ruin the calculation."

"Hey, Howard, can I see my dad's book again?" He handed it over and I flipped through, looking for the page I remembered. "I think Dad wrote about the park in his book. They had to reroute roads and stuff to get it exactly how Dr. Underberg wanted. . . ." I found what I was looking for and started reading. "'*Town Hall meetings from this time indicate that there was much debate over Dr. Underberg's specifications. He would only donate the money under the conditions that the park meet the following qualifications: 1) perfectly round, 2) precisely fifty meters from end to end, and 3) in the exact spot he specified.*'"

"That's got to be it," said Howard. He leaped up and snatched the book out of my hands, as if I was going to keep it.

And that was probably why Fiona had been so interested in the park the other day. She knew Underberg had some kind of treasure, but without the last page of the diary, she had no idea about the riddle, and no clue that Solar Park was only the beginning of the trail. "So if the park is the starting point for the map, we have to . . . uh, find X." I looked at Savannah helplessly.

She was entering numbers into the calculator app on Howard's computer. "If the sun is fifty meters across, then the relative distance to Pluto is . . ." She punched a button. ". . . about two hundred and twelve kilometers."

"No 'abouts,'" said Howard. "We need the exact number, because Pluto's going to be very small."

"How small? What size is Pluto really?" Savannah asked.

"Two thousand, three hundred and sixty kilometers in diameter." This time, when Howard rattled off the exact number from memory, Savannah didn't so much as smirk. She was already deep into her calculations, punching in numbers.

"Eight point four-eight centimeters," she announced. "So about three inches."

"Like an orange," Eric pointed out.

"Or a doorknob," said Howard.

"Or a soda can," Eric said.

"Or a fist." Howard was really getting into it now.

I closed my hand into a fist. All the hair on my arms stood on end and I swallowed. "Or . . . a battery."

"What?" asked Savannah.

I flipped to another page in Dad's book. "The prototype for the Underberg battery," I explained, pointing at the diagram in Dad's book. "It was supposed to be small enough to hold in your hand."

Howard frowned. "You think the treasure is a battery?"

"Not just any battery," I said. "A hundred-year battery. It was going to revolutionize the world, end the energy crisis. It was going to change everything!"

"Then why didn't it?"

I remembered what Dad had said the other day. "Because there were people out there who had a lot of power and money because the world didn't have a battery like that. And they made Dr. Underberg and his battery disappear."

"*They* again?" Savannah asked.

Howard thought about this for a minute. "That seems stupid."

"It's because it is," Eric said. "There's no proof that battery ever worked, but Dr. Underberg kept trying until they fired him."

I whirled to face him. "Since when do you know so much about it?"

"I live in our house, too." He shrugged. "I know what's in Dad's book. I just came to a different conclusion than you guys did."

I'd show him. I'd show them all. If we found the

battery, it would be a hundred times better than a statement from the diner owner. We could prove the battery worked, that Dr. Underberg wasn't a crackpot, and that all Dad's theories were right.

"Dad's book never mentioned anything about this riddle," I said. "Do you think he just thought it was scrap paper, with all the random numbers?"

Eric considered this. "I'm sure if Dad thought this had any potential, he'd be tracking it down—and dragging us along. Should we ask him?"

"No way!" I shook my head. "If he finds out Fiona's been snooping, he'll go into security mode. And even worse, if he decides to trust her and tells her what we've discovered, she'll—"

"Be gone for good?" Eric suggested. "That is what you want, isn't it?"

I looked away. That was one goal, at least. But it also meant Fiona would get to . . . whatever it was first. I was pretty sure she had no intention of sharing the treasure if she found it. After all, she'd already stolen from Dad.

Eric sighed, letting his head fall back in frustration. "Oh no. You think there's *really* something to find there. Something that will maybe prove Dad was right?"

"And you don't?" I asked.

Eric gave me a pitying look. It's weird the way he looked so much like Mom sometimes. "Gills . . . even if you're right about Fiona—and I kind of believe you are—even if she is only dating Dad because she wants this piece of paper . . . that doesn't change anything. All it means is that Fiona is as gullible as Dad is. It doesn't make Dr. Underberg any less crazy, and it doesn't make Dad any . . ."

He trailed off, but I knew where he was going. It didn't make Dad any less wrong.

The morning Mom walked off our campsite, we heard our parents arguing. "I refuse to sacrifice my career on the altar of your paranoia," she'd told him. Mom left Dad because she didn't believe him. But Eric and I were still here. Mainstream phase or not, my brother hadn't given up on Dad entirely.

My throat felt too full of words to speak.

"Think about it," Eric said. "If Dad thought there was anything worthwhile on this page, it wouldn't have been filed away with a bunch of scraps. It's just Dr. Underberg being delusional. Come on. Even Dad thought this was nothing."

Even Dad.

But Fiona didn't seem to think so. She wanted this piece of paper for some reason. Maybe it did lead to the battery. Maybe it was a wild goose chase. The only thing I knew for sure was that Fiona didn't have the map.

We did.

FAKE SCHOOL PROJECTS

HOWARD WENT TO THE DOOR OF THE BEDROOM. "NATE!" HE CALLED.

Savannah mouthed *Nate* at me.

"Can I borrow your GPS?" He turned back to us. "My dad and brother have one for hunting trips."

Private Pizza—Nate—appeared at the door with a device that looked like a large cell phone in his hand. "What are you guys doing?"

"School project," Eric said.

"A mapping project," I clarified. "We, uh, need the GPS to get exact measurements."

Nate leaned against the doorjamb and looked at each of us in turn. "What are you guys mapping?"

"Pollution," I said, at the exact same time as Eric said, "Bird migration."

Nate snorted.

"We're making a scale model of the solar system based on a fifty-meter-diameter park in Reistertown," Howard said.

"Oh," said Nate, as if it suddenly all made sense. "That's cool, bro."

Howard turned to Savannah. "You have that exact number?"

"What number?" Savannah smoothed her hair down and giggled in Nate's general direction.

Howard groaned, then shoved past her to his computer. "I need the exact relative distance from the sun to Pluto—" While he furiously pressed the keys, Savannah pushed away from the desk.

"Geez, chill out. It's just a calculator."

I shook my head at her. Seconds ago, she'd been the one doing all the math.

"So, Nate," she said with her most winning smile. "What grade are you in?"

"Eleventh," he stated flatly.

"Cool."

Nate said nothing. Eric shot me a look, which I ignored.

"Okay. 212,306.84 meters," Howard announced.

"That should be close enough to find the treasure. I'll just make a line from the center of that park . . ." He picked up the GPS and started punching in coordinates.

"What direction are you using?" Eric asked.

Howard paused and looked up. "Huh?"

"North, south, east . . ."

"Oh." Howard lowered the machine. So he hadn't thought of *absolutely* everything, even if he had the measurement down to the atom.

I read from the riddle. "'Follow the path I've laid for you, in the direction marked by the birth of ice.'"

"This doesn't sound like a school project," Nate observed.

Howard shut the door in his brother's face.

"That was rude!" cried Savannah.

"Shut up, Sav." I didn't have time for her crush right now. We were so close to solving this. "'The birth of ice.' That sounds cold, doesn't it? Maybe it's north."

"There's ice if you go far enough south, too," said Howard. "Like the South Pole."

"Duh," Savannah grumbled.

"Well, two hundred and twelve kilometers doesn't get us that far south," I said.

"212,306.84 meters," Howard said. "And it doesn't go north all the way to the arctic circle, either." He showed me the GPS. "Just most of the way through Pennsylvania."

"Please don't tell me we're going to draw a two-hundred-kilometer radius around the park and search the whole orbit of our imaginary Pluto," Eric begged.

"212,306.84 meters," Howard repeated. "But I agree, that would be ridiculous."

"Yeah," said Savannah. "*That's* the part of this that's ridiculous."

I sighed and looked down at the map. It was out there somewhere. All we had to do was figure out Underberg's code. *For those who trust me it shall not be difficult to reach safety, for you know my heart.*

No one knew Underberg like Dad did. No one trusted in the truth of his story more than us. Every other part of the riddle had to do with his biography: his twin, Pluto; Solar Park . . . If the truth was out there, there was no one on Earth better suited to finding it than my dad.

We just had to get to him before Fiona did.

WHEN SAVANNAH, ERIC, and I pulled our bikes up to the house that evening, we found Dad in the yard, airing out our pup tents.

"You going camping?" Savannah asked.

"Gills," Eric whispered, stricken. "Do something."

I wasn't sure exactly what he wanted me to do. If Dad had decided to take us all off grid, it wasn't like I could change his mind. Maybe he'd noticed that the strand of my hair I'd so carefully trimmed down to appropriate Dad length and placed back in the Underberg file wasn't his, despite them both being brown. Maybe Fiona had done something else we didn't know about.

On the other hand, Dad wouldn't be spreading out our brightly colored tents on the lawn where they could be seen by everyone from nosy neighbors to passing spy satellites if he was afraid *they* were watching. But then, what was he up to with this very public display?

I put the kickstand down and approached. "Hey, Dad," I said, taking care to keep my voice light. "Are we going camping?"

"Nah, just making sure everything's in working order before I store it for the season," he said. I looked at my brother, who had slumped against the porch railing in relief. "Hello, Savannah. Are you staying for dinner?"

Savannah looked scared. I didn't blame her. "No thanks, Dr. S."

"Gillian, honey, can you grab that corner over there and pull tight?"

As I knelt to help Dad check the seams on the tent, he called to Eric. "Son, can you check the batteries on the head lamps?"

"Sure thing!" Eric called, happy to help now that he was sure he wouldn't be dragged away from his precious video games. He started unloading the flashlights and head lamps from the box on the porch steps, clicking each on and off. Savannah sat on the porch and wrapped an arm around the railing, watching us. She jerked her head in Dad's direction. "Ask him about the ice thing," she hissed at me.

Fine. "It's too bad we all lost out on Dr. Underberg's batteries, huh, Dad?" I said, trying to keep my tone as casual as possible. "We'd never have to worry about replacing them."

"True," Dad said, working his way down the long side of the tent. "It's a sad statement, isn't it? How much humanity as a whole loses out when scientists and . . . other people are silenced by their enemies."

"That's so true, Dr. S," said Savannah. "Like when that scientist, um . . . got iced?"

Really, Sav? That's your best shot?

Dad gave her a quizzical look, then chuckled. "Iced? You watch too many cop shows, Savannah."

I sneaked another look at Eric, who was giving me a warning shake of his head. But I was well beyond warnings. I'd already messed with the security on Dad's filing cabinets, and recruited Savannah and Howard into this treasure hunt. If there was something to find out there, I needed a few hints.

"Is there anything else he invented?" I asked carefully. *The birth of ice, the birth of ice* . . . "Some kind of cool . . .

refrigerator? Or what is it called when you freeze people and then bring them back to life?"

"Cryogenic freezing?" Dad sat back on his heels, a wistful look on his face. "Who knows, sweetheart? Who knows what we lost when we lost him? Dr. Underberg was a brilliant man, dedicated to the betterment of the human race. He fought to end the nuclear arms race, to create clean, renewable energies, technologies that would help humans live with fewer resources or in places we never thought we could: deserts, under the sea, even in outer space . . ." He trailed off. "The possibilities are endless."

I slumped. And what were the possibilities regarding ice?

"But Underberg thought it was all just a dream. He was certain humanity would destroy itself before we ever had a chance to progress that far. You don't know what it was like, to live during the Cold War. I hope you guys never do. Every day people like Dr. Underberg were certain we were about to get bombed into extinction by the Russians, or vice versa. Even when I was younger, that possibility haunted us." He sighed. "Do you remember when we went to visit Underberg's Solar Park the other day?"

I perked up at the words. Out of the corner of my eye, I saw Eric and Savannah lean in, too.

"There was that plaque there, with his speech from the dedication. Let me see if I have this right," Dad said.

"Something about how *the human race holds the power to bring itself into the light or into the darkness.*"

"*To let the sun rise or set on the face of history,*" I continued. I'd seen that plaque a million times.

"That's the one." Dad moved down to the other end of the tent, and as soon as his back was turned, Eric lobbed the head lamp into my lap.

"Hey!" he whispered as I scurried up to meet him on the porch. "Isn't that what the riddle said? Something about the sun setting on the Earth?"

I nodded, surprised that he'd actually memorized it. What's more, he was out here, listening to me and Dad talk instead of rushing through his chores, then beelining for his video games. I couldn't remember the last time that had happened, but I certainly wasn't going to complain.

Whatever we were looking for, we had to be on the right track. The last line of Dr. Underberg's speech on the Solar Park plaque was about how his dream of a better future had become a reality. It sounded like he was talking about building a nice park for his hometown, but what if it was something more? What if he was talking about a battery that would help fix the environment and end wars over oil?

"Just don't let this one blow it with all her gangster talk." Eric gestured to Savannah. "*Iced?* Really?"

She glared at him. "You have a better idea?"

"How could anything possibly beat mobsters and cryogenics?"

I giggled and she turned to me. "Are you seriously taking his side?"

"He does have a point," I admitted. And I'd be more than happy to take his side now that he was finally taking mine.

"Gillian, we're following a treasure map written by a mad scientist to a model of Pluto. Nothing is off-limits."

"Okay. You have a point, too." I smiled at her, but she sniffed and looked away.

Eric rolled his eyes and began putting our camping supplies back in the crate, then suddenly froze. "Gills," he whispered. "It's degrees!"

"What?"

He was crouched on the porch, his old compass cradled in his hand. "Degrees! Like degrees of temperature. Ice freezes at thirty-two degrees."

The birth of ice . . . that made sense. "But how does that help?"

He showed me the face of the compass and pointed to a ring of tiny numbers marching around the outside. "Don't you see? Directions have degrees, too. We use them in sailing. Like zero degrees is due north and one hundred eighty degrees is south."

"So what is thirty-two?"

"Kinda north by northeast . . ."

"Wait," I said. "That's Fahrenheit. Wouldn't a scientist use Celsius or something? Zero is the freezing point of water in Celsius."

"So that would be north," Eric said. "By degrees." Which led us back into northern Pennsylvania.

Savannah mumbled something.

"What?" I asked.

"Oh, now you want my opinion?" she snapped. The light was failing but I could see well enough to catch the spark of anger in her eyes.

"Well, if you have actual information to give," Eric said.

"As a matter of fact, Eric, I do." She straightened. "The Kelvin scale—scientists usually use that. And the freezing point of water in Kelvin is 273.15 degrees."

"Hey, Dad? We'll be right back. Have to make a phone call." I raced up the steps and into the cottage, with Eric and Savannah right behind.

"Noland residence," said the pleasant-sounding woman who answered the phone.

"Hi, Mrs. Noland," I said. "Can I speak to Howard? This is Gillian Seagret. From school," I added.

"Howard?" Mrs. Noland said. "Really?" But she got him anyway.

"Am I on speakerphone?" he asked when he came on the line.

"Yes." I pressed the button.

"Who is there?"

"Me and Eric and Savannah," I replied.

"No one else?"

"No one else, Howard," Sav said, annoyed. "Just tell him."

"Do you have your GPS? Try plugging in the distance at the following angle . . ." I trailed off and looked at Eric for help.

"273.15 degrees," Eric said. "It should be slightly north of due west."

Howard was silent on the other end for a second. "That's the Deep Creek Lake area," he reported.

Eric and I stared at each other. He groaned, but a thrill shot through my body. Deep Creek Lake was where Dad had taken us when we went off grid. I bet it was because the area had something to do with Dr. Underberg.

"That's like an hour away," Eric said. "It's way too far for our bikes."

"We could tell Dad it was for a school project. The bird . . . pollution thing."

"I'll back you up, Gillian," said Savannah, her voice soft. "If we find something, fine. If not, we tried."

"It won't be easy," Howard said over the phone. "It'll be really small. Three inches."

"If it's even there anymore," Eric pointed out.

I looked at Eric, willing him to understand.

He took a deep breath. "I just don't want you thinking you can save the day. And I really don't want Dad to get all paranoid, which you know he'll do if he figures out why we're really out there."

"I'll ask my brother to drive us." Howard's voice broke in over the phone. "Tomorrow's Saturday."

Savannah gave a little hop and clapped her hands together. "Yes! That's an amazing idea! Thank you, Howard!"

"What are you going to tell him?" Eric asked. "I don't think he buys that we're doing a bird poop project."

"Oh, hush," said Savannah, smiling like it was her birthday. "We're in."

We made arrangements for Nate and Howard to pick us up in the morning, then went out to tell Dad about our new "school project."

"Deep Creek Lake, huh?" he asked, packing away the last of the camping gear. "What a coincidence. Fiona was talking about it today, too. That's actually what reminded me to check on our camping gear."

"Really," my brother said flatly.

"Yep," Dad said. "She's a pretty good researcher, for a beginner. She told me something even I didn't know—apparently, Dr. Underberg's father used to have a cabin out there."

"Really?" I said, my tone far more interested than Eric's. If Fiona was asking about the forest, maybe she knew another way to get to the treasure without the missing diary page. What if we'd gone through all of that trouble to calculate the location and it was really just an old family cabin? Worse, what if I dragged everyone out there and Fiona had already taken the battery?

"She said it's impossible to find, though."

That was a relief.

"The road doesn't even exist anymore."

Nonexistent road, check. Good thing we had the exact coordinates.

"Did she, um, have any idea how to find it?" Eric asked.

"No. Seemed pretty frustrated, too." Dad shrugged. "Maybe we'll go look for his cabin next summer."

Or maybe we'd find it a lot sooner than that.

THE MISSING MOON

WHEN NATE'S RED PICKUP PULLED IN TO OUR DRIVEWAY ON SATURDAY morning, the General Tso's Pizza sign was nowhere to be seen. I almost missed it. Savannah was already waiting with us on the porch, adjusting the zipper of her pink velour jacket and smoothing her hair. I think she'd even put on mascara. I was just wearing jeans and a long-sleeve top. Eric had found a bit of rope and was practicing his sailing knots, which was something I hadn't seen him do since Dad sold off his dinghy and made us live in a tent.

Savannah, Eric, and I approached the truck as Howard got out of the passenger side and pulled the seat forward so we could all climb in back. "I read the Underberg book last night," he said instead of greeting us. "All of it—even the parts that aren't about the space program."

"Yay?" I climbed in the backseat.

"You know, Howard," Savannah said sweetly, "if you want to talk to Gillian about the book, I'd be happy to sit shotgun and let you have my seat."

No! I mouthed at her. I could already imagine thirty miles of space talk.

"Forget it," said Nate. He was sitting up front, his hands draped casually over the steering wheel. "Howard sits up here. I need him to navigate."

Savannah pouted, then hopped on the bench next to me. Eric shook his head and climbed in last.

On the road, Savannah leaned forward between the two bucket seats and tried to talk to Nate, who mostly grunted one-word replies. Meanwhile, Howard peppered me with questions about Dr. Underberg, and what, precisely, we were looking for.

"But the author of the book"—no matter how many times I reminded Howard that the author was my dad, it didn't seem to sink in—"didn't discover why the government buried all the information about Underberg and his battery. The story has no ending."

"That stuff is classified," I said.

"You can still make an educated guess."

I wasn't so sure about that. Everything Dad wrote was

fact, and he'd still gotten in plenty of trouble.

Eric stared out the window as the fields flashed by. "Great. So the publisher didn't pull Dad's book because of a conspiracy. It was just that it sucked."

"Did not!" I snapped.

"It doesn't make sense," Howard said. "If the battery was going to save all this energy and money and help the environment and everything else, why didn't the government get behind it?"

"Dad says people in power sometimes work against the public's best interests," I said.

"That doesn't make sense," Howard insisted.

"But that's how it works anyway," Nate broke in. "In history class we learned how Henry Ford and other car manufacturers convinced President Eisenhower back in the fifties that highways were the best way to escape a nuclear attack."

"Probably better than hiding under your desk," said Eric.

Nuclear attack again? Was every decision made by the government in the twentieth century because people were afraid of getting nuked? I looked out at the pale blue sky. I couldn't imagine living under such a shadow.

"Whether it actually would work is beside the point," said Nate. "It got the government to build highways instead of public transportation systems. Trains and subways might save energy and money, just like that battery, but it didn't help Ford sell cars."

"So whoever buried the Underberg battery had something they wanted the government to use instead," I said.

"It still doesn't make sense," Howard said. "And it isn't about space, either."

I bit my tongue. Why did everything have to be about space with him? I know he'd helped us, and that he was the reason we even had a ride today, but, honestly, a little bit of Howard went a long way.

"I mean, that puzzle you found was clearly astronomical, but Underberg wasn't an astronomer. He did do some rocket science, but he mainly worked on life support for the astronauts. Not just suits, but everything that had to do with living in space, eating, breathing—"

"Pooping," Nate volunteered. Savannah sat back in her seat, wrinkling her nose. I snickered. Oh no, her idol said the P-word.

"And the military," Eric added. The submarine research had always been my brother's favorite part. "He built things for guys living in subs at the bottom of the Pacific for months and months."

"All kinds of survival stuff. Astronauts, submarine stuff, nuclear war preparations . . ."

"So why did he stop?" Nate asked. "Did they find out he was a Russian spy or something?"

"No!" I practically shouted. "Underberg hated the Russians. He thought they were going to destroy the world with nuclear bombs. You know, if the USA didn't do it first."

"Sounds like a good cover story to me." Nate pulled off the road and into a service station. "I need to fill up. You each owe me two bucks for gas, by the way."

I got out of the truck on the driver's side to give Nate six dollars. Since this whole trip had been my idea, the least I could do was pay Savannah's and my brother's way.

"You're the ringleader of this operation, huh?" he asked as I handed over the money. "Why don't you tell me what this is really all about?"

"What did Howard say?"

"Nice try. He said you were trying to find a scale model of the solar system built by a crazy Cold War scientist." Nate rolled his shoulders. "Howard doesn't lie—not to me. But though my brother might do that kind of thing for fun on Saturdays, I don't know what the rest of you are doing out here. It's not a school project. That much I know for sure."

I looked away. Off in the distance, a dark SUV was coming down the road, kicking up dust across the asphalt.

"Hey." Nate waved a hand in front of me. "My brother—he doesn't have the easiest time of it at school. And if you three are messing with him—"

He might have said something else. I'm not sure. Because that SUV pulled in to the parking lot, and sitting in the front seat was none other than Fiona Smythe.

I SCRAMBLED BACK into the cab of the truck before she could see me. "Eric! Head down!"

Eric, with all the training of a sailor who knows to duck when a boom comes flying at him, flattened against the seat.

"It's Fiona," I whispered. "She just pulled up."

Savannah leaned over me to see out the window. "Oh, she's even prettier than you said. Except I don't know about her fashion sense. What's up with the black jumpsuit? And who are the two guys in the car with her?"

Nate stuck his head back inside. "So, you were telling me how this is totally a school project and you aren't about to get my brother into trouble . . . ?"

"Fine." I slid even farther down in the seat. "The woman in that SUV is my dad's girlfriend, and we're pretty sure she's been stealing stuff from him, and that crazy Cold War scientist we were talking about? She's on a hunt to find the lost prototype of his hundred-year battery and we want to get there first."

Nate blinked at me. "See? The truth wasn't so hard." Then he shut the door again.

"Sav," I hissed. "What's happening?"

"She's getting out of the car and coming over," Savannah said.

Oh, no. She'd seen us. She'd seen us and she knew.

A second later, I heard Fiona's smarmy voice floating above us. "Excuse me, young man? Can you help us? We seem to be a little lost."

"Sorry, ma'am," Nate replied. "I'm not from around here."

"Have you heard of Charon Way? It's the street I'm looking for, and I don't see it listed on the map."

"Nope," Nate said. I peeked over the side of the window. Fiona was indeed wearing some kind of weird military-style black outfit, with a utility belt and everything. The two men with her were dressed similarly, and their vehicle was crammed full of boxes, wires, and ropes.

Howard was mumbling something under his breath.

"What?" I whispered to him, ducking back down.

"Charon," he repeated. "It's the name of Pluto's largest moon."

"Really?" I asked. That couldn't be a coincidence. Maybe that was the road that Fiona had been asking Dad about. We were so close. I couldn't let Fiona find that battery first. I strained to hear if Fiona and Nate were saying anything else.

"Though, really, they're more like binary dwarf planets because—"

We were saved from hearing the *because* as Nate got back in the car. "All right, Howard," he said. "I'm going to drive now, and you're going to tell me where, and blondie here is going to make sure the SUV doesn't follow us, and the other two are going to keep their heads down and explain to me exactly what is going on. Got it?"

"Yes," we all said, though with varying levels of enthusiasm.

Savannah leaned over me and squeaked in excitement. "He likes my hair."

"He *described* your hair," Eric corrected.

"Shut up, you two," I snapped at them. "Nate, what else did she say?"

"That she was looking for a road that didn't seem to exist."

So I'd been right. Charon Way was the road near Underberg's old cabin. Fiona was closer on our heels than I'd have liked. Still, she didn't have a precise location and we did. All we had to do was follow the directions on Howard's device and we could find it, road or no road.

Eric gave Nate the short—and extremely skeptical version—of my theory about Fiona and her activities. "So then we went and looked up the torn-off page and we found that riddle, and we gave it to Howard—"

"Howard," I said. "Which way to get to the location you marked?"

"It's south of here," he said, pointing to the left. "There doesn't seem to be a direct road. Must be in the woods somewhere."

Perfect.

Once we were sure we'd left Fiona and her companions behind, Eric and I sat up again.

I looked out the window at the trees flying past, just a short field of grass away. In there, somewhere, was Dr. Underberg's secret. His "last and lasting gift to mankind." I *had* to find it before Fiona did. If she got her hands on that prototype, I knew she'd never show Dad. His last chance at proof would be gone. My eyes roamed over the grass and brush streaming by, when I saw something that didn't belong.

"Nate!" I cried. "Stop!"

He pulled over and I tumbled out of the car almost before it came to a halt. There, sticking up from the weeds around the soft gravel shoulder, was a broken wooden pole. I spread the stalks of grass around the base, kicking until my foot hit something hard.

There. I pulled the object up. It was an old rusty road sign. The only letters I could make out were *HARO AY.*

CHARON WAY.

THE BATTLE OF THE BOULDER

"CHARON WAY," HOWARD FILLED IN BEHIND ME.

"Yeah, that part I figured out all on my own." Howard wasn't the only one around here who could work out riddles.

Eric was kicking at the dirt on the shoulder. "And here's the missing road." He pointed into the field. "Look, you can see where it used to go."

"So right down there"—I pointed—"is where the old Underberg family cabin is. Or was. Or something."

Nate was still behind the wheel of his truck, watching us from the window with wary eyes. "Okay, kids, this just went from interesting weekend science project to interesting start of a horror movie. Back in the car."

"No way!" I cried. Not when we were so close. The grown-over road beckoned.

"Yes way," said Nate, in the tone you hear from babysitters and summer-camp counselors. The one that says *I'm totally your friend, except when I'm handing down the discipline.* "Finding a model solar system is boring but harmless. Getting chased by people wearing jumpsuits and driving unmarked black SUVs down a nonexistent road to an abandoned cabin is—well, maybe exciting, but definitely not harmless. I'm not putting any of you in danger."

"Nate," Howard protested, turning to his brother. "You *promised.*"

Nate's expression was unreadable, but he stared at his brother for a full two seconds. Howard, surprisingly, stared back.

Right away, Nate's expression softened. "Okay. But you guys have to swear that you'll do exactly as I say."

We all nodded.

"And that the second I say we're going home, we go home."

We all nodded again.

He sighed. "I'm going to regret this. I knew as soon as you two girls showed up at the door I was going to regret this. Get in."

We got in, and Nate backed up and turned down the overgrown road, driving slowly as we rumbled over the thick grass.

"If I hit anything, you all owe me big time."

"Stop here." Howard tapped the GPS. "We're less than a kilometer from the location. It's right in the woods."

As we got out of Nate's truck, I looked back at the road. Were we far enough in to conceal the truck from Fiona and her friends if they drove by? I hoped so.

We picked our way through the tall grass of the field toward the trees. There were signs posted there showing the boundary of the state forest and telling us that hunting and fishing were not allowed. We kept going, silent except for Howard's regular updates on how close we were to the target.

"Ah, this brings me back," Eric said. "Dust? Check. Boredom? Double check."

"Yeah," I replied, "but last summer, we were just wandering around this park. This time we're going somewhere."

"Somewhere," Eric echoed skeptically. "Everywhere is *somewhere*."

"You're such a party pooper," Savannah said to him.

"Two hundred meters," Howard intoned, eyes glued to the screen. My heart was racing, even though we were walking at a nice, steady pace. We trailed after him, over roots and fallen logs and ditches and hills. "One hundred and fifty. Keep your eyes peeled. Remember, we're looking for something really small, like a tennis ball."

"How about a squirrel?" Eric suggested. "That's the right size."

It wasn't a squirrel. It was the battery. I just knew it.

I surveyed the forest. There was no road—abandoned or otherwise—back here, and no sign of a cabin, even as Howard announced we were one hundred meters away from our destination. Only a football field's distance. We should be able to see some sign of a cabin now, right?

"Twenty," said Howard. "Fifteen. Ten."

Ahead of us, a massive boulder rose out of the earth. We'd passed several others on our path, but this one was by far the biggest—almost the size of a tool shed. Howard walked right up to it, pressing the GPS into the stone. "That's odd."

Savannah snickered. "Walking into a giant rock?"

"The location is a half meter in," he said, tapping the stone. "In there."

"Maybe the boulder *is* the treasure," Eric said.

"No," said Howard. "It's supposed to be as small as a tennis ball, remember?"

Or a battery.

But my brother didn't buy it. "Maybe it's a space rock. From Pluto."

Howard shook his head. "A meteorite would have left a crater, and probably blown all these trees outward around the impact site, like in Tunguska."

"The Tunguska Event," I corrected, "was *not* a meteor impact site. There was no debris or crater, and witnesses say the sky glowed for days after—"

"Are you kidding me?" Howard said. "*Another* conspiracy theory? I can't wait to hear what you think Tunguska was."

I shrugged. "Lots of possibilities. Hydrogen explosion, electricity experiments, extraterrestrials . . ."

"Aliens?" Howard blurted. "That's nuts. And inaccurate. Soil samples taken from the impact site showed large amounts of iridium, which is consistent with—"

"Guys," Eric broke in. "I was joking. It's not a space rock. It's a wild goose chase."

I looked at the boulder with dismay. We couldn't dig under there. And there was no sign of a cabin, abandoned or otherwise. Maybe we were wrong about the riddle. Or the math. Maybe Fiona had a better idea of where the treasure was, or *what* the treasure was. . . .

Or maybe it was all a joke, just like Eric thought.

Savannah had been pretty quiet this whole time, not even trying to flirt with Nate. Now she laid her hand on my shoulder. "Don't give up, Gillian. Let's look on the other side. Maybe he was off by a few feet, or there's a clue carved into the stone or something."

"Oh, goody," Eric said, in a tone that meant the opposite. "Another clue."

"That's a great idea!" I said, brightening. We started around the side of the boulder, and I brushed away leaves and dirt as I went, looking to see if there were any markings cut into the stone.

On the opposite side of the rock, there was a massive, perfectly straight crack, running from the ground to a few feet above my head. "That's weird." I ran my fingers along the crack, but couldn't feel anything else.

Eric scrambled up the side of the boulder, wedging his fingers and toes into cracks and divots as he went. "The crack makes a right turn up here," he said. "A perfect ninety-degree angle."

Even weirder. I raised up on my toes, hopping in excitement as I watched my brother brush debris from the line of the impossibly perfect crack. Could this be another clue? I should have brought the Underberg book. What if this rock just led to another riddle, the way the granite block in Solar Park did?

Nate hurried around to our side of the boulder, his eyes wide. "Okay, time to go."

"Already?" I said. "What, you saw some dangerous-looking squirrels?"

"No," he replied. "The chick from the gas station and her friends. They're just over the rise."

I caught my breath. Fiona. Were they following us? Or following steps of their own? And if so, what else did they know that we didn't?

"Hey, Gills," Eric called down.

"Shh!"

He slid down the side and landed lightly on his feet on the dirt. "Sorry. I just thought you'd like to know that your space rock?" He swept away a curtain of moss. "It's a door."

Eric was right. There, clear as day, was a rectangular outline formed by the cracks in the stone. I reached up with trembling fingers to trace the outline, while Eric started feeling around inside the crack on the right side. He tugged and tugged, and, impossibly, the rock shifted. The crack widened, revealing a dark hollow that smelled of rot and glowed with dim red light.

My breath caught in my throat. I had no explanation for this. I'd been looking for a cabin. A battery in a box or on a shelf. But this . . .

"It looks like the gates of hell," Eric said softly.

"Fitting," said Howard. "Pluto was the god of the underworld in mythology."

"You swore," Nate reminded me under his breath. "You swore when I said to go, you'd go."

I stared at the entrance, afraid to blink, as if it would suddenly vanish. This was real. There *was* a treasure. It was right in there.

We should have brought Dad. Dad would know what to do. But there must have been some small part of me afraid this was just one more wild goose chase. I hadn't wanted to see that look of disappointment on his face if there'd been nothing there, like Eric had thought.

But now? Now, I'd give anything to see him tell us what in the world we'd just found.

"Another fifty meters," said a strange voice, not nearly far enough away to suit me.

Nate cursed.

"Should we run?" Savannah whispered, her eyes wide.

"Too late," Nate said under his breath.

"Hello?" came the voice again. Deep. Rough. Close. On-the-other-side-of-the-rock close.

We all froze.

"Is anyone there?"

Nobody on our side of the rock said anything, moved anything, maybe even *thought* anything, just in case.

On the other side, I heard footsteps and then a harsh, feminine whisper. Fiona. "Get out your gun."

I swear my heart stopped, and I don't care what Howard might say about it being scientifically impossible.

Gun. The word was a drumbeat in my head. *Gun.* Nate

was right. We should have left.

Somehow, I heard Nate hiss, "Inside," and then he was shoving us all into the darkness.

"No—" Sav protested as we jostled and squeezed our way in. All our efforts at silence had ceased, but the only sounds I heard were the shouts from the other side and the horrible grinding as Nate and Eric threw themselves against the stone door, trying to shut it and keep Fiona and her friends out. I saw a glimpse of Fiona's face glaring at me, then a flutter of hands in the crack of light.

Fiona cried out, "It's his kids. They found it—" and then a massive clang as Eric threw down some sort of metal bar across the door, shutting us inside.

Wait. There was a metal bar? *Inside* the boulder?

"They have a gun. They have a gun." Savannah was hyperventilating beside me.

I blinked, trying to adjust my eyes to the red glow. The inside of the rock was hollow, a sort of metal cage with the form of the boulder arcing just beyond. Tiny red pinpricks of light glowed from every crossbar of metal. There was nothing else inside. No box. No shelf. No battery.

"What is this place?" Nate asked.

"Oh my God, oh my God," Savannah blubbered.

"This can't be it," Howard was saying, still clutching tightly to the GPS. "It was supposed to be small, the size of a tennis ball."

"It's pretty small," Eric pointed out. We were all pressed together inside the space, clinging to the center as if afraid the metal box around us might electrocute us.

Outside, there was a commotion.

"What do you mean you can't get the door open again?" Fiona was shouting, her voice shrill. "I'm so close. I will not have the Seagrets get there first."

Get *where*? The boulder? I had half a mind to let her know that there was no treasure inside this rock. The other half, of course, wanted to shout out to her that I knew she'd been messing with my dad all along, so there!

But as for treasure, there was . . . um. Metal. A boxy metal cage with red lights. I looked around, following the grid of red lights that outlined our new space. What little illumination came from the red lights showed my friends' frightened faces and the rough, hollowed-out rock wall beyond the cage. Nothing remotely interesting, except . . .

There, opposite the door, embedded in the grid at about waist level, was one big red light, several inches across. A button. And Howard was staring right at it.

"The size of a tennis ball . . . ," he murmured, reaching out.

"Howard," Nate warned. "Don't touch anything."

Howard pressed the button, which promptly blinked off. There was the sound of whirring, of engines coming to life, as one by one, the lights went off all around us, then blinked back on a sickly greenish white. Everything shuddered, and a clanking groan filled the space as sheets of metal rose from the floor beyond the metal cage to enclose us and block out the outline of the boulder. I felt my stomach push up against my chest.

We were going down.

THE WORLD BELOW

I CAN'T TELL YOU WHO STARTED SCREAMING FIRST. TRUTHFULLY, IT might have been me.

But after a few seconds of shrieking ourselves hoarse, we sort of tapered off. After all, it wasn't a roller coaster, dropping us down into nothingness. More like . . . an elevator, clanking us down in slow, steady fashion. And who screams in an elevator?

This one apparently came complete with elevator music. A tinny, tinkling melody started playing, and we all quit shouting "Help!" and "Stop!" And "Howard! What did you do?"—that one was Nate and Savannah combined—to listen.

We were only a few stories down when the music was replaced by words.

"*Greetings, survivors!*" said a cheery man's voice.

Survivors? It was tough to see my friends' faces in the pale running lights. But since we'd all gone from screaming our heads off to shocked silence, I imagined they were making the same face I could feel I was. Eyes wide, mouth wider.

The voice went on, as calm and carefree as ever:

> **Congratulations on escaping the attack, plague, or natural disaster that has brought you here. Our condolences on the family members and/or appendages you may have lost during the end of the world.**

"The end of the world?" Savannah choked out.

"Appendages?" bleated Eric.

> **Rest assured, you have reached safety.**
>
> **We would like to take this opportunity to remind you that pets, plague-infected persons, enemy combatants, and firearms are not permitted entrance. Please terminate or discard these items before your descent.**

The music started up again, no doubt meant to accompany our efforts to do whatever it might take to . . . discard our pets or plague-infected loved ones. Down and down we went, as the music looped through the speakers and echoed up into the endless tunnel that we could still make out beyond the metal grid at the top of the elevator. We all stared up into the shaft as it receded into shadow and we descended deeper into the Earth.

"What's happening?" Sav asked. "Where are we?"

We all looked at Howard, but he was staring through the grate above our heads as if it would provide some sort of answer.

"Gillian?" Eric prompted.

I shook my head. This wasn't in Dad's book. I don't think this was even in Dad's *world*.

Finally, with another enormous grinding of gears and screaming metal, the elevator touched the ground. The music morphed into a brassy little fanfare, like we were about to meet a king, and the disembodied voice said:

Welcome . . . to Omega City.

"Oh," said Savannah, Eric, Howard, and I in unison. "*Omega.*"

Wait . . . Omega *City*?

"This means something to you?" Nate asked. But no one answered, because just then, the doors slid open.

Howard was the first to peek out. "There's nothing here," he said flatly.

I pushed past him and out the door. "That's impossible." And I wasn't about to trust anything Howard said after his little button-pressing escapade.

We were standing on an odd sort of platform, an artificial cement island in the middle of a vast underground lake, like a giant dock. About ten yards in front of us I saw black waves lapping the side of the platform, and distant drips and splashes resounded through the chamber. If there was an opposite shore, I had no idea how far away it was. To our left and right on the platform were several other cylindrical elevator shafts, just like the one that had taken us down. They all wound upward and disappeared into the inky blackness high above. The ceiling—if that's what it was—appeared so far away that I couldn't see it at all. In fact, all I could see were tiny twinkling lights, like stars, far, far away.

A wave of dizziness washed over me, like the whole thing was about to tip over and spill us into the black hole over our heads.

"What," Nate said, though it sounded more like a gasp, "is this place?"

"It's Omega City." I tried to calm my nerves. The others had joined me on the platform. I put my hands out to the side for balance.

"Yeah," Eric said softly. "Didn't you hear the guy on the elevator?"

I was racking my brain, but I knew Dad had never mentioned Omega City before. Whatever this place was, no one knew about it. No one but Dr. Underberg, Fiona . . . and us.

But what kind of city was underground, in the middle of nowhere? And why didn't this place look like a city at all?

Greetings, survivors.

We all stopped moving as that weird voice echoed through the cavern. Floodlights blinked on, lighting the ground around us in a circle of bright white light.

You have arrived at the Omega City Welcome Center. Please prepare for your decontamination showers. This step is a prerequisite for entrance into the city. It will rid your person of any chemical contaminants, diseased cells, or radioactive dust you may have acquired on the ruined surface of the Earth.

"I don't like the sound of that," said Eric.

At the count of five, your shower will commence. For your safety, please remove all electronics, infants, and corrective contact lenses.

Five.

Four.

"Where is this shower?" Savannah asked frantically.

I looked around. I didn't see anything that looked like a shower head.

Three.

Two.

Just then, a panel opened at the base of our elevator shaft and what looked like a small cannon emerged.

One.

Begin decontamination showers.

A blast of heat and water and blinding light hit me all at once. Howard was knocked off his feet by the wave, and his GPS went clattering out of his hands and over the side into the black water. Savannah and Eric tried darting to the side, but the cannon just followed their movements. I couldn't even see Nate. I fell to my knees and cowered as steamy water pummeled my skin. It was like standing in front of a heated fire hydrant. Pulses of light rained down from above—white, red, yellow, white, red, yellow.

"Make it stop!"

After a few moments, it was over, and we crouched there, dripping wet and blinking at one another. My skin tingled and steam rose from my hair and clothes and everything smelled like industrial-strength cleaner. I'd never felt cleaner, or more gross.

"Everyone okay?" Nate asked. Savannah and I nodded as he and Eric helped Howard to his feet.

"The GPS!" Howard cried. "Oh, Nate, Dad's going to kill me."

"No," said Nate. "He's going to kill *me*. I managed to get myself and four twelve-year-olds buried alive." He started squeezing water out of his shirt.

"To be fair," I said, "your brother is the one who pushed the button."

Nate glared at me. "And who dragged us out here in the first place?"

I looked away.

"Okay, that's it," Nate said. "We're getting out of here before that thing decides we're ready for our delousing."

"What," asked Eric, "is *delousing*?"

"You don't want to know," said Nate, and turned back toward the elevator.

Savannah was holding her sopping pink hoodie away

from her body, but she scurried after Nate. "Come on, Gillian. We found . . . well, whatever it was Underberg was talking about in his diary. Now let's go home."

"How?" Eric asked. "Aren't Fiona and those guys just waiting up there for us?"

Nate looked at the endless elevator shaft. "Okay. We'll take one of the other ones. There have to be a good half dozen, see?" He started striding toward the next one, across the damp cement floor, with Savannah hot on his heels. Eric shrugged and jogged a few steps to catch up. The floodlights, I noticed, followed their every move. Just as the cannon had.

"Um . . . guys?" I said, my eyes on the lights. Why were they watching us?

And who were *they*?

Despite my recent steam bath, a full-body shiver started in my toes and went all the way to the tip of my ponytail.

"Howard," Nate barked, marching along. "Let's go."

Howard was standing where they'd left him, on the very edge of the platform, where the floodlights didn't reach. "The lights in the ceiling," he said softly, almost to himself, "are constellations. It's like a planetarium."

"Isn't that nice," his brother said. "Now it's time for you to keep *your* promise. I said we're done here. We're going home."

Eric turned and looked at me, and I saw the same sentiment echoed in his eyes. "You made your point, Gillian. There's something here, okay? Now let's go and tell Dad about it."

Something, sure, but . . . *Omega City*? This was light years away from a prototype on a dusty old shelf. I turned around, looking from platform to elevator shafts to dark lake. It was too much to take in. I should have brought a camera. But I wasn't even sure I could photograph what I was seeing, let alone try to explain it to Dad.

And the elevator message—*Greetings, survivors*—and all that other stuff about plagues and attacks. We were back in Cold War, they're-going-to-nuke-us-all territory. Was this the treasure the riddle was leading us to? It sure didn't look like a city. Underberg's last gift to mankind—was it a bunker of some sort? A refuge from the nuclear disaster he'd been so certain was going to befall humanity?

And if so, maybe he could have thought about putting a few cots in for sleeping? Or how about a couple of shelves for canned food? I hugged myself and toed the cement floor. Decontamination showers but no towels? Lights but no people?

Or at least, no people we could see.

I squeezed the water from my ponytail and hurried after the others. The first few shafts Nate approached were empty of elevators, and there was no call button or anything to get them down there. But on the far side of the platform, next to the wall of the cave, he found another type of elevator. Unlike the one that had brought us down, this elevator wasn't connected to a solid tubelike shaft. Instead, the elevator itself was a solid metal box affixed to a rail along the rock wall. I paused at the entrance.

"We have no idea where this goes," I said, pointing up at where the metal rail and its accompanying service ladder vanished into the gloom.

"It goes," Nate stated as he ushered the others inside, "to the *surface of the Earth*. After that, I don't care. Now get in."

I got in, and saw the others frowning at what looked like a control panel.

"It's in gibberish," said Savannah.

"Russian," Howard corrected. "They use the Cyrillic alphabet—"

"How do you know that?" Eric asked. "Wait, don't tell me. You read cosmonaut textbooks."

"That's a great idea. But, no, I just see a lot of Russian writing in space books in English. I'm working on my Mandarin, too, since the Chinese space program . . ."

Oh, no. Here we go again. Why did everything have to be a five-part essay with him? The one good thing about getting back to the surface was that we wouldn't have to deal with his weirdness anymore.

"Can you read the instructions, Howard?" Nate broke in, frustrated. I was relieved I didn't have to be the one to say it.

"Maybe." Howard stared down at the funny letters. "This one says *close,* and this one says *up.*"

Why was there a Russian elevator in Dr. Underberg's survival bunker? He was a Cold War scientist. He hated the Russians and thought they were going to start the war that would destroy the world. There was no reason he'd put any Russian technology here, unless . . .

"Wait," I said, and my hand shot out to stop Howard.

But it was too late. He pressed the buttons anyway. *Again.* Sure enough, the doors closed and the elevator started lifting.

"Phew," said Nate, slumping against the wall.

I wasn't relieved. I was furious. "Why did you do that?"

"To make us go up," Howard said matter of factly.

"Dr. Underberg wouldn't want to help any Russians who made it down here, not if he thought they were to blame for the bombs or the war or the plague or whatever." I wanted to shake some sense into Howard, but I settled for stomping my foot against the metal floor and giving him a death glare.

"Um, what are you saying?" asked Savannah, as the box lifted us higher and higher.

"Yeah, Gills," said Eric, sounding panicked. "What are you saying?"

"If Russian spies made it to this place, he'd never want them to be able to get back up and tell people what they'd found here," I argued as the elevator shot upward. "He'd try to kill them first."

Greetings, comrades.

"Oh," said Howard.

"No," added Eric.

Nate cursed, again.

THE IMPOSSIBLE COMET

THE MAN'S VOICE WAS NOT SO CHEERY THIS TIME. INSTEAD, IT WAS stern, scolding. Threatening.

> **Your infiltration of Omega City has been noted. Steps will be taken to neutralize any damage you may have done during your visit, and/or any attempts you may make to alert our enemies to our presence. At the count of five, a canister of nerve gas will be released into this chamber. You will all be dead in thirty seconds.**
>
> **If you have received this message in error,**

please press the cancellation key now.

"Cancellation key!" Nate shouted. "Find it." We all started frantically searching the control panel, as if the Cyrillic letters would suddenly make sense now that our lives were on the line.

Five.

"This one says *stop* in Russian," said Howard. "That's similar to cancel."

"Good enough!" cried Nate.

Four.

"No!" I screamed, yanking back his arm before Howard could push yet another button. "Just stop, Howard! Think! This is a trap built for Russians. Why would he make it something the Russians would do? That button will probably release the gas right away."

Three.

"What are our options, Gills?" Eric asked as both the Nolands glared at me. "English speakers trapped in this thing are just going to press random buttons. They have no idea what any of them say."

"We're going to die, we're going to die," breathed Savannah.

Two.

Random buttons. I stared at the panel. Exactly. I shoved Howard aside and slammed my whole arm against all the buttons, making sure to cover every one.

Ooooonnnn . . .

The voice trailed off. I waited for the hiss of nerve gas. Would we smell it before it killed us? Had I just sentenced all five of us to death in a metal box hundreds of feet below the earth?

Well, at least we didn't have to worry about burial.

Seconds passed. Ten, fifteen . . . all the way past thirty, while we all stood there, cringing.

"I think you stopped it, Gills," Eric said at last.

I did? That seemed . . . convenient. Maybe it was a slow-working nerve gas. Maybe we'd all drop dead in twenty minutes.

And if we didn't, could I still kill Howard for getting us all into this mess?

"I think she stopped everything," Nate said. "We aren't moving anymore." He pried open the elevator doors a crack and peeked out. "Yep. Dead stop."

"I can try to get it moving again," Howard suggested, turning back to the control panel.

"Don't touch anything!" I screamed at him. "You and your buttons! You sent us down here! You almost got us killed! Stop pressing buttons! What's wrong with you, you freak!"

Howard flinched as if I'd hit him, then backed as far into the corner of the elevator as the space allowed. Savannah and Eric were gaping at me. Nate was staring daggers.

I swallowed thickly. "Howard, I'm sorry—"

He said nothing. His brother just snorted at me. "Forget it. He's not going to say another word."

"Howard . . . ," I tried again. I felt like that decontamination shower must have washed away all my good sense. A few days ago, I thought Savannah had been out of line to call him a freak, and here I was doing the same exact thing.

Then again, here he'd almost gotten us all killed.

I closed my eyes. No. *I* was the one who'd almost gotten us all killed. I was the one who wanted to find Dr. Underberg's treasure. Howard may have pushed the button but before he did, we were just trapped inside a boulder, waiting for Fiona to catch us. If people were going to be mad at someone, it should be me.

Because I was following a crazy old man's directions into the center of the Earth. Who was the freak now?

"Gillian's right about one thing," said Savannah, breaking the silence. "We shouldn't touch anything else. There could be more traps."

"So what, you want to just sit here?" Nate asked. "Forever?"

Eric peeked out of the open door. "I think we can climb down. We're only about three stories up. There's a utility ladder on the side of the rail here."

I shuddered, and not just because I was still soaking wet. Climb three stories straight down to a cement platform? On a ladder? In the dark?

All at once, Howard pushed away from the wall and climbed out the door.

Nate reached for him but he jerked out of his brother's reach, stepped onto the ladder, and carefully started climbing down.

I bit my lip as Nate turned back to me. "You're next, boss lady," he said, clearly still angry.

I guess I deserved that. I couldn't blame Howard for getting us into this mess. After all, coming out here had been my idea.

The rungs of the ladder were sturdy and wide, and if you didn't look farther than the next step, you could almost pretend you weren't swinging over your death-by-cement-floor. Eric came down after me, then Savannah, and finally Nate. By the time we got to the bottom, we were all out of breath. Eric splayed out on the concrete floor in the glow of the floodlights, and the rest of us did the same. Howard kept a little way away from us, staring up at the fake starry sky.

"My cell phone's useless," Nate said at last. "Maybe it was the shower, maybe it's the fact that we're a mile underground." He groaned and rubbed the heels of his hands against his eyes. "I can't believe this."

Neither could I, but for a whole different reason. I looked up into the blackness. This was Dr. Underberg's—all of it. And Dad didn't know about it. No one did. Maybe no one had been here in decades. Maybe this—not the battery—was the reason the government turned on him. And sure, it was super creepy and obviously deadly and awfully cold. But Omega City was *his*—it was where all his inventions must be hidden. Waiting. I could feel it.

I felt a tug on my ponytail. "Hey." I turned my head to see Nate beside me. "Look," he said softly, his expression tired. "I need to talk to you." He drew me a few feet away and lowered his voice. "I know he's not the easiest person, but Howard . . . he doesn't handle stress like other people. He shuts down. And we can't afford that right now."

"That wasn't stress," I said. "That was a Cold War booby trap built for Soviet spies. And I handled it a lot worse than Howard."

Nate chuckled. "True. But on the other hand, you did save our lives."

I snorted and gestured to our surroundings. "Saved them for what?" Like he'd said, we were buried alive. Right now, our only option was to go back up to the boulder and confront Fiona.

And her guns.

"Is there anything I can do to make up with Howard?" I asked Nate. If anyone would know, it had to be his brother.

Nate cocked his head and looked at me, his hair falling down over his cheek and shading his brilliant green eyes, and I suddenly understood why Savannah got all weird whenever he brought us pizza.

"No one has ever asked me that before," he said. "I wish more people would. It's better when you figure out how he works."

"What do you mean?"

He shrugged a shoulder. "How his brain works. My father—he can't understand, because he can't make Howard care about what he thinks he should, but as soon as you try to see things from Howard's perspective, you see it's not worse or better, it's just . . . different."

"Space." I nodded. "He likes to talk about space."

"Yeah," said Nate with a weak smile. "You pretty much can't go wrong with space."

Space I could do. I stood up, hating the way my damp jeans felt sliding across my legs, and went over to Howard. Out of the corner of my eye, I saw Savannah and Eric at the edge of the water. Eric was nudging something with his foot.

"Hey, Howard," I said as I sat down next to him. He didn't move or acknowledge my arrival in any way. I stared up at the fake sky. "What constellations do you see?"

"Why does your brother call you Gills?"

I blinked. That was unexpected. But any words were good words, I guess. "Um, it's a nickname."

"No," he replied. "A nickname is like Nate for Nathaniel, or Howie." Howard frowned. "My dad likes to call me that."

"I'm sorry?" Okay, so he didn't *always* want to talk about space. "I'm also sorry for what I called you. I didn't mean it. I was just scared. And taking it out on you."

"Gills is not a nickname of Gillian," he said as if he hadn't heard. "It doesn't even make the same gee sound."

"That's actually how it started," I said. "Someone called me Gill-ee-an instead of Jill-ee-an, and Eric thought it was hilarious."

"Also," Howard continued, "it makes you sound like a fish."

I sneaked a glance at him. He was grinning.

"Are you making fun of me?" I asked.

He looked directly at me for possibly the first time ever. His eyes were green too, just like his brother's. "You deserve it." Then, just as quickly, he looked back up at the ceiling. "I wasn't looking at the constellations," he said. "I was looking at the comet."

"The comet?" I narrowed my eyes.

He pointed. "See? It's moving. Down."

I followed his finger and found a new light in the sky, brighter than the others, swinging a bit and definitely moving down the side of our elevator shaft. I stared in horrified fascination as it got closer and brighter.

"Howard," I whispered. "That's not a comet." It was a figure, all in black except for a head lamp, and it was rappelling down the side of the shaft.

"Kids!" said the comet. "I'm coming down to get you."

Savannah jumped to her feet. "Yay! We're saved!"

The floodlights veered in wild arcs and zeroed in on the figure.

Just then, I heard a massive whirring sound, and a few seconds later, a strong wind wafted over my face, lifting the ends of my still-damp hair. I looked at Howard, who raised his hands in defense.

"I didn't touch anything this time."

Far above us, the comet started careening around.

Whoever it was had clearly lost his footing on the elevator shaft, and was swinging from his rappelling rope.

"What did you do!" he cried. It was definitely a he.

"Clint!" Fiona's voice echoed down from the ceiling.

The wind had increased to a roar, blowing my hair around and plastering my wet clothes to my skin. I had no idea where it was coming from. Above us, Clint—or whoever he was—slammed back against the elevator shaft. He was close enough to see now, as he gripped the shaft and his safety line with his legs and one hand, while with the other he started fumbling with something strapped to his waist.

"Are you okay?" I screamed above the wind.

"Don't move," Clint cried, and pulled out his gun. "Or I'll shoot."

12

THE MIDNIGHT SEA

I IMMEDIATELY DUCKED, THOUGH THE SECOND I THOUGHT ABOUT IT, IT seemed pretty silly. If the guy threatening to shoot you is directly above you, you're the same size target standing up or crouching down.

Howard hadn't moved. "He must think we know nothing about guns," he said. "My dad hunts. There's no way he can hit us from that distance swinging around like that."

"You are *so* missing the point," I hissed at him. "There's a man with a gun who has just threatened to shoot us."

"And he's getting closer every minute," Savannah added. She'd put her hands over her head like a character in an Old West holdup.

"Look, man," Nate called up to Clint, his hands also in the air. "We're not trying to cause trouble here. We didn't mean to . . . trespass or whatever."

"This place isn't his," I said. "It's Dr. Underberg's."

Nate glared at me, then returned his attention to the weirdo in the sky. "So we'll all just go back up the way we came and I'll take the kids home, okay?"

Clint gestured with his gun. "Get in the elevator. We'll meet you up top."

"You heard the man," said Nate. He started herding us toward the elevator shaft. "Howard," he said to his brother, "I know you think now's the time to play elevator games. But don't talk about them."

"Okay. I won't." Howard nodded his head once and marched toward the elevator.

"Excuse me?" I crossed my arms. "The whole reason we're down here is because we were running away from them. You want us to surrender?"

"Gillian," Savannah said, her pitch getting higher and more frantic. "Come on. He's getting closer."

"Listen," said Nate. "This is pretty simple. They have guns and we're trapped underground. So go."

I started stomping toward the shaft. "Wait! Where's Er—"

Nate shoved me hard in the back. "Shut it."

I blinked up at him. What was going on?

We walked around the shaft to the back, where the door was. I couldn't see Clint dangling down from the sky anymore. I expected Nate to lead us back inside the elevator but instead he pressed us all up against the sides of the shaft. He looked at Howard and nodded. "Elevator games, bro."

Howard ducked his head in the door and pressed the button, then whipped out again before the doors shut. I heard the engines start to lift and understood. We were sending the elevator back to the surface . . . empty.

"Wait," Nate whispered over us. We were shoved together closer than we'd been even in the elevator. Savannah was panting short, scared little breaths, and I don't think it had anything to do with being in Nate's bear hug.

For a few moments, all I could hear was water lapping against the sides of the platform and the blood roaring in my ears as I peeked out from under Nate's arms in search of my little brother. Where was he, and what would Fiona do to him if she caught him?

Just then, his head popped up over the platform at the edge of the water. Was he swimming? No, he wasn't wet—just damp, like the rest of us. He grinned at me and beckoned. Had he found another way out?

I wrenched my neck looking up at Nate in confusion. He winked. I turned back to Eric. *Now,* he mouthed. Nate gave me a little shove.

Ducking under Nate's arms, I bolted blindly toward my brother and catapulted over the ledge, holding my breath like I was about to plunge into the lake. But instead I fell onto a soft, springy platform—a woven fabric float spread between two inflatable pontoons.

Leave it to my brother to find the only boat on an underground lake.

The catamaran was grimy and wet, but I was already a mess from the shower, so I didn't much care. Eric was still examining the skies, waiting to see if Clint was looking. He made another signal at Nate, who sent Howard over, then Savannah, and then sprinted and made the leap himself. One by one, they bounced onto the fabric, splashing dark water up over the pontoons.

"Any second now, they're going to realize we're not in that elevator," Howard mumbled. "And now they have an easy way to get down here."

Savannah hugged her knees and bit her lip.

"How did you do that?" I asked Nate.

"I told you. I know how to talk to Howard."

"I can't believe you didn't make us get on the elevator," I said.

"I want us out of here," Nate replied. "But I don't have a good feeling about people who've threatened to shoot us twice. When people have guns, you run in the other direction or you're meat. We have a half-dozen deer heads on the wall at home that can tell you that."

"Or would," Howard added, "if they weren't dead. And deer."

Either way, we were still here, which meant we still had a chance to find something that could help my dad.

"We have to find another way out," Eric said. He pointed to a big metal pole sticking out of the catamaran's frame. "The sail's folded up inside there. There wouldn't be a sailboat on this lake unless there was something to sail *to*, right?"

"Why would there be a *sailboat* on an underground lake?" Savannah asked.

The weird wind picked up again.

She swept her hair out of her face and smiled sheepishly. "Oh."

Eric quickly cranked out the sail, which, thank goodness, was black, like the pontoons, the float, and the lake itself. "Downwind's that way," he said, pointing out over the water. "I suggest we try it."

I've been on enough boats with my brother to know the drill. Do as he says with the ropes, stay out of the way of the jib. The little catamaran didn't seem built for five passengers, but Nate and Howard flattened themselves out on the float, I pushed us away from the platform, and soon enough, we picked up speed and left the cement island far behind. Even in the darkness, I could see the size of Eric's smile. I used to complain about all the time we'd spent at my little brother's regattas. Now I was grateful he knew what he was doing.

"I don't even see that guy anymore," Howard said, staring at the sky. "Do you think he went back up?"

"Yes. I'd rather go down in an elevator than on a rope," Savannah said. "Especially in this wind."

"Yeah," said Eric. "This underground wind." He gave me a look that was halfway between determined and bewildered, but I had no idea where the wind was coming from, either. Darkness fell all around us as we got farther from the lights on the platform. If there was a distant shore, I couldn't see it. I really hoped Eric wasn't sailing us into the center of the Earth.

I didn't know what to think. On one hand, why would someone put a sailboat here if no one was meant to sail? On the other, Underberg had an elevator filled with Cyrillic buttons meant to trap Russian spies. I tried to remember if he had anything against yachtsmen.

"That sound is getting louder," Nate said after another minute of sailing through blackness. It was. The whirring, which had been a low grumble on the platform, was now a pounding roar.

"And what's that glow?" Savannah added. I felt her arm move as if she was pointing ahead of us. Sure enough, a faint orange light, like the beginning of a sunrise on the horizon, was growing stronger along with the noise. It all seemed to be coming from ahead of us. When I looked back down at the others, I could even make out their features in the darkness.

"Um . . ." Eric frowned. "I think I may take the sails down. I don't know if I like where we're headed."

"Smart move," Nate said, rolling his eyes and flattening against the float.

Eric and I lowered the sails, but the boat still moved at a decent clip.

"That's interesting," Eric said, looking over the side of the port pontoon.

"What is?" I asked.

"There seems to be . . . ah . . . a current?"

"Like a river?"

"Yeah." His frown deepened. "Or, you know. A drain."

Savannah whimpered. "A *drain*?"

Uh-oh. "No," I said, patting her on the arm. "It's a river. I'm sure it's a river."

"Yeah?" she replied. "A river to where?"

"Look at it this way," Eric added, still clearly thrilled to be at a tiller once more. "At least we're away from Clint and Fiona. And . . . that third guy."

"But away *where*?" Howard asked.

I was back to looking ahead of us, where the weird orange glow had grown strong enough to make out what we were heading toward. A massive, curving wall. And right in the middle was a giant, whirring fan that had to be several stories high.

"Good news," I said to the others, pointing. "It's not a drain. It may slice us to pieces, but it's not a drain."

Everyone shot up, no longer worried about wind resistance. If anything it might help. Nate said, "It looks like an exhaust turbine. Probably pumping in fresh air for the chamber. . . ."

"No." Eric was shaking his head. "If we're heading toward it, that means it's pulling the air, not pushing it. It's sucking whatever air is here deeper into the ground."

"Like maybe there's even more to this place?" Nate asked.

Savannah shrugged. "Well, that platform wasn't much of a city, was it? Omega *City*, remember?"

"So then what's this supposed to be?" Nate snapped. "Omega Lakefront Property?"

Howard was peering at the turbine. "We're not going to get sucked into the fan. There's a ledge just in front of it. We can stop and get out."

But as we got closer, we saw that the ledge was really just the bottom frame of the giant turbine and it was about eight feet higher than the water level. I wasn't sure how we'd be able to get up there—not that we'd want to, seeing how it came with the risk of getting ourselves sliced to pieces by the blades of the fan. The outer wall of the chamber seemed to be covered in concrete and as Eric steered us close I saw a set of stairs built into the side of the wall, going from the turbine ledge down into the water. The water here glowed golden, like a swimming pool at night. I leaned over the side of the boat and saw the steps going down the side of the wall, deep under the remarkably clear water. At the bottom of the lake, about seven or eight feet down, was another glowing orange light set into the wall over what was unmistakably a door.

The water level in this chamber must be a lot higher than Underberg had ever intended.

"Look!" Savannah cried over the roar of the fan blades. She pointed. Over to the left side of the wall, right above where that door was, was a large metal cage, half submerged in the water. "I wonder if it's another elevator."

"I'm done with elevators," said Howard.

"Maybe there's a button inside that can stop the fan," she clarified. "Like a control panel."

We guided the boat along the wall until we hit the cage. Up close, it looked like those freestanding cage elevators you sometimes see at construction sites, with four wire-grid walls, a wire ceiling, and a solid metal floor. I could see the rail it was attached to descending along the wall down to the underwater landing. The door on the side of the elevator seemed to be stuck closed but when I looked inside, I saw a blinking panel of buttons that still sat above the water level. A laminated sheet was posted to the top of the panel. I reached between the bars and tore the paper free.

The others gathered around me as I squinted down at the page in the orange light. One side of the sheet looked like a schedule of some kind—maybe meant to assign times for the fan to be on or reversed or whatever. But the other side had a diagram showing dozens of chambers sitting on the other side of this wall, all neatly labeled and with arrows and other color coding that showed air, water, and electricity flow.

On the top it read *Omega City*.

My eyes widened as I took it all in. This wasn't some little bunker. This was a whole underground world. And it was only a few yards away.

Nate jabbed the sheet, where a bunch of little red signs pointed the way to exits. "Look. Exits marked. We just have to get in."

"And how do you plan to do that?" Eric asked. "That door is underwater. Chances are whatever's on the other side is, too."

The recorded voice bounced around the cavern again.

You have arrived at the Omega City Welcome Center. Please prepare for your decontamination showers.

"Uh-oh," said Savannah. "They're here."

"Maybe the water cannon will wreck their guns," said Eric.

I listened, but I didn't hear any screaming. Maybe the water cannon didn't have enough pressure for another shower so soon? A moment later, a distant shout floated across the water. "Kids?" Fiona.

"Where did they go?" came a male voice, echoing the way only a vast underground cavern could. "They didn't just swim off this thing, that's for sure."

There were more shouts, but we couldn't make them out over the roar of the fan above us.

"Maybe they're hiding in another shaft." Fiona again. "Find them. Now!"

In the orange glow emanating from the water, my friends' faces were filled with terror.

"We have to stop that fan," Savannah said. She rattled the locked door of the cagelike control booth. "Open up, you stupid thing."

I looked through the metal grid inside. The bottom of the booth, sitting in about two feet of water, was rusted and broken, leaving a huge gap where the metal had rusted out and fallen away. "I bet someone could swim up into that hole."

"Someone really skinny," said Nate.

Everyone got quiet. Everyone looked at Savannah.

"Oh, you have *got* to be kidding me," she said.

"It's not like you aren't already wet," I said.

"And the water looks pretty clean," Nate added. "I mean, we can see all the way down. It's probably a reservoir or something. You won't get any weird disease."

"Are you up to date on your tetanus shots?" Howard asked her.

"Look!" yelled one of the guys across the water. "Ropes. They must have taken a boat."

"Find another," came Fiona's voice.

"We need to stop the turbine," Nate said. "Now. I'm not going to fit in that hole. Please, Savannah?" I think it was the first time he'd used her name.

Savannah sighed and clenched her jaw. Then she pulled off her hoodie and handed it to me with an annoyed look. "This is your worst idea of all time."

"Agreed." I stuck the map in the waistband of my jeans. "I owe you. I really owe you."

"Yeah. You owe me a whole new outfit." Savannah tied her long hair in a loose knot, took a deep breath, and jumped off the side of the boat. We saw her form, white tank top and pink pants, ghostly in the water, and then she disappeared beneath the elevator. A second later, her blond head broke the surface of the water inside the elevator. For a second she just treaded water, half in and half out of the elevator.

"Try not to cut yourself on the metal," Howard said. "Tetanus."

"You think?" Savannah swiped her wet hair off her face. Gingerly, she pulled herself up onto the broken floor, then stood, her legs braced wide to avoid the hole. "Okay. I'm in. Now what?"

"What do the controls say?" I leaned over the top of the cage, trying to read the panel through the bars. The pontoons butted up against the metal grid and the water inside sloshed around Savannah's thighs. I hoped she wasn't going to get electrocuted in there.

"They aren't marked. Wait, this one has an arrow." She pressed it and the elevator shuddered upward.

I lost my grip on the cage and stumbled back, falling against the float of the catamaran as the broken-bottomed elevator lifted up out of the water with the awful sound of shrieking metal. The catamaran pitched wildly from side to side and we all held on tight to keep from being thrown off.

"Gillian!" Savannah shouted as the booth kept rising. She flattened her body against the wall and jammed her fingers through the bars. "The floor! It's crumbling!"

Nate made a leap for the bottom corner. He missed, but the move sent the boat directly under the elevator. The metal mast banged against the booth and Savannah wavered on her feet. Above us, there was a horrible crash, and then a big section of the jagged, broken bottom of the cage swung free over our heads like a trapdoor. A giant, sharp, very deadly trapdoor.

"Stop! Stop!" Savannah jabbed her free hand against the buttons. Far above us the turbine shuddered and groaned, its ancient blades screeching and—marvelously—beginning to slow.

"You did it!" Eric cried up at Savannah. Nate hooted his approval and I pumped my fist in the air.

But we celebrated too soon. The elevator stopped, and started lowering again.

"Um . . . Savannah?" I said, as it clanked its way back to the surface of the water. "Stop the elevator."

"I'm trying!" The elevator was dropping in fits and starts, the broken edge of the cage zipping back and forth over our heads. Eric tried to push our boat away from the cage as it descended so the hanging bits wouldn't pierce the pontoons.

"I'd get out now," Howard suggested.

Savannah shrieked in frustration. She was trying to ease herself through the hole but every movement of the elevator sent the sharp, broken edge of the cage swinging wildly back and forth. If she dropped out now it was likely to cut her in two.

"Help me!"

Nate tried to grab for the broken edge and hold it out of her way but only succeeded in pulling the edge of the catamaran under the elevator just as it dropped back into the water. Rusty froth churned up through the grates as the elevator juddered into the lake. There was a horrible tearing sound and the catamaran tilted wildly to the side, spilling us all into the water.

I surfaced, spluttering, and looked around. Grab for the wall? The elevator? The swiftly sinking boat?

"Help!" Savannah screamed, and I realized she was still trapped. "The boat! It's blocking the hole to get out!"

The cage was still lowering into the water, dragging the tangled rubber of the catamaran with it. We swam to the booth, tugging on the door, the walls, the ceiling, anything. Savannah was up to her waist in the water, then her chest.

"Gillian!" She was treading water now, her round eyes as huge as dinner plates. "Please."

I reached for her through the bars, as if I could pull her through by force of will alone. "Hang on!" I shouted, though for what I didn't know.

Our fingers touched. She grabbed my hand around the grid. The water slipped to her neck.

"Take a deep breath, Savannah!" I called to her as she pressed her face against the ceiling grid, her fingers straining against the metal bars. And then those, too, slipped beneath the dark surface of the water, and that was the last I saw of my friend.

13

CAGE MATCH

"SAVANNAH!" I DOVE UNDER, TRYING TO PULL AGAINST THE ELEVATOR AS if I could lift it out of the water like the Incredible Hulk. Eric yanked me back.

"Gills!" He shook his head and gestured behind me. "Help Nate."

The Noland brothers were tugging on the half-sunken catamaran, trying to untangle it from the broken edge of the elevator cage. Eric and I paddled over and started tugging, too. But even as I pulled with all my might, there was a stopwatch going in my mind. Ten seconds. Twenty. How long could people hold their breath?

Nate dove under as the rest of us kept yanking on the

mess of sail and float and torn rubber. Twenty-five seconds. Thirty.

"Pull harder!" I screamed.

"It's—" Howard puffed, tugging. "Hard—to get—leverage."

Forty seconds. My best friend was dead. I'd dragged her along on this journey to the center of the Earth and then I'd let her drown. I screamed, tugging as hard as I could on the material.

Nate burst to the surface, Savannah limp in his arms. They were both covered in scrapes from the broken bottom of the cage.

"Quick! Help me get her on the ledge!" We swam over to the steps and pulled Savannah up on the flat surface near the now-stopped turbine. She instantly began coughing, spitting up water and slime. Her arms were covered in messy scratches, and there was a nasty, deep-looking one across her torso, right where her shirt was nearly torn in two.

Nate thumped her on the back. "Get it all up."

She clutched her shirt together with both hands and retched.

"Those cuts look pretty bad," Howard said. "Lockjaw is, of course, the most well-known symptom of tetanus, but there are others . . . such as drooling, excessive sweating, and uncontrolled urination."

Savannah glared at him with bloodshot eyes. "Gross. Shut up, Howard!"

"Also irritability."

Savannah leaned over and threw up all over Nate's shoes.

He jumped back so hard, I thought he might fall in the lake. "Eww, watch it."

Savannah groaned and fell back into my lap. "Someone kill me."

"No way," I whispered, hugging her close. "We just saved your life."

For a few moments we all sat there, catching our breath and wringing out our clothes. I cradled Savannah's head in my lap, smoothing her wet hair out of her face, while she scrubbed at the cuts on her arms and body with her ruined hoodie.

Savannah was okay. She was okay. But I wasn't going to risk anyone's life again. Not hers, not the Nolands', and certainly not my baby brother's. I didn't care if the battery prototype was somewhere in the city. Nate was right—we needed to find the quickest way out of here. Now.

I pulled the laminated map out of the waistband of my jeans and ran my fingers over the figures on the page. Omega City could wait for experts. We should go home.

After a moment, Savannah rose up on her elbows,

coughed a few times, then cleared her throat and turned to me. "What now?"

I clenched my jaw. "Find the exit."

Nate breathed deeply, then smiled. "Finally, you're listening to reason." He pushed himself to his feet, wincing a little.

"Are you kidding?" Savannah asked hoarsely. "I didn't nearly get myself killed just to leave."

"The important part of that sentence is that you nearly got yourself killed," Nate pointed out.

"We're never going to see this place again, you know," she said to me. I looked at her, stricken. "We're going to go up, tell the authorities, and then that's it. It'll be all over the news—not our secret anymore."

"Sounds good to me," said Nate.

"And not your dad's, either," she added. That made me hesitate. I figured if the mainstream media started taking Dad seriously, it would be a good thing. But what if they bypassed him entirely? I wanted Dad to be vindicated, but what if that only happened if he was the one to bring Underberg's inventions to light?

"I agree with Savannah," Howard said. "I hate that I do, but I do."

"At the very least, we should see if we can find some sort of first aid station," Eric added. He pointed at the blood staining Nate's and Savannah's clothes.

I checked out the map. "Right here, the first building on the diagram is a mess hall. There might be something there." And we could kill two birds with one stone. Fix up Savannah, and search for the prototype.

"Either way, we should keep moving," Eric said. "Fiona and her friends may have found another boat."

I helped Savannah to her feet and together we eased across the ledge to the turbine. There wasn't a lot of room between the blades, but we could get through if we threaded single file through the lowest two blades.

Except none of us moved. What if it started up again while we were inside?

Then again, what other choice did we have? The boat was sunk, and Fiona and her friends were after us. This was the only way out.

I squared my shoulders. "Okay. I'm going in." I took a deep breath. The blades didn't move. I touched one. It felt gritty like rust beneath my fingers. It was hard to believe a few minutes ago it was slicing through the air so fast it was a blur.

"Are you going to do it?" Howard asked.

"Yes," I said, trying to convince myself as much as Howard. I closed my eyes and ran between the blades, forcing my feet to a halt after a few steps so I didn't careen off the ledge on the other side.

Eric slammed into me from behind, then caught me by

the back of my shirt as my arms pinwheeled over empty space. "Watch out, Gills—whoa."

Whoa was right. Below us spread an enormous cavern, vaguely lit by massive blue floodlights focused up on the carved rock walls. It wasn't quite as big as the lake chamber, but what it lacked in size, it made up for in sheer insanity. I gasped, but there was no way to breathe it all in.

This, without a doubt, was the *real* Omega City.

The ledge we stood on was about twenty feet off the ground. Below me, a maze of boxy buildings like giant multistory trailers, some connected by walkways, some by tunnels, spread out along the ground. Many were underwater, or nearly so, while others remained above the water level. Some of the buildings had fallen over or collapsed on themselves, and debris the size of trucks floated in the submerged sections.

More tunnels led from the buildings in and out of the rock walls, which curved upward into a point like we were standing beneath a vast tent made of stone. All around the perimeter of the cavern and above me I could see windows or even buildings set into the walls. Everything was lit blue, like some strange, subterranean twilight had fallen over this vast, silent space.

Nate, Howard, and Savannah met us on the ledge. In the eerie blue light, I could see their mouths open, their eyes wide. Eric looked the same and I'm sure I did, too.

Dad's book had been full of wild theories, but even he had never dreamed of a place like this.

"Do you think anyone is here?" Savannah asked.

"No." I shook my head. There couldn't be. The lights and the cannon and the turbine must work on timers, or motion detectors, or something. How could anyone be here if the place looked like this? "It was built for survivors of a disaster, just like that recording in the elevator said. For the end of the world—a war or a comet or . . ."

"The Yellowstone supervolcano?" Howard suggested.

Nate had said that during the Cold War the government built the interstate system—tens of thousands of miles of highways—to help people escape from a nuclear disaster. Was a place like this what they were meant to be escaping to? If something bad happened to the world above, were we supposed to find this place?

Except it wasn't built by the government. It was built by Dr. Underberg.

"This is what Dr. Underberg meant when he wrote about his last gift to mankind," I said. "It's not the battery, it's a whole city. Omega City. The last city."

Eric, of course, looked skeptical. "But it's in ruins."

"Yeah." I shrugged. "Kind of like everything else connected to Dr. Underberg." I consulted the map and pointed. "The mess hall is down there." Thankfully, it was in an area of higher ground.

We took another set of stairs bolted into the wall down to a raised walkway. Below the walkway, the rough rock ground was covered in puddles, but the ramp to the first of the elevated, trailer-like buildings was dry.

On the metal door was a large Greek omega symbol painted in red, and then a number 1. On the map the building seemed to contain several smaller apartments—the mess hall, a hair salon, even a grocery store. We'd surely be able to find something to treat Savannah's and Nate's wounds inside.

"Go ahead, Gillian," said Nate. "I think this just became your party."

I turned the handle and opened the door. Fluorescent lights flickered on.

But the inside of the building looked like a bomb had gone off.

THE VERY MESSY MESS HALL

LIGHT FIXTURES DANGLED FROM THE CEILING, LETTING OFF EERIE FLICKERS, and the halls were clogged with debris, loose paper, broken furniture, and some kind of unidentifiable black sludge.

"We're not going in there, are we?" Savannah asked. "It's disgusting."

I glanced pointedly at the tattered, bloody remains of her velour pants and her vomit-spattered shirt.

"You're right," she admitted. "Can't get worse." She stepped inside.

We skirted the mess, trying to find our way through the tangle of hallways to a place where we could get our bearings.

The whole time I could hardly keep from squealing. Dr. Underberg had built this. And he couldn't have done it alone, either. There had to be hundreds of people: construction workers, electricians, plumbers. People put this massive project together . . . somehow.

And now, it was nearly destroyed. What had happened here? How did my dad not know any of this? How come no one knew? If people had helped Underberg build this city, there had to be lots of people who knew about it—unless the government had iced them, too.

And yet, we'd been to other war bunkers before. There was one under Parliament in London that was a museum now. There was another out in a hotel in Virginia that was originally built for Congress. The government kept a whole missile launch station in a hollowed-out mountain in Colorado.

If this was here, a little more than an hour from our house, how many more were there? And if we didn't know about them, then who were they built for?

We found the mess hall, which featured a smattering of metal folding tables and chairs scattered haphazardly—some overturned—on a wrinkled linoleum floor. Overhead, foam ceiling tiles lay crookedly around a grid punctuated by burned-out fluorescent lights. One wall featured a cafeteria-style opening and buffet stations, and from what we could see of the kitchen beyond, the industrial-sized stainless steel ovens and refrigerators and storage containers were all open . . . and empty.

Eric pulled the first aid kit off the wall near the light controls. "Score." While my brother started sorting through the bandages and ointments, I went with Howard to look around. In a pantry off the kitchen we found a jumble of items that must have spilled from the racks on the wall, including flashlights, whistles, water bottles, a few military-style freeze-dried foods, and, yes, some packages of patented, Underberg-brand astronaut ice cream.

But nothing that looked like the prototype for the Underberg battery. Oh, well. Probably a long shot that he'd keep it in the mess hall, anyway.

"Strawberry? Chocolate?" I called to the others.

"No vanilla?" Nate called back.

"Don't worry—you can have your pick." I'd had no idea astronaut ice cream came in so many flavors. I gathered an armful of the stuff and went back to the tables.

"Is there anything else in the storage room?" Savannah asked, wincing as she dabbed a peroxide-soaked cotton ball against her arm. She was still clutching her clothes together with her injured hand. "Like maybe an extra T-shirt?"

"No shirts," said Howard, emerging with a bunch of shrink-wrapped packages. "But I found something even better." He tossed a pile of them on the table. "Space suits."

I looked at the little folded packages, each about the

size of a cereal box. These were certainly not space suits. Across the table, Eric ripped one open, and shimmery silver material slid out of the package and into his lap. He lifted it up.

"No way," said Nate. "We'll look like extras from a bad sci-fi movie in these."

Howard read off the label of his. "Waterproof, fireproof, tear-proof, and soil-resistant."

"Just resistant?" Eric asked. "Come on, Underberg, don't let us down now."

I turned my package over in my hands. "Omega City Utility Suit" was printed at the top in bold black letters, right above another omega symbol. Below that was typed the following:

MADE BY THE ARKADIA GROUP

Below that was another symbol, like two upside-down Js crossed over a map of the world. Actually—I peered closer—they weren't Js at all. There was a little extra hook on the tail end of the J.

A shiver rushed across my skin that had nothing to do with my wet clothes. I'd seen that J symbol before, on Fiona's arm. At the time I'd thought it was an initial, but maybe it was her company logo. Maybe Arkadia Group was the name of the development firm where Fiona worked. If so, then maybe Nate had been right that Omega City belonged to them and we were the ones who were trespassing.

But that couldn't be right. If Omega City was theirs, they certainly weren't taking care of it very well. And it didn't explain Dr. Underberg's diary or the treasure map we'd used to get here. My dad had never mentioned or written anything about an Arkadia Group. Underberg worked for the State Department and NASA.

Then again, Dad hadn't known about this city, either. Maybe he'd gotten all kinds of things wrong about Underberg's life.

No. I refused to believe that. No one knew about the city. Back at the boulder, Fiona had worried that Eric and I would find Omega City before she did. So she couldn't work here—she didn't have any idea where this place was. Even if the Arkadia Group had made these suits for Dr. Underberg, that didn't mean they knew what he'd done with them. Maybe he'd just bought them and put them here. My fingers trembled as I pulled open the packaging. What if Dr. Underberg had *literally* put them here? What if he'd touched this very suit?

"At least they're dry," Eric said. He peeled off his shirt.

"Eww, Eric, don't change in front of me!" Savannah covered her eyes and grimaced.

"Would you say that if I were Nate?" he teased.

Nate looked scandalized by the idea.

Savannah didn't answer, just frowned down at the suit in distaste. "They look so baggy."

"Beggars can't be choosers, Sav," I pointed out.

She bit her lip. "I'll put it on if you do."

I was on board with that. After all, silly or not, at least the jumpsuit was dry, and I couldn't say the same for my jeans and T-shirt.

Savannah and I retreated to a space behind the empty fridges in the kitchen area while the boys used the mess hall to change. It wasn't easy getting my damp jeans off, and I actually had to have Savannah help. She held up her pink velour outfit, which now looked like a giant used dishrag. "This was my big Christmas present," she said. "I saw it in a magazine and spent weeks begging my mom for one."

"I'm sorry, Sav," I said. I mean, I didn't understand who'd spend a hundred dollars on a pair of sweatpants, but I did know how much she loved them. I'd done my fair share of begging for presents over the years.

She shrugged, balled it up, and tossed it in a corner. "I don't think Nate even noticed."

The silver suit weighed practically nothing, and closed with a silent zipper. They only came in one size, and after you put it on, you folded and zipped portions near the ankles, knees, sides, elbows, and shoulders to make it fit you perfectly. There was even a zipper near the neck, but I'm not sure what it was for since the collar didn't seem adjustable. Not to say they were skintight. Once we'd adjusted our suits to fit according to the directions on the package, they were still a little loose, more like a mechanic's one-piece suit and less like some kind of space-age leotard. Still, they were dry and warm, which was an improvement. I almost hated putting my wet sneakers on again afterward. Too bad there were no space-age boots lying around on the broken, dangling shelves. I did, however, find a toiletry set, and Savannah was able to brush her teeth and rinse her mouth out.

"How do you feel?" I asked her.

"Like I swallowed a bunch of water from an underground lake and then threw it all up again." She stuck out her tongue. "I may pass on the ice cream."

By the time Sav and I had gotten back to the boys they'd left a pile of crumpled ice-cream wrappers around their table, and on top of the jumpsuits, they each wore a rainbow mustache of sticky powder.

"Here," Howard said to me, handing over another ice cream. "I saved you a lemon-lime. It's definitely the best flavor."

"Thanks," I replied, surprised. I guess he'd forgiven me for the whole "freak" thing. Maybe almost dying a few times makes name-calling seem like no big deal.

Nate shrugged. "I liked mint chocolate, actually." He tore into another packet.

Savannah sighed, looking at her options. "Can you imagine actually living down here and eating freeze-dried food every day? It's disgusting."

"I think it's awesome," said Howard. He was hungrily eyeing the rest of the shelves.

"Better than pizza," Nate said. "I think I could go the rest of my life without eating another piece of pizza. Especially that nasty sesame chicken one you guys always order." He made a face.

"You say that now," said Eric, his mouth full of freeze-dried ice cream mush. "But try a few months of this and you'll change your tune. Believe me, I thought I'd never get enough s'mores, but you go camping with my dad for a month or two and the very thought of marshmallows will make you want to vomit." He shot a guilty glance at Savannah. "Sorry."

After I was done with my ice cream, I pulled the comb out of the toiletry kit. "Come here, Sav. I'll braid your hair." Right now it looked like it had been attacked by a particularly excitable rat.

"Ladies," Nate said. "We don't have time for hairdos, okay?"

I glared at him. Savannah finger-combed her hair and looked down.

"Hairdos?" I snapped. "Are you serious right now?"

"Yes," he replied. "We have no idea when those people with the guns are going to show up again. We can't sit around forever. We have to get out of here."

"You *so* don't have a sister, do you?" Eric asked wearily.

"It takes two minutes to get her hair safely out of the way of anything that might catch in it," I said. "How long have you been sitting here shoving ice cream in your face?"

Eric held up his hands. "Look, we're fine. We're still resting, and everyone wants a snack, anyway, am I right?"

Howard was fiddling with something on the arm of his suit. "Yeah. I wanted to try one of those MREs."

"What?" Savannah asked.

"Meals, Ready-to-Eat," he explained. "They even have a chicken and dumpling."

"Don't do the dumplings," Eric warned. I had to agree with him. Dad made us eat the occasional MRE when we were off grid, and the dumplings tasted like burnt water. I could only force it down on nights when Dad's culinary experiments were worse than usual. "But if they have a beef teriyaki, that's not too bad."

"Trust me, kid," said Nate. "Howard won't eat anything labeled teriyaki."

"I don't think he should eat too much of this stuff no matter what flavor it comes in," I said. I was combing through Savannah's hair as we talked, the lemon-lime ice cream tucked away in one of my utility suit's many zippered pockets. "We have no idea how long it's been down here. Maybe it's all gone bad."

"I thought that was Dr. Underberg's thing," Nate said. "Howard said he invented food that never went bad."

"There's no food that *never* goes bad," Howard said. "Except honey."

"That's a myth," I said, braiding. "Only if it's sealed and stored in dry conditions. And doesn't have botulism in it."

"So the honey thing is a myth, but Tunguska was aliens?" Howard asked. "Maybe you should make up a list so we can follow which crazy theories you actually believe."

I snapped a rubber band around the end of Savannah's braid. "We've now spent more time discussing food we don't need to eat than we have on girly hairdos. Satisfied, Nate?"

He laughed. "Okay, you win. But *now* can we go?"

"Sure." I pulled the map and the lemon-lime out of my pockets and walked over to the table. "According to the diagram, the fastest route to an exit from here is like this." I traced the line through three buildings and connected pathways to one of those little red Exit symbols.

Eric looked over my shoulder. "Look at all these rooms."

Honestly, I was trying not to. The battery could be in

any of them, and we were heading straight for the exit.

"What do you think they're all for? A.T.R. . . . F.L.F. . . . E.M.O. . . . S.I.L.O. . . ."

"I don't know and I don't care," said Nate. "Just find the one marked e-x-i-t."

I pointed at another building marked Comm. "I wonder if this stands for Communications. Maybe we should try to call the police or something."

"And say what?" Savannah asked. "Help! We're trapped in weird city a mile underground and being chased by creepy thugs with guns?"

"It's the truth," Eric pointed out.

"I wonder if Omega City phones are unlisted," Howard said. He was twisting in his suit now, running his hands along the seams and trying to reach for something at the small of his back.

"Do you have ants in your pants or something?" I asked him.

"This suit is wired," Howard said. He held out his forearm. "Look: a control panel."

"Does it have a silence setting?" Savannah deadpanned.

"I'm not sure. . . ." Howard started jamming buttons. Oh, great. More buttons for him to press.

"She's joking, bro," said Nate.

"Oh." He frowned. "It does have a warming setting . . . a cooling setting . . . water lines, I think?"

"Think later," his brother said. "We should go, before those guys catch up to us. Everyone grab some of those flashlights and a bottle or two of water. The last thing we need to worry about is dehydration."

"I think it's the last thing you *should* worry about." I shrugged. "There's water everywhere here."

"Not potable."

"What's potable mean?"

"*Drinkable.* And you aren't keeping up your end of the deal. What did I say on the drive out here?"

I hung my head. "When you say go, we go." But things had gotten . . . well, really weird since then. How could Nate keep playing camp counselor when we were stuck in a secret underground city with Fiona and her friends?

Nate shoved a bunch of first aid supplies in his pockets and we all picked up flashlights. They were perfectly normal little mini lights, about the size of candy bars and made of metal in primary colors. There wasn't even an Omega symbol on them, like the suits. I scanned the shelves for anything that looked like Underberg's work. Nothing, except the ice cream. Normal first aid kits, normal flashlights, cool suits that were made by some other company. . . . No giant hundred-year batteries or unimaginably awesome lost pieces of tech like Dad used to tell me about. Maybe all those naysayers had been correct—maybe Underberg was a fraud, and his marvelous inventions weren't all that marvelous. Maybe this city didn't even belong to him.

After all, could any man build a city—even a small, secret city—all by himself? This was probably a government installation of some kind. Or maybe it did belong to whoever Fiona was working for. Maybe the only part Underberg had played in all of this was building his own secret entrance near his cabin. Maybe that's the bit Fiona had been looking for.

Then again, it had been easy to find Underberg's entrance from the inside: it looked like a giant elevator shaft. It was only from the outside that it had been disguised. *My last and lasting gift to mankind.* One that would only be useful if mankind itself were on the brink of destruction.

Dr. Underberg had a hand in creating so many things to help us survive, but this city was proof that someone, at least, was sure we would fail.

Armed with water, flashlights, and the last of the astronaut ice cream, we headed off toward the nearest exit. The path led out of the mess hall building and onto another raised metal walkway. This one was a lot more rickety and sagging, and in some places we had to wade through knee-deep water and across rusted-out sections. The eerie blue glow cast an endless twilight around us, enough to see by, but I still clutched my flashlight. We skirted another building marked **Ω2**—showers and sleeping quarters, according to the map—and headed toward one of the chamber's side walls. As the stone started arching over my head, I got that weird topsy-turvy sensation again. I knew I was on solid ground, but I felt like an ant crawling up a wall. I had no idea which way was which and I was afraid I was going to slide right off the edge.

I forced my attention onto the map in my hands until the dizziness faded. "It should be right here."

Only a few more minutes and we'd be safely above ground. The city, and everything inside it, would be nothing but a memory.

"It is," Nate said. His voice sounded odd. "But . . ."

I looked up. In front of us stood an elevator shaft. The doors at its base were broken open, and the elevator itself lay smashed to smithereens inside.

GUNS, WORMS, AND STEEL

AT THE SIGHT OF THE WRECKED ELEVATOR, THE BOTTOM DROPPED OUT of my stomach. Forget an ant crawling up a wall. I was an ant in a snow globe, and some cruel giant was shaking me. I grabbed on to Eric's silver sleeve as if I was going to fall.

"Gills?" He steadied me. "Are you okay?"

"She's claustrophobic," Nate growled. "Perfect."

I wasn't claustrophobic. That was about being afraid of closed spaces. I wasn't afraid. I was dizzy. There was a difference. I shook my head. *Stop it, Gillian. The ground is beneath your feet.* "I'm fine."

"Now what?" Savannah asked, looking at the wreckage of the elevator. "Is there another exit?"

"Five more," said Howard, sneaking a peek at my map. His flashlight roamed the page, the grimy metal walkway, the dark water surrounding us on all sides. The walkway seemed to sway like a rope bridge in high wind.

Nate kicked at the broken elevator doors. "What are the chances those are a bust, too?"

"Gillian?" Savannah touched my shoulder. "You look kind of green."

"We shouldn't have eaten those ice creams," I muttered through gritted teeth. "I told you guys." The ground. Was beneath. My feet.

"There have to be stairs, right?" Eric asked. "There are always stairs. In case of emergency power failures . . . and . . . stuff."

"Oh, sure, because this place was obviously built to some kind of code." Nate rustled his hand through his hair. "Okay, what are our options? Gillian? You still good with the map?"

I gave a firm nod. The map might be the only thing I was good with right now. Every time I looked at its neatly drawn, flat black lines, the flipping feeling stopped. "There are other exits, but I'm not sure how easy they are to get to. Like this one—" I pointed at another red mark on the diagram. "That may be underwater. Maybe it would be better to try to get to the Comm station." I pointed at the room marked Comm on the map, which was on an upper level, set not in the cavern but somewhere within the rock wall to our left.

"Deeper into the city?" Nate asked, annoyed.

"We have to go deeper in either way," I said. "And look—the Comm room is on the way to the next exit." All the other elevator shafts marked on the map were set farther into the rocks, rather than in this big cavern.

Nate sighed. "I swear . . . I should have turned around when I realized you were lying about the whole school project thing. I never should have let you guys come this far."

"You were the one who shoved us all inside that boulder," Savannah pointed out.

I stared at her. Savannah was actually disagreeing with Nate?

"What?" She shrugged. "It's true."

"Well, I didn't expect it to deposit us in some inescapable underground doomsday deathtrap."

"Trust me, Nate," said Eric. "No one did. Not even Gills, and she believes everything."

"Not the thing about the honey," Howard piped up.

Nate swiped his hand across his body in a cut-it-out motion. "Okay. Enough. No more arguments, no more finger-pointing. We're getting out of here. Shut your mouths and follow me."

He took off toward the Comm room and we fell into line behind him.

"I think I'm officially over my crush," said Savannah, trudging along behind me.

"Sure," said Eric, who was bringing up the rear. "No one's as cute not holding a pizza."

Nate yanked open the door of the next building and marched inside. Dutifully, we all followed. Whatever had happened to Omega City to cause all this damage, this building seemed even harder hit than the one containing the mess hall. The lights in this building were out, except for an occasional ceiling emergency light that cast the entire space in a dim red glow. The beams of our flashlights bounced off cracked walls and collapsed doorways. The hallways sloped at slight angles, and the carpets squished beneath our feet as we walked. Everything smelled like mold. We passed dark doorway after dark doorway.

Oddly enough, I felt better. See? It wasn't claustrophobia, no matter what Nate said. Claustrophobia was fear of tight spaces. Everyone knew that. And this little trailer building—well, it was much smaller than that enormous cavern. I took a deep breath and shook off my unease. We'd just . . . get to the exit. Get home. No more problems.

"Gills . . . ," Eric whispered, his voice shaky. He crowded up close behind Savannah and me. "Why am I in the back? It's always the slow gazelle that gets eaten by the lion."

Savannah elbowed him until he stopped stepping on

her heels. "It won't be a lion here, Eric. It'll be a giant earthworm."

"Gills!" my brother cried, reaching for me.

I stopped short. "Worms, Sav? Really? You had to bring up worms?"

"It's not my fault he reads too much sci-fi."

I pushed them both ahead of me. "Here, Eric. I'll take the back."

I was used to Eric's overactive imagination. When we were camping, he'd gotten his hands on some stupid horror novel and wouldn't go to the bathroom alone for a week. You haven't had fun until you've been forced to listen to your brother pee on a tree from a foot away.

Besides, back here no one could see me consulting the map for every room we passed. C15 was a broom closet, C17 was a bathroom, and C23 looked like a classroom, with wooden desks bolted to the floor and a cracked chalkboard hanging at a crazy angle. I almost stopped the others, thinking they'd enjoy a glimpse at a trashed schoolroom.

C27 was marked M.B. on the map, and when I flashed my light into the room, I saw bunk beds and footlockers. Men's Bedroom, maybe? I ran the beam of the flashlight over the walls and caught sight of an empty gun rack. Military Bedroom? Of course, that made sense. They'd need to have some sort of protection in the city. But once I started thinking about guns, the image of Clint dangling from the sky and threatening to shoot us filled my mind. Where were they now? Were they still chasing us? Inside like this, we had no way of knowing how close they might be.

Now I was the one running to catch up to the others.

At the end of the next hallway, we hit a dead end. The floor tilted sharply downward here, and the rest of the hall was above our head, revealing sheer blasted rock edges and busted wiring. Nate didn't even seem fazed. He simply boosted Howard up, then turned to help Savannah. Eric came next and then it was my turn.

"This takes us back out of this chamber," I said to him as he held out his hands for me to step into.

"I'm hoping it takes us out of the ground."

"You know I didn't plan on this," I said by way of apology. "Fiona, or the elevator, or . . . I don't know. I thought it was just a little cabin or something." He lifted me up. I grabbed Eric's hand and stepped onto the higher level, and Nate hefted himself up behind me.

"I know. But here we are," he replied flatly.

Yeah. Here we were. In Dr. Underberg's greatest creation—well, what was left of it, anyway. Dad wouldn't be rushing us through this thing as quickly as Nate was. Dad would want to stop and enjoy every part.

Well, unless Fiona decided to chase Dad around with goons and guns, too.

I consulted the map again. "The Comm room is over

there, but this looks like a flight of stairs." I pointed to a series of hash marks on the diagram.

"What's this thing over by the stairs?" Howard asked. The beam of his flashlight circled around a large fan-shaped room marked M.T. After what I'd seen in the C-block with the gun rack, I wasn't sure I wanted to know.

"Military Training?" I suggested, a little nervous.

"Like maybe a gun range?" Nate asked.

I hoped it wasn't a gun range. There was an outside and two inside ones in our town, and they were always packed. Only one pizza-slash-Chinese delivery place, but three gun ranges. People around here liked shooting more than eating.

"Maybe we should check it out," he suggested. "If there are any guns in there, we can at least put ourselves on equal footing with those guys."

"I don't know how to use a gun!"

"I do," Nate replied. "Howard does."

"That doesn't comfort me," Savannah said.

"If I had a gun," he said, "I could protect us."

"If you had a gun," I replied, "you could hurt someone."

"I'm a really good shot!"

"In the dark?" Eric asked. "In a hallway?" My brother had a point. I'd seen the movies. Bullets bounced off rock walls. We'd all end up shot.

Nate was breathing hard. I could hear him panting. I pointed my flashlight down at his hands, which were clenched into fists. He saw the beam of my light and quickly crossed his arms over his chest. I lowered my flashlight as all that astronaut ice cream turned into a leaden lump in my stomach. He wasn't supposed to be scared, too.

Then again, we'd left all our "supposed tos" up on the surface. Down here, there were entirely different rules. Nate had helped us escape Fiona. He'd saved Savannah's life. If he was being a little grumpy right now, there was a good reason.

But that didn't mean we should arm ourselves.

"No guns," I said to Nate. "You're not the only one who gets to make rules."

"You gonna tell that Clint guy to follow your rules?"

"No. Guns," I repeated. "All in favor?"

Eric and Howard raised their hands. Savannah sighed and followed suit. I turned my flashlight back on Nate.

He rolled his eyes. "This is not a democracy."

"Why not?" Howard asked. "Dr. Underberg didn't die and make you King of Omega City."

Nate turned toward his brother. "Did you just make a joke?"

Howard looked at his feet and mumbled something I couldn't quite make out.

Something changed in Nate's face, and when he spoke

after another minute, his tone was completely different. "Okay. You guys win . . . no guns."

I was going to say something, but he kept going.

"Now let's get to that communications room before we wish we needed them."

I could live with that.

We started off again, though this time, the mood was a little lighter. The rooms off this hallway were way larger, and the doors were, too. Through one, I saw giant glass-walled refrigerators and wire shelves that made me wonder if it was another grocery store, or maybe a medical storage facility. I'd pause outside every doorway for long enough for Nate to growl something about "staying close" or "keeping together." If only we had a chance to explore. Inside one of these rooms could be the prototype for the battery. I couldn't imagine what Dad would say if I brought it home to him.

But we didn't pass anything that looked like someplace a world-changing battery prototype might be stored. In another room we saw barbells, rings hanging from the ceiling, even a pommel horse. It was eerie to look at the benches and weights in these dark rooms: neatly stacked, totally unused, and covered with a layer of dust and grime.

"Weird," Eric said as his flashlight bounced off the wall. "No treadmills or stair machines."

"Dr. Underberg must have been old school when it

came to training," Nate suggested.

"Dr. Underberg built this thing decades ago," I said. Or at least someone did.

The beam of Eric's flashlight traveled over rows of free weights and moldering wrestling mats, then bounced off the figure of a man.

I gasped. Savannah clapped a hand over her mouth. Eric dropped his flashlight, which promptly turned off. I heard him gulp and scramble for it.

"It's just a wall poster," Howard said. "Look." He aimed his light. Half of the man's body was translucent, showing muscles and joints and bones. The paper was yellowed with age, and its edges were torn.

Nate clapped Savannah on the shoulder. "Don't worry about it. I keep waiting for a dead body to show up, too."

"Waiting?" She shuddered.

"Okay. *Dreading.*"

"Can we please stop talking about dead bodies and guns and underground monsters?" Eric said. He was swinging his flashlight at every shadow in the room. "Just in general?"

"So it's fine for a video game but not real life?" Savannah asked.

"Yes!" Eric shook his head at her, incredulous. "In real life you don't get to press reset."

At last we arrived at the door to the fan-shaped M.T.

room. The door to our left was shut and marked with the word *Balcony*.

Nate paused. "Can we at least check out what's inside?" I wasn't going to argue after we'd explored all the other rooms. Nate opened the door and we all stepped into the darkness.

It wasn't a gun range.

A slightly sloped floor covered by row after row of plush red seats overlooked a wrought-iron balcony. Beyond it, I caught a glimpse of a high, arched opening and long red curtains. We all knew instantly what we were looking at, because we were used to seeing this in the dark.

"M.T.," I said softly. "Movie Theater."

We went down the aisle to the edge of the balcony and looked out over the auditorium. It was a giant black lake, its surface as still as glass. If there were seats on the lower level of the theater, they had to be underwater.

"Cool," Eric said. He dropped something over the side and ripples spread out over the space, as the plop echoed from drowned velvet curtain to drowned velvet curtain.

"It's just a movie theater," said Howard. "We have those on the surface, too."

"How would you feel about a movie theater in a spaceship?" Savannah asked.

"Don't be silly!" he scoffed. "That's not remotely practical."

Neither was this. I gripped the elaborate wrought-iron curlicues of the balcony. Luxurious red velvet seats in the end-of-the-world-shelter movie theater? And here I'd been dreading a gun range. I thought back to those military barracks I'd seen in the C-block. How small they were compared to the classrooms and the gyms and this enormous theater. I thought back to that recording we'd heard in the elevator. *Firearms not permitted.*

This wasn't a place for an army. This was a place for people. For people to eat and sleep and work and learn and, yeah—even watch movies. For people to live, even if the world above had died.

"Thanks, Dr. Underberg," I whispered softly, so no one else could hear me. "I knew you wouldn't let me down."

But someone had let *him* down, that much was obvious. Omega City lay in ruins, and Dr. Underberg had disappeared. Why did no one know about this place? Why wasn't anyone taking care of it? I wished Dad were here. He'd be able to fill in the blanks and explain to us what all this meant. If it even was Dr. Underberg's. Maybe we were passing by all kinds of important clues without even knowing it.

The next room was the one marked A.T.R., and after the wonder of the movie theater, we couldn't help but drop in. Unlike the other rooms in this building, A.T.R. smelled of bleach. The floors and walls were tiled, and a long line of enormous lockers stood against the far wall. We started walking in when Nate stopped short. "Careful!" he shouted. "There's a drop-off." He aimed his flashlight down.

Sure enough, in the center of the room was an enormous tiled pit, with a large drain at the very bottom.

"What is it?" Savannah asked.

"Looks like a swimming pool," Nate said. He pointed his flashlight to a ladder attached to one of the walls.

Eric laughed. "The driest place in this city is a swimming pool?"

"I guess we're above the flood level here."

"How does A.T.R. mean swimming pool?" Savannah asked.

I wasn't sure, but I couldn't imagine what else a room like this might be used for. Nate was right, it looked just like when they drained the pools at my old school for cleaning. And the smell—that wasn't bleach. It was the remnants of chlorine. There were large, rusty metal hooks on the wall. Maybe they'd once been used for pool cleaning equipment.

All in all, this wasn't half as interesting as the movie theater. At least, that's what I thought until Howard opened one of the lockers and a person fell out.

UNDER PRESSURE

AS THE MAN FELL TO THE FLOOR WE ALL JUMPED BACK, OUR SHOUTS OF surprise echoing around the darkened room.

I'll give Eric credit—he held on to his flashlight this time. "Wait a second." He stepped toward the slumped figure. He shined his beam over the figure. "It's a space suit," he announced.

No one moved.

"An *empty* one," he clarified.

We crowded around and examined the suit. Big puffy arms and boots and gloves and helmet and all. I'd seen them in cases at the Air and Space Museum, but I'd never touched one before. It was heavy and bulky, which I guess made sense, given that people would mostly be wearing them in zero-gravity conditions, but the actual material was thinner than I would have thought. Imagine having only a quarter inch of material between you and the vacuum of space.

Considering I had a good mile of rock between myself and the surface of the world at present, it seemed really minuscule.

Howard started examining all the pieces, comparing them to Z-series or constellations or I'm not entirely sure what else. However, it was clear he was much more excited about this suit than he'd been about anything since . . . well, since the last suits we'd found.

Finally, he said, "Wow! I think this is a Galaxy series! I thought they canceled this prototype because of heat transfer problems?"

"Maybe they canceled it because it was connected to Dr. Underberg, same as everything else?" I suggested.

"Maybe they canceled it and Dr. Underberg got it on the cheap," Eric replied.

"Maybe none of us are astronauts and so looking at a space suit isn't nearly as important as getting out of here?" asked Nate.

But no one was listening. It was a space suit! And if there were space-suit prototypes in here, then that meant the battery prototype might be here, too. I opened up the other lockers, but there was nothing more than some random tubes, hoses, and air tanks.

"Hey, Howard," I asked, "don't astronauts train in swimming pools?"

"Yes. They simulate antigravity conditions—"

I tapped the map. "A.T.R.: Astronaut Training Room." Only, why would they need astronauts in Omega City? If you were worried about survival, the space program would probably be the last thing on your mind. NASA wasn't even focusing on manned space travel these days, that's how low a priority it was for them.

Then again, those always had been Dr. Underberg's two great loves: space and survival. I looked around the room. If Omega City was really his, it would make sense he'd want to train astronauts. Even if we descended into the Earth, he wouldn't want us to give up on the stars.

"Astronaut Training. Brilliant deduction," said Nate, steering me around by the shoulders. "Now let's go."

But I wasn't the problem. The rest of us headed out into the hallway, but Howard didn't budge. He just sat there on the tile, the space suit pooled in his lap, examining every inch.

"Howard." Nate waved at him.

He unscrewed the helmet.

"Howard!"

He paused, helmet poised over his head. "Come on,"

he said. "Please? I've never actually touched one before."

"Right, he has time to play dress-up but I can't braid my hair?" Savannah asked.

Nate sighed and rubbed his temples. "She's right, buddy. Let's go."

Howard looked longingly at the suit as his brother led him out to us. Savannah gave an annoyed grunt, but I totally understood how he felt. Howard getting to touch an actual space suit was like me visiting Area 51.

Or like now, I guess. Like visiting Omega City. I couldn't stop running my fingers over the lines on the map. Had Underberg really designed this place? Every detail felt like him, but if he'd made it, how come Dad never knew? How come no one did?

The map indicated we needed to go down a set of stairs and then up again into another rock chamber to reach the Comm room, so we headed in that direction. But when we got to the spot where the staircase was supposed to be, we found nothing left but a long, dark shaft. Nate and Eric aimed their beams down the shaft, where I could just make out water far beneath us.

Nate was teaching us all kinds of new swear words today.

"Now what?" Savannah asked when he'd finished.

Eric stood, looking down at the water, then abruptly swung his flashlight around to Howard. "How do the astronauts breathe when they're in training?"

"What does that matter?" I asked.

"Do they use the suits, are there tanks, what?"

"They use the suit apparatus," Howard said. "But they're usually assisted in the water by scuba divers—"

"Oh, no," I said, holding up my hands in a T symbol. "Time out, no way. Don't think what you are thinking."

"You think there's scuba equipment in those lockers by the pool?"

"Eric," I insisted. "No."

"There is," said Howard. "I saw it. So what?"

"Gills, let me see the map."

I shook my head but he snatched it out of my hands and pointed out the fan shape of the movie theater. "Look, there's a hashed line down here by the stage in the movie theater. That's got to be another exit." He traced his finger through that hashed line, through several more rooms and over to the stairwell. "All these rooms are connected and I bet they're underwater. Still, we can get to the Comm room by scuba diving."

"I don't know how to scuba dive," said Savannah. "Don't you need to take classes or something?"

"We have—Gills and me."

Getting certified had been Eric's tenth birthday wish. He'd made us take all the specialty courses: night diving, cave diving, even rescue diving. But neither of us had been since before the divorce. And we'd never done it without a grown-up before.

"That doesn't really help the rest of us," said Nate.

"If we can get to the Comm room, we can maybe call for help," Eric argued.

Nate looked doubtful. "You want me to let the two of you strap on God-knows-how-old scuba equipment, dive off the balcony of an underwater movie theater, and go someplace I can't follow you? I don't think I can allow that."

I nodded eagerly. "Yes! I agree with Nate!"

"I don't like the idea of us separating," Savannah said. She was holding her flashlight like a prayer candle, and it cast her cheekbones in ghostly planes. "What if something happens to you two?"

"Something's going to happen to all of us if we don't get out of here," said Howard. He was looking at the map. "I don't see another way through to the exit."

Eric folded his arms. "I'll listen if anyone has a better idea."

Nate was silent for several seconds, and much as I hated to admit it, I couldn't think of an alternative, either. We couldn't get to the next exit from here, and we had no idea how close Fiona and her friends were.

"Are you sure, Eric?" I asked. "It's going to be really dark down there."

He gave me a disgusted glare. "Are you seriously trying

to psych me out of saving all our lives?"

"No—I just . . ."

"I'll have you with me," he said. My throat grew tight. "I won't be scared. We can do this, Gills. Together. Like we used to."

We used to have Dad . . . and Mom. We used to use brand-new equipment. We used to not be trapped in an abandoned underground city.

But *not* diving wasn't going to fix any of that. "Okay," I found myself saying.

Nate shook his head. "I can't take care of you if I'm not with you."

"You can't take care of us, period," said Howard. His brother looked at him, stricken. "I'm sorry, Nate, but you can't. You know you can't. This isn't like at home."

Nate said nothing.

"Should we take another vote?" Eric asked.

"I vote no," said Savannah. She grabbed my hand. "Don't do it, Gillian. It's dangerous. You could drown." Her eyes were wide and fearful in the dim light. I remembered what she looked like, caught in that elevator as it went underwater, and my stomach turned over on itself.

I knew how the vote would go. Eric and Howard wanted us to dive. Nate and Savannah didn't. I'd be the deciding vote. And I had to get us all out of here. Somehow.

"It's dangerous here, too," I said. "We have to try."

We returned to the astronaut training room and found the best two sets of scuba equipment we could—inflatable vests, masks, head lamps, breathing equipment, and air and depth monitors. They didn't seem quite as modern as the ones Eric and I had learned on, but it was the best we could do. The air pressure in the tanks seemed okay and we tested all the valves and tubes thoroughly. There were no wet suits but Howard showed us how to set our silver jumpsuits on "warming."

"Won't these short out when we get in the water?" Eric asked.

"It says they're waterproof." Howard shrugged.

We lugged everything back down the hall to the movie theater balcony and put it on. As Eric helped me assemble the pieces, we rehearsed all the diving details I hadn't bothered thinking about in a while: stuff like descent and ascent times, clearing our ears, signals to our partner, and how to make sure we were taking big enough steps off the side of the boat—um, or balcony, in this case—so as not to catch on the tanks we were wearing on our backs. We put on flippers and stuck our sneakers in the pockets of our suits. We went over the map again and again until it was burned indelibly in our brains. We needed to go down through the door of the theater, through one hallway to a large chamber marked *P*, into the stairwell and out through a lower level, through another hall, and up another set of stairs to the Comm room. Reluctantly, I handed my precious diagram to Savannah.

"Please don't die," Nate said, once we were ready.

"*Please,*" Savannah added.

"And you guys stay here," Eric said, setting the timer on his dive watch. I used to make fun of him for wearing it around the cottage. Now I was grateful. "Hopefully, we'll be able to get in touch with you from the Comm room, but if we can't, stay here and at least we'll be able to find our way back to you or send help."

Nate looked grim. "For how long?"

"What?"

"An hour? Four hours? How long should we stay? When should we start freaking out?"

"We're not already freaking out?" Howard asked. "I thought that them strapping on old scuba diving equipment and leaving the rest of us here with no escape route was us freaking out."

Savannah bit her lip. I wasn't sure if she was keeping herself from snapping at Howard or whimpering in fear.

"At least an hour," I said. "We'll know by then if we can get a message out."

"And what if Fiona and those guys show up?" Savannah asked.

"We'll hide behind the seats," Nate assured her. "Don't worry. As long as we're together, I'll keep you safe."

Once upon a time, Savannah might have fainted dead away at the prospect of Private Pizza saying something like that to her. Now she just looked unsure.

There were probably more plans we should have made, but I knew if I spent any more time thinking about it, I'd never be able to get in that water.

I hugged Savannah, waved to the Nolands, and lined up next to my brother on the edge of the railing. He took a big step off the balcony, and when he cleared out of the way, I followed him into the depths.

UNSEEN DEPTHS

I SPLASHED DOWN INTO COLD BLACK WATER, THEN BOBBED BACK UP, fitted my regulator in my mouth, cleared my mask, and pulled it down over my eyes. Far above me, I saw the others' flashlights, up on the balcony. I waved to them, but I couldn't tell if they could see. Eric, his face distorted by the equipment, made the OK signal at me. I returned it, he pointed his thumb down, and under we went.

Scuba diving takes a lot of precision, but when you get your balance right, it's pretty easy—you feel weightless. No wonder they used it for astronaut training.

I'd scuba dived in the dark before. But that had been in class, with Eric and my parents, in a cave that had been certified completely safe for beginners. The abandoned movie theater was nothing like that.

Hand in hand, we kicked our way down the aisle, our head lamps roving over row upon row of empty seats. In places, the velvet or the carpet had torn and pieces drifted up toward us like ghostly arms of seaweed. We avoided these as we floated over the chairs and to the stage up at the front. There, my head lamp cast a giant shadow of Eric's profile on the glowing white movie screen. I laughed, and bubbles escaped my regulator.

Eric gave his shadow bunny ears, then moose antlers. He turned his arms into Godzilla and pretended to make it eat his flipper. You'd never guess he was the same boy who'd freaked out over giant earthworms. This is what happens when you get my brother in the water. I wondered if the others were up on the surface watching this. If they could even see us fooling around when they were trapped up there.

I grabbed his arm and pointed to my wrist. *Time, Eric.*

Okay, he signaled back. At least he wasn't afraid of the shadows. As for me . . . well, the nice thing about being underwater is you can't fall. Besides, the bubbles always go up.

Together, we floated over the stage and behind the screen to the movie theater's back door. Eric turned the doorknob and swung it open, sending some grit on the floor swirling into little eddies. Eric swam through the doorway and I followed.

By now, the others would see the lights passing out of the room and know we'd at least made it to the next chamber.

I tried not to think too hard about how that meant that if something went wrong, there'd be no way for them to reach us, but the fact loomed up, even larger than the walls of rock separating us from the surface. My breath sped up in my regulator and I reminded myself to calm down. We needed to conserve our air. I checked the pressure gauge—still at seventy percent.

I shut my eyes. Up on the surface, Dad was waiting. I imagined his face when we told him what we'd found, and what it would mean for his research. I held the image tight in my mind as I opened my eyes and swam on.

We headed single file down a narrow hallway and then out through another door. This one was a much larger chamber, and when we entered, my jaw dropped so suddenly I barely hung on to my regulator. It was a parking garage. On the map, it had been marked with a simple *P*, just like on a map at the mall. But I'd never seen a parking garage that looked like this.

The beams of our head lamps bounced off windshields and metal hoods and darkened red taillights. Through the murky water, we could make out the giant shapes of submerged vehicles. From tiny golf carts to giant cement mixers, backhoes and diggers and flatbeds and four-wheel ATVs, there had to be at least twenty vehicles parked in this chamber, end to end, like cars packed into a ferry.

This was not like scuba diving with my parents. This was more like dreams of flying.

We floated over the hoods of frozen pickups and by the windows of big rigs, glancing in at their unused, drowned gearboxes and headrests and cup holders. I couldn't imagine how such big machines had gotten here in the first place. There had to be some kind of giant elevator or driveway or ramp or something that could have let such big vehicles get all the way down to this level. Maybe there was even an alternative route to the surface. But though Eric and I made a full circuit of the chamber, I didn't see any kind of entrance or seam cut into the rock walls. Enormous metal plates reinforced the chamber in places. Maybe behind one of these plates there'd once been an opening, but now they were all bolted shut.

We gave up and continued our search for the exit. Eric's dive watch showed we'd been under for fifteen minutes. My pressure gauge now read 2500 psi, which meant the air was fifty percent gone.

Finally we found a door marked with a stair symbol. We opened that one and swam into a stairwell, where we found the cracked remains of the collapsed staircase we'd been trying to reach from above. I glanced up at the surface glittering at the end of my head-lamp beam. That meant we were more than halfway to the staircase we needed.

My breath shuddered in my regulator. More than halfway there, and half my air gone. Could we still make it there and back?

Eric must have sensed my fear, since he squeezed my hand as we slowly went deeper, clearing our ears and checking with each other as we descended one flight, then another. We passed through an open door into another small, narrow hallway.

I gestured to Eric. *You go first.*

He cocked his head at me as if to say, *You sure?*

I waggled my arm through the air like a snake. "Worms," I gurgled through the regulator.

Bubbles erupted from his face as he laughed. But he still went first.

There were more dark doorways, more black, underwater rooms. Some were bare, some filled with crates or mechanical equipment I couldn't identify. One had an examining table, another what looked to be a pretty elaborate dental chair, with a lamp and a drill arm and everything. Shards of metal flashed on the floor as I cast the beam of my head lamp across the room. I peered closer, only half surprised to see scrapers, picks, and even one of those little tooth mirrors scattered across the underwater floor. Guess it was a dentist's office—or had been, once upon a time.

Finally, we hit the end of the hallway. Here was another

door with a stair symbol on it, but though the knob turned, we couldn't get it open. Eric tried from above, then even let some of the air out of his vest, put his feet on the floor, and shoved against it as hard as he could. He turned to me and lifted his hands in defeat.

I checked my pressure gauge: 1700 psi, or two-thirds of the tank gone. We were losing air faster than I'd have liked. According to our training, we should surface when we still had about 500 psi left, or the pressure in our tanks would be too low for us to move air out of them when we breathed. And now I saw our mistake. The way above had been blocked—we should have realized the lower passage might be too. And we'd already used over half our air, which meant we wouldn't have enough for the return trip.

Which meant there was no way back to Savannah and the others.

I exhaled in a rush of bubbles through my regulator. *Okay, Gillian. Think.*

We could go back to the stairwell with the collapsed staircase. At least there we could breathe. We could call out to the others. They'd probably hear us. But then what? We'd be trapped at the bottom of the stairwell.

Every way I looked, I saw the walls closing in. Even my head lamp couldn't shine a way through the darkness surrounding us. I lost track of my breaths as I tried desperately to think of an alternative.

I didn't even realize I'd been drifting until my tank thumped loudly against the wall of the hallway. I wheeled my arms through the water and knocked my head lamp askew.

My breath in my regulator went wild.

I felt Eric still me, straightening my head lamp. He made the OK symbol in front of my mask. I nodded, miserably, and answered him. *OK*.

But I was *not* okay. I was miles below the Earth, dead-ended in an underground chamber with my brother and two ancient scuba tanks. And even my friends who *could* breathe on their own were trapped while lunatics with guns were looking for them.

Great idea, Gillian. Just get the pizza delivery guy to drive his little brother, you, and two of the people you love most in the world out into the middle of nowhere to look for something bad guys with a lot of power are willing to ruin lives over. Ignore the fact that when Fiona comes looking for Omega City, she brings two burly dudes, at least one gun, and a whole truck full of equipment. There's no way this could all go wrong.

Eric tapped the pressure gauge dangling off my BC. 1500 psi. Less than a third of my air was left.

I held my breath, which was something they taught you never, ever to do while scuba diving. Then again, they also taught us not to dive in unexplored caverns, so it wasn't like we were really following directions, anyway. I breathed in, as slowly and calmly as I could. *Think. Quickly.*

I opened my eyes and looked at my brother through the lenses of our masks. His eyes were wide and scared, too. I gestured to his pressure gauge and he held up five fingers. Fifty percent. Okay, at least he was doing better than I was.

Behind him I saw a pair of metal double doors with a button box on the outside. An elevator? If it was stuck on this floor, we were done for, but what if it wasn't?

This was our only option. I didn't need to think about Dad's research right now. Not with my brother floating in front of me, breathing ancient air and looking nervous, even behind the scuba mask.

I signaled for Eric to wait and swam back down the hall to the dentist's office. I grabbed a handful of metal implements off the floor, then swam back and shoved the thin end of a few of them inside the crack between the doors.

Eric got the picture quickly. We used the metal sticks as leverage to widen the crack, then pushed our hands in, tugging with all our might. The doors ground and squeaked against their runners, but opened. Eric eased into the empty shaft and aimed his head lamp up, while I crossed my fingers that the elevator car was higher than the water level. I caught the flash of his light against the surface of the water, several stories up.

He looked at me, a question in his eyes. I gave him a

thumbs-up, which in scuba language doesn't mean "okay." It means *let's go up now.*

It was tight quarters in the elevator shaft, what with our tanks and all, but we wrapped our arms around each other. It was like Eric said. We wouldn't be afraid if we were together.

I checked my pressure gauge. Only 750 psi left—the red zone. I hugged him tighter. It would be okay. All I had to do was go up.

Up.

We started to ascend. One story. Two. Numbers were painted on the inside of the elevator doors. The ascent was agonizing, but Eric, of course, made us follow guidelines, going slowly and stopping to readjust to the pressure. I refused to look at my pressure gauge. Three. Was the air inside my regulator getting thinner? Was I breathing more than I should? Would I have any warning or would I try to breathe in and find nothing to suck? We passed the door marked 4, and then hit the surface.

I instantly ripped the regulator off my face and breathed in real air. Above us, my head lamp illuminated an endless shaft with no elevator car in sight. I quickly looked back at the water level before I started getting dizzy again.

Air. Real air. I was happy staying here forever, now that I knew I'd have something to breathe.

"What floor are we going to?" Eric asked, bringing me back to reality. Right. Bobbing in an elevator shaft was not a permanent option.

"Six." I paddled over to the ladder built against the wall. "But we won't be able to climb up with our tanks on."

"If we climb up," he said, "will we be able to open the door from the inside?"

Another good question. We probably should have saved the dental tools, but it was too late to go back for them now. I didn't have the air and I doubted Eric did, either. Eric unhooked himself from his tank and it bobbed away from him, kept afloat by the inflated vest.

I did the same and grabbed the rungs of the ladder. "Kinda slippery."

I kicked off my flippers next, then went up a few rungs, hooked my arms around the ladder, and slipped my shoes back on. Eric followed. The ladder wasn't so bad, as long as you just stared at the rung in front of you and tried not to think about anything else, like your soaking shoes or your cold, slippery fingers, or what might be waiting when you got to floor six. Also, there was real air to breathe. That was a definite plus. I concentrated on that: breathing and climbing.

This was the only way. Up one rung. We'd figure it out when we got there. One more rung. Wouldn't Dad be proud? Another rung. Check that Eric was still right behind me. Think about how, if we fell, at least it would just be splashing down into the water.

You know, as long as I didn't slam against the wall.

When we got to the floor marked six, the door was indeed shut, and I saw right away that there would have been no point bringing along those dental tools. We'd never be able to pry the door open while dangling off the ladder.

"What's the holdup?" Eric asked from below.

Four feet higher, near the top of the door, was an old rusty lever that looked like it was supposed to be attached to something. I looked at it. The handle part had a wide base. I wondered if it was somehow supposed to connect with the actual elevator door when it hit the floor. I pushed on it and the doors groaned, which seemed promising. I threaded my feet through the rungs of the ladder, holding on for dear life, and tried again, this time with both hands.

Nothing happened.

"No!" I shouted at the lever. "Open up, you stupid thing! Open!" I banged on it with my hands. "Open! Don't you see, you're the only way out!"

My words echoed up and down the elevator shaft, and I clamped my mouth shut, embarrassed. I was screaming at a piece of metal. First Howard, now inanimate objects? How low was I going to sink today?

"Do you want me to try?" Eric asked from beneath my feet.

I rested my forehead against the lever in despair. "Sure. Why not?"

It moved beneath my brow. The doors slid open. I nearly fell off the ladder in surprise.

"Hey!" Eric called out happily. "You did it!"

No, I most certainly hadn't. I'd barely touched it this last time. Had I loosened it with all the banging? I touched the lever softly, but it seemed as firmly stuck in the open position as it had been in the closed position before.

Eric shoved on my legs. "Move. Let's go."

Right. Escape. I wedged myself between the two doors, in case they decided to shut as mysteriously as they'd opened, and held my hand out to Eric. "Come on."

That's when the doors started to push back together. Hard. I braced my feet and hands against one side and wedged my back against the other. "Hurry!" I screamed. "I can't keep it open!"

Eric looked panicked. "How? You're blocking the door!"

I shifted my feet to leave him a little space. "Crawl under my legs." The doors pressed against me. "Quick. I can't hold it much longer."

He scrambled underneath me as I locked my legs and arms, trying to keep the elevator doors apart. They were going to slam on me the second I tried to move. I would have to jump.

Eric hugged me around the stomach. "I'll pull. Count of three."

"One," we said together. "Two. Three!"

I jumped and Eric tugged and we both went sprawling across the silent hallway of level six. The doors slammed behind us.

"Phew," I said, and let my head fall back.

"Yeah," Eric agreed. "Can we just stay here for a minute?"

I wanted nothing more, but we had to think about Savannah and the Nolands. I sat up and rubbed the sore spot on my butt where I'd fallen to the linoleum floor.

Level six looked like a dry version of the hall we'd just left, but it was lit by those same orange and red emergency lights. And unlike the hall where the movie theater and the astronaut training room were, this one didn't smell like mold. There was a stale, dusty scent in the air, more like an attic or a box you haven't opened in a while.

Eric stood up and tried the elevator buttons, but nothing happened. The water below had probably shorted out the whole system.

"I figured," he said, though he sounded bummed. That would probably be too easy, right? An elevator right there to take us to the surface.

Well, easy, after almost getting drowned a few times.

We walked down the hall, lined with doors that seemed to be bedrooms, kitchens, and living spaces, until we reached the end, where on the final door was painted four letters in bright red stencil: *Comm.*

We'd found it.

VOICES FROM BEYOND

I TRIED THE DOOR, BRACING MYSELF FOR ANOTHER BATTLE, BUT IT opened easily. The inside was dead black, and though I flicked all the switches on the wall near the threshold, the overhead lights didn't seem to be working. I wondered if that meant the machines before us were dead, too.

The room was filled with boxy, off-white computer monitors, sound boards covered with metal switches and plastic buttons, grimy keyboards, dusty speakers, old-fashioned black telephone receivers, and even cassette recorders. There wasn't a flatscreen or flash drive in sight. What space wasn't taken up with these machines was stacked floor to ceiling with videotape cases marked with neatly typed labels that read things like *Plague, Famine, Fertility Problems,* and *Revolt.* Another shelf held more recordings. *US History, Vol. 4–12,* I read on one, and *Beginner Agriculture* on another. Then I found the mother lode. Row after row of tapes sat on a shelf labeled *From the Founder* in handwriting I recognized well.

Dad. Would be. In heaven. For a minute, I completely forgot we were supposed to be trying to find a way to escape and just stared in wonder at this wall of pure history. It was like the first time Dad had taken me to the big reading room at the university library, and I'd seen that massive wall of dusty leather books. No, it was a hundred times more exciting, because I knew exactly what I'd find on each and every one of these videotapes.

Dr. Underberg. It was his city, after all.

"I knew it," I whispered to the tapes on the wall.

"This is wild," Eric agreed. He walked over to one of the sound boards and flipped a switch. The board lit up, buttons and lights blinking red, green, and yellow. "At least this works."

"Yeah," I murmured, distracted as my eyes roamed the shelves. There was enough information here for Dad to write a hundred books.

"Um . . . Gills? We were trying to contact the outside world?"

Oh, right. Quickly, I turned on as many of the machines

as possible. I picked up the phone, hoping to hear a dial tone, but I got nothing. I booted up the computers, but they just showed blue screens and command prompts. I couldn't even find a mouse.

"I think Omega City was built before Windows," Eric said.

"What do you mean?"

"The computers—never mind. Look, it's another map." He pointed down at the display board in front of him. It was illuminated in a rainbow of colored lights and when I joined him at the panel, I could see that this diagram put the sketch we'd found by the turbine to shame. Here was the entirety of Omega City laid out before us, level by level, chamber by chamber, and apparently system by system, too. There were different system maps, color coded for Communication, Electric, Atmospheric Control, and Water/Sewage, and overlaid on the general white outline of the chambers. According to the key, rooms that were marked with green lights were "operational" while those in red were listed as "offline."

"Should be blue for 'underwater,'" Eric snarked. And most of the city was, in fact, in red. This place was huge. I couldn't imagine what it must have been like when it was all working as designed.

"Here's the theater." I pointed at the spot on the map. The lower level was listed as red on the Communications map, obviously, but the higher one was still green. "Find the intercom controls."

On another board, we found a massive panel of switches. I sat down on the wheeled desk chair in front of the panel and flipped the one marked MT Balcony.

"Hey, guys. We found it. Can you hear me?"

"Gills, turn the mic on."

There didn't seem to be a switch on the microphone itself, but I found one labeled Master Control on the panel and flipped it. The next time I pressed the button for the balcony and spoke, I could hear the faint echo in the microphone that meant it was transmitting my words.

"Guys? It's Gillian. Can you hear me?"

Silence. Was there an intercom button on their end, too, or was it only one way?

"We found some more maps here so we're plotting out an alternate route to the exit for us." I looked over at Eric for help. He gave me two thumbs up, grinning.

"Um, we're fine here?" I added. "It's nice and dry. And those suits were really warm. You were right, Howard." I hesitated again. "I hope you guys are fine, too. And, um, I hope you can hear me. Otherwise, I'll feel dumb."

Okay, that was awkward.

"Gills, look at this." Eric was rummaging in one of the crates near the floor. "Walkie-talkies!" He turned a set on. "Testing, testing."

A lot of good those did us, since we were standing in the same room. If only we'd had them back at the movie theater. And they weren't going to help us contact the outside, either.

"See if you can get online or something," I snapped.

"I don't think these computers are hooked up to the internet, Gills," he said. "I don't think they're even in color. They look like they're from the eighties."

"Find something that says 'outside line,' then. Maybe we can call 911."

"Okay," said Eric. "But you're going to have to be the one talking to them, because there's no way I'll be able to bring myself to tell them a story that starts with us crawling inside a boulder and getting shot at with a water cannon."

But try as we might, there didn't seem to be any connection to the outside world. Some communications room. It was all well and good if the world truly did come to an end, but what about the rest of the time?

"Hey, Gills." Eric was studying the map panel. "Check it out. These are the air vents." He pressed a button on the panel, and little dotted blue lines started marching around the screen, showing the path of air from one chamber to another, from room to room to room.

"Did you just turn the turbine back on?" I asked him.

He bit his lip. "Um . . . maybe?"

Maybe he'd made mincemeat out of Fiona and her

goons. Except, they had to be farther than the turbine now, right? Still, even if they were in the city, there was no way for them to guess which way we'd headed or where the others were hiding. We'd be safe for a little while.

I really wished I could talk to Savannah and the Nolands.

"But that's not the point. Look at this." He traced a line of dots across the map, from the hall outside the Comm room and straight across the map, across the entire chamber to C-block, over where we'd seen the classrooms and the military barracks. "We didn't go up those stairs, way back at the entrance, because it just led to this room here." He pointed at a room marked O.D. "But the air vent goes to that room. I wonder if we could crawl through and bring everyone else back like that."

"Crawl through the vents?" I shook my head. "That sounds really dangerous."

"*That* sounds dangerous?" Eric blinked in disbelief. "After swimming up elevator shafts and Russian gas traps and everything we've been through? At least we'll be above the flood waters. Come on, let's go check out the size of the vent."

So we went outside and pulled the grate away from the vent. It wasn't actually too bad—about the width of a doorway, but square, so it was the same height. Not that I was thrilled about the idea of getting trapped in an even smaller space than we already were. We shined our lights down the tunnel as far as we could, and saw nothing—no spiderwebs, no collapses, and most of all, no water. There was a soft breeze, though, which must mean the turbine was doing its job.

"I think it'll be okay."

I stepped back. What if we got trapped in the tunnel, not able to stand or move or run if we had to? Maybe I should tell Eric that if there were worms, they'd definitely be in there. And what about Nate? Somehow, I didn't get the sense he'd be thrilled about crawling into some tunnel.

"Gillian?" A crackly voice floated out of the Comm room. "Can you hear me?"

"It's Savannah!" We sprinted back inside.

The blinking light was coming from the room marked Gym. I leaned over the microphone. "I'm here. We're here."

"Thank goodness!" Savannah let out a big breath. "It's so good to hear your voice. Nate's been freaking out. Are you okay?"

"We're fine. The phones don't work, though. We're trying to figure out a way to get you up here."

"Yeah. The intercom button thingy didn't work where we were, so we moved."

"Eric thinks you can crawl through the vents and meet us."

There was nothing but silence on the other end of the line.

"What vents?" Nate asked at last. If he was scared, I couldn't hear it through the intercom.

"There are—air vents. Nice ones. Big."

"*Nice* air vents?" Eric said, making a face.

I ignored him. "We can see the whole layout of the city from here—what parts are okay, what parts are flooded. What systems are working . . ."

"How does that exit we're heading to look?"

I checked the map. Green. "It looks fine. We just have to get you guys up here."

"So what's the story with the air vents?"

Eric cut in on the microphone. "It's not so bad. You just need to go to the room marked O.D. on the map. It's right down near the C-block. You see it?"

Nate's voice crinkled through the speakers. "Yeah."

"Observation Deck," Howard piped in. "That's probably the Observation Deck."

"And then find a way to crawl up into the air vent."

"Yeah," said Nate. "That's the part where you lose me."

"You want to get out of here, don't you?" Savannah's voice filtered through.

Eric started giving out detailed directions about when they should turn and what other air passage intersections they might pass, but I stopped him with a hand over the microphone.

"They'll never remember all that," I whispered. "They'll get lost."

"We can still hear you," Savannah said, annoyed.

"I'll remember," said Howard. "I've been working on my memory palace."

"What's a memory palace?" Savannah asked him, and then they all started talking at once, and I couldn't make out any of Howard's explanation or exactly what Nate said to get him to shut up and focus.

Eric ripped off a sheet of paper from a notebook and started scrawling directions. "Okay," he said. "This is what we're going to do. We're going to give them the first few directions, then I'm going to get in and meet them halfway."

"You are not!" I exclaimed, grabbing his arm. "We don't split up."

"Too late," Nate said over the speaker.

That was different. Eric and I had been together, and so had the Nolands and Savannah. I wasn't sending my baby brother off alone. Nate of all people should understand.

Eric handed me a walkie-talkie. "We'll be in contact the whole time. I won't get lost—you'll tell me where I am."

He wanted me to sit here and listen to him getting trapped in an air vent over a walkie-talkie? Dad would kill me if anything happened to Eric on my watch. "You don't know the conditions of those tunnels. You don't know what's inside them."

"Yes we do." Eric tapped the blue dots on the screen. "Air."

Air . . . and collapses and drop-offs and spiderwebs the size of beds and bat colonies and . . . sure, giant worms. Why not? They had to like air vents. It was nice and dark inside them. I opened my mouth to say all of this to Eric when Savannah's voice came out of the speaker again.

"Are you guys still there?"

Oops. I'd been silent for too long, thinking about what it would mean to let my kid brother—and he was, even if he never acted like it—crawl away into a dark tunnel without me. "Yeah. We're here. Sorry. We're . . . figuring stuff out."

"Don't you see, Gillian?" Eric asked. "This is the best way. The safest way."

"Splitting up again?" I felt my eyes burning. "Eric, you didn't even want to be in the back of the line before. Now you want to go off alone?"

"Honestly? I'd rather go off alone than sit here alone."

"Why is that?"

He gestured to the Plague shelf. "This place is creepy."

"This place is awesome!"

He nodded. "Exactly why I think you should stay and I should go."

I had no argument for that.

"Besides, one of us has to stay here and man these controls, give us backup info. You can tell us where to go if Howard's memory palace is more like a shack." He switched on our walkie-talkies. "Testing?"

"One two three," I answered glumly.

"Okay, guys," Eric said. He gave them the first set of directions and they repeated it back. Savannah even made a little jingle out of it.

"*Up past two, turn right. Over past three on left, then turn left. Straight past five on right, turn right.* We can do this." I wondered if she was trying to talk herself into it, too.

"And I'll meet you there and bring you the rest of the way in," Eric said. He stuck his walkie-talkie into yet another pocket of his utility suit, then tugged at the zippers on the wrists. "I'm still not entirely sure what these are for." He unzipped them and some crumpled silver material slipped out and dangled from the cuffs.

"Gloves." I unfurled them. The palm and fingertips of each glove had little bits of rubber on them, like the bottom of a sneaker. "I bet they're for traction."

"I wish I'd known about this when we were climbing up the elevator shaft. Maybe they'll come in handy in the tunnel." He tugged them on.

I started thinking about drop-offs again. And about Dad, who had no idea his kids were trapped underground. And about Eric leaving me alone in this room. I clutched the walkie-talkie to my chest. There was no point in panicking. We had too much work to do.

Eric and I hugged, and then I saw him into the tunnel. I watched the shape of his body, silhouetted against the head lamp, all the way until he made his first turn. Then I returned to the Comm room to wait.

"How you doing, Gills?" came my brother's voice.

I depressed the button on the walkie-talkie handset. "Fine. Trying not to think too much."

"How's that going?"

"Not well."

"Want me to sing? I bet it'll be like singing in the shower. Good echoes."

"Please," I begged. "No." Eric was many things, but musical was not one of them.

Ignoring me, he busted out with a truly atrocious rendition of a pop song. Then he tried "Singin' in the Rain." When he got to "Supercalifragilisticexpialidocious" I turned the volume on the handset to low and went looking for a distraction.

Fortunately, the Comm room provided that in spades. There must be hundreds of videotapes, but I knew precisely where I wanted to start. On the Founder Message shelf, I picked the one marked *Monthly Message 1* and stuck it in the VCR. The machine made a few unpleasant grinding sounds and started to play.

At first it was nothing but shots of waving fields of grain and seagulls soaring over sunlit beaches, set to melancholy music, and then, a man's voice.

> **Earth . . . how beautiful it once was. How perfect. Able to sustain such vast quantities of life, able to recover from everything we've done to it. We shall not abandon our mother.**

It was the same voice we'd heard in the elevator, and back on the entrance platform, and in the Russian box. This was the voice of Dr. Underberg himself. My mouth dropped open in awe. Dad would be going nuts, listening to this. But before I could watch any more, the singing on Eric's end stopped. I paused the video.

"Everything okay?" I asked into the walkie-talkie.

He made a terrible sound, something between a cough and a minor explosion.

"Eric!" I cried.

"Sorry," he said. "There's—" Another exploding noise. "Dust."

Just dust? Sneezing sounded seriously dangerous in a metal tunnel. Better him than me. "*Gesundheit,*" I said, and went back to the video. Finally I could get some answers about Omega City. This place was unbelievable and utterly secret. How could it be that my father, who had spent years studying Underberg, didn't even know about it? He couldn't have built it single-handedly. When I pressed play, the image melted away to a scene of a middle-aged Dr. Underberg sitting on a bench in Solar Park. He addressed the camera directly:

> **Those of us who have chosen to remain, while so many others have left, deserve praise for our loyalty. We shall not discard our home like it's nothing more than a broken cocoon.**

What was that supposed to mean? If he was talking about Mother Earth, where else were you going to go? It wasn't like there was a secret base on Mars or something.

Wait. *Was* there a secret base on Mars?

> **My friends, it is clear that our lust for violence and bloodshed is what is tearing our world to pieces. We must band together, as people of Earth. For now, we truly are a people . . . of Earth.**

"Gillian? Calling Gillian Seagret. Respond at once."

I paused the tape again as my blood ran cold. I knew that voice. Even through the tinny echo of the speakers, I knew.

Fiona.

SPEAKER OF THE LOUSE

"GILLIAN, IT'S FIONA. I KNOW YOU CAN HEAR ME."

How did she know where I was? How did she know I was alone? My gaze flew to the intercom panel, where an orange light blinked.

"Turn off the master control, Gillian. What we have to discuss is not for everyone's ears."

I caught my breath. The master control? Did that mean that my conversation with Savannah and the Nolands had gone . . . oh, spitballs. It had gone *everywhere*. It was like the school's PA system—the office could contact individual rooms, or they could turn on every speaker in the whole school at once. And that's what Eric and I had done.

Eric! We'd sent him into the vents and then, thanks to the master control, we'd given out directions to Fiona and her friends.

"Gillian, I will not ask you again. We know where you and your friends are now."

What choice did I have? I flipped off the switch marked Master Control. This time I could hear it, the faint, echoing blip of feedback resounding down the empty corridors. We must not have heard it before because we'd closed the door behind us. I dropped my head into my hands. We were done for.

"Very good, Gillian. Now, flip on the switch marked L1, and we can talk."

I ground my teeth together but did as she said.

"Hello?"

"Good." Fiona cleared her throat. "I have to say I underestimated you, Gillian. You and your brother. You're clearly much more resourceful than your foolish father."

"Don't you talk about my dad!"

She chuckled. "You're very sweet. But, Gillian, you and I both know what he's like. He had in his possession for years the location of this place, and he never even figured out what it took a twelve-year-old girl a day to find? He's too academic. Too impractical. He doesn't deserve Omega City."

"And you do?" I rolled over to the map to track down

a room marked L1—but I couldn't find anything like that. Where was she? If they were far enough away from us, there was a chance Eric and the others could get back here before they were caught. The good news was, Fiona's men wouldn't find it any easier to get up here than we had, and Clint and the other guy wouldn't fit in the vent as easily as my friends did.

She was silent for a second. "You don't even know where you are, do you, Gillian? What the Omega City was built for? Such a shame. Allow me to enlighten you."

"I don't care what you have to say." Okay, that was a lie.

Fiona sighed into her mic, and it echoed loudly around the room. "I think we've gotten off on the wrong foot. Whatever you may think, I'm not your enemy."

"Oh no?" I started ticking off reasons on my fingers. "You're lying to my dad to steal his stuff. You have Dr. Underberg's diary, which means you must have been one of the people who broke into our cottage and flooded everything to destroy my father's research. And you've been chasing me and my friends. With guns!"

"I apologize for that last one," Fiona said. "Had I known that it was you in the woods, I never would have told my men to use their weapons. You're just children."

Except the way she said it, it wasn't like she was being kind to kids. It was more like she didn't think she needed guns to stop us.

"Clint shouldn't have threatened you like that, back on the entrance platform. No wonder you ran. Really, Gillian, this is all a misunderstanding."

"It was a misunderstanding when you flooded our house?"

Fiona seemed to hesitate for a moment. "How perceptive you are. And yes, in a way it was. I was following orders from my boss."

"I don't think that's an excuse."

"Neither do I," she replied. "That's why I quit."

"Hey, Gills," Eric's voice came through the walkie-talkie. "You still there?"

I swallowed, flicked L1 off, and depressed the button on the handset. "Yep."

"Okay. You just went quiet. I was worried you got caught."

I hesitated. Should I warn him? Would it make him panic? "I did. Kinda. Fiona contacted me through the intercom."

"What?" I heard a thump, as if Eric had jumped up and hit his head on the inside of the vent. "I'm coming back!"

"No!" I cried. "Go get the others. They're coming for all of us."

"Gillian," said Fiona calmly. Dangerously. "It's important that you're listening to me."

"Leave her alone!" Eric yelled. Oh, no. He needed to get

to Savannah and the others. He couldn't do anything to help me from there—and more important, Fiona could do nothing to hurt me while I was still up in the Comm room.

"Eric," I said firmly. "She's just a voice. But those men coming for Savannah and the Nolands are real. Now hurry!" I put down the walkie-talkie and turned the microphone back on. "I'm listening, Fiona."

"I don't deny that I was part of the team who raided your father's office and sabotaged his research two years ago," she confessed. "I was . . . working somewhere else then, and my bosses thought it was a good idea."

It was like she'd punched me in the stomach. How could Fiona—how could anyone—just sit there and say something like that! She'd ruined our lives, and she was talking about it like it was some vacation she took one time. "Who are they?"

"People you don't want to mess with, kid. Trust me. Actual bad guys."

"Who?"

She ignored that. "That's why I left them. That's why Dr. Underberg did, too, long ago. I don't want to hurt anyone, Gillian, don't you see?"

"No," I admitted. "I don't see. I see guns and lies."

"I'm not lying to you. I don't want to hurt you or your father. I don't want to hurt anyone. That's why I don't work for the Arkadia Group anymore."

Arkadia Group? I looked down at my silver suit. "The Arkadia Group are the people who hurt my father?"

She sighed. "You're wasting my time, Gillian. I'd be happy to explain everything to you once we're safely out of the city."

"Explain now," I snapped. "Why are you people after my dad?"

She hesitated again. "They didn't want him snooping."

That was only half an answer. "And you?"

"Oh, darling, I don't care what some little historian does," she replied simply. "I just wanted the directions to the Omega City."

A lot of pieces clicked into place for me then. Like how Fiona had been waiting for us at the diner when the owner suddenly changed his mind about talking to us. Maybe she'd threatened him before we'd arrived. And how Fiona had gotten so frustrated at the granite slab in Solar Park. She knew she'd been looking for some kind of rock connected to Dr. Underberg, but she had no idea which rock it was, and Dad couldn't help her. She'd acted like she was Dad's only friend, but she'd been working against him all along.

There was a huge racket on the walkie-talkie. "Gillian!" I heard Savannah's voice. "We're here!"

"Great!" I said. "Hurry back!" I needed a plan. I needed to know exactly where we were going the second they got here. And I needed to make the plan without Fiona knowing.

Fiona was still talking on her end. "What do you see in this city, Gillian? I see the life's work of a great man."

"You plan to ruin that, too?" I started tracing lines on the map to the exit. It looked pretty straightforward.

"No. I plan to celebrate it. Do you know why Dr. Underberg built this place?"

"Because he was afraid we'd start a nuclear war and blow everyone to pieces?"

"Yes . . . that. But more than that. He was afraid that there was no place for survivors to go. During the Cold War, sometimes people built backyard bunkers. Little spaces the size of schoolbuses that could protect one or two people for a month or so. And at the same time, the government was building massive ones—Greenbrier in West Virginia was meant to hold Congress. The NORAD facility in Colorado was built for the military."

"I know about them." What did she take me for? Dad had taken us on tours of them, way back when we were a whole family. Before Fiona and whoever she worked for had wrecked our lives.

I scanned the space for a backpack or a tote bag or something. I could collect all these videotapes and carry them with me. I could bring them home to my dad. We might not get our hands on the battery, but we could finally have proof again that he'd been telling the truth all along.

"But where were the normal people supposed to go, Gillian? People who weren't military or government, who didn't have top secret clearance? Dr. Underberg wanted to save them."

I stopped what I was doing as her words sunk in. I'd been right all along. Those hundreds of empty seats in the movie theater . . . those classrooms and the gym and the parking lot filled with empty vehicles. He was making a place for the normal people, the people like me and my family and friends.

I thought of his writing in the diary, his "last and lasting gift to mankind." I looked at the tape and its grainy image of sunlit seashores and misty forest-covered mountains Dr. Underberg probably put in there because he thought anyone watching these tapes had seen them nuked out of existence. The only weapon I'd seen in this whole place was that trap for Russian spies on the entrance platform. *Enemy combatants and firearms are not permitted,* as the recording in the elevator had said. The same one that said *Welcome, survivors.*

That's what Dr. Underberg had always been focused on. Survival. Survival for soldiers in war, for sailors at the bottom of the sea, for astronauts in space . . . and for normal people who needed shelter when things went really, really bad up top.

But there was one thing I was absolutely sure of: office-flooding Fiona and her gun-toting goons were *not* normal people. They were . . . well, *them*.

"I want to help people, too," Fiona insisted. "All those amazing inventions of Underberg's—they disappeared along with him, and that's not right. But"—her voice dropped—"they're here. His wonderful battery? What if it's hidden right here?"

Yeah, what if? But I'd been all over this city and the only stuff I'd seen was out-of-date gym equipment and old computers. If the prototype was here, Underberg had hidden it well.

"Think about what the discovery of his battery would do for the energy crisis. What his nonperishable food could do for millions of starving children around the world. What his smart fabric could accomplish in hospitals, or for sports. The list goes on and on."

Smart fabric? I brushed my hands over the sleeves of my silver suit as a chill shivered my skin. I was sure if I could see my arms, they'd be covered with goose bumps. This suit said it had been made by the Arkadia Group. But was it still Dr. Underberg's invention?

"And that's what you're trying to do?" I asked. "Bring Underberg back into the world?"

"Yes!" She sounded relieved. "We're on the same side, don't you see?"

I remembered what she'd said, back at dinner with my dad, about what a great man Dr. Underberg was. At the time, I just thought she was buttering him up, but maybe she'd been telling the truth. But if that was the case . . .

"Then why didn't you just tell my father what you were looking for?"

"Well . . . I wasn't sure how he'd react, was I? He's been so burned by the whole situation. I wasn't sure he'd take kindly to my search."

Something about this didn't make sense, but I couldn't be sure what it was. And then it hit me—she had been very clear about wanting to know everything Dad knew about Underberg. She'd wanted to see all his research. And Dad had been excited about every morsel of attention. He'd been thrilled to see a young, attractive woman with a steady job and no trace of an aluminum-foil hat interested in his work again. He would have handed her whatever she wanted, had she asked him. But instead, she'd kept secrets. She'd even sneaked into his files. And she'd never let him know that her goal was to bring Underberg's celebrated technologies back into the world.

"You don't want to rediscover his inventions," I realized aloud. "You want to steal them."

She was quiet for a very long time. "Aren't you clever."

"Yeah, I am. And you're not going to do it. Underberg has, like . . . patents or whatever on his work. That means you can't claim it."

She laughed. "Are you seriously trying to tell me what patents are? Little girl, I do this for a living."

I scowled at the speaker, flicked the microphone switch off, then turned the walkie-talkie back on. "Eric?"

"Coming," he said, sounding out of breath. "Gills, there's someone behind us. We can hear them in the tunnel. Get ready to run."

It must be Clint and the other guy. And they knew at least the first half of the directions. They probably even knew Savannah's little jingle.

"Hurry!" I gave up looking for a backpack and started shoving tapes into the pockets of my suit. I could only fit a few, though. I rushed over to the desk with the lighted maps, scanning the surface for a hard-copy version of the detailed schematics on the screen, but found nothing.

That's when I realized Fiona was still talking to me.

"—not like they will let anything patented by Dr. Underberg come to market. They'd prefer that he and everything he stood for be completely forgotten."

As Eric would say, who are *they*?

"And," she went on, "since he's not around to make any money off his inventions anymore—well, isn't it better that people be able to have these things than not? I can bring them to the market, and Underberg can't. It's as simple as that." She paused. "Gillian? You're still there, aren't you?"

I lunged at the switchboard and turned on L1. "Yep. Right here." And still very busy thinking Fiona was a big, stinking liar.

"I don't think you realize the precarious position that I'm in!" she said. "Look at your father—the Arkadia Group didn't even want a biography about Dr. Underberg out because it would compromise their goals."

"What goals?"

She ignored me. "Think about that for a minute, Gillian. They wrecked your father's whole career over a book. Not even an invention. I'm taking on a lot of risk here."

"Excuse me?" I asked, incredulous. "You want me to feel *sorry* that you're a thief?"

"Who cares who invented it?" she cried. "You don't know who gets the money for every single thing you buy. You're wearing sneakers constructed by some child in Cambodia that cost your dad more than that kid makes in a year. Tell me, is that fair?"

"No," I said. "But neither is what you're doing. And you're the one I can stop right now."

"Don't play games with me, little girl," she said. I wished she'd stop calling me that. "I've gotten the better of smarter and more powerful people than you. You will meet us at the turbine at once, and you will bring with you everything useful or interesting you have found in the city."

Didn't she mean in *the Omega City*? I was sick of listening to her. She didn't know the first thing about this place. She was no better than a pirate.

"Then what?" I snapped. "You'll pay us with treats? We're not golden retrievers you can just send off to fetch you things."

"I pay my golden retrievers in steak," she replied coldly. "Believe me, I can make it worth your while. You don't want to live in that hick town forever, Gillian. Don't you miss your old home, your old school? I know Eric wants his sailboat back."

How dare she? For a second, I wished I could look at her perfect, awful face. Glaring at a speaker didn't really have the same oomph. Then again, her being somewhere else in the city meant I could say whatever I wanted. "You ruined my dad's life and now you want to pay us off with a *sailboat*? No way, lady."

"I'm really tired of arguing with you, Gillian. I've tried being nice, but you're not getting out of here unless you help me."

Oh yeah? We'd see about that. I wrote down the directions to the nearest exit and repeated them back inside my head. I could do this.

"You will bring your friends and any technology you may have picked up with you to the turbine."

This was Fiona's weakness, I realized. She may have wanted all of Underberg's cool lost tech, but she was not about to get herself drowned or crushed by wandering around inside the ruins of Omega City. Not when she could get a bunch of kids to do it for her.

"You want it?" I said. "Get it yourself."

"I will ask you one more time. Bring yourselves and any items you find to the turbine, or I will seal off the exits and leave you and your little friends down here. Forever. You have one hour."

There was a blip, as if the link was cut, and I was alone in the silent Comm room. I looked at the frozen image of Dr. Underberg, staring out from the past.

"Don't worry, sir," I said to the screen. "I won't let you down."

BLIND FLIGHT

"GILLIAN!" ERIC AND SAVANNAH BURST THROUGH THE DOOR, BOTH YELLing their heads off. "Let's go! Those guys are in the tunnel."

I wiped the tears out of my eyes and wheeled the chair around. They were a mess—sweaty and breathing hard, with long streaks of dirt marring the shimmery silver of their suits. Savannah's hair was frizzing up around her head like a white-blond puffball, and where their faces weren't flushed from exertion, they were covered in dust.

"Wow!" Howard was right behind them. "Look at all these tapes." He grabbed one labeled *Space and Near-Planet Colonies.*

"Take it with you," Eric said. "Take whatever you

want." He started filling his pockets with his own collection of videotapes and other records.

"Nate's trying to screw the grate back in," Savannah said. "He thinks it might give us a little extra time."

I opened my mouth to speak, but no sound came out. I knew I should tell them what Fiona had said, what she'd threatened to do. I knew we should take a vote, just like we had with the guns.

Nate poked his head in the room. "We gotta go, guys. I can hear them back there. They don't fit quite as well as we do, but they're still moving."

I took a deep breath, and it all poured out in a rush. "Fiona says if we don't turn ourselves in to her at the turbine in an hour she's going to seal us all in here to die."

They all stared at me, wide-eyed.

"Are you serious?" Savannah whispered.

I nodded, miserable, and tucked my chin into my chest. Of course they were going to vote to surrender. If I spent a few seconds thinking about it, I'd do the same. And then Fiona would steal all of Dr. Underberg's inventions and Dad would still be ruined and this was all for nothing.

Nate pursed his lips. "Well then, we'd better hurry."

"Yeah," Eric agreed. "We only have an hour to get to that third exit."

"More like fifty-eight minutes," Howard said. "But yeah."

I raised my head, looking at them in amazement.

Savannah grabbed my hand and squeezed it. She was wearing her suit's silver traction gloves. "You've plotted the way, right?"

I pulled out my directions. Then I heard it—the sound of thumps and grunts and echoing, metallic curses. Fiona's men.

"Now or never, Gills," Eric said.

Okay, then. I clutched Underberg's treasures through the silver material of my pockets. "Now."

WE RACED DOWN corridors and up flights of stairs. Thirty seconds after we'd left the Comm room, we heard the clatter of metal.

"They kicked down the grate," Nate panted as we ran up another set of stairs. "Run!"

So we ran, as quickly and quietly as we could. With any luck, the men wouldn't guess what way we'd gone.

One more hallway filled with intriguing doors I didn't have time to explore and we burst into another stairwell. Right on the other side of this landing, according to the map, was the elevator for the third exit. Nate and Eric sprinted over to the doors, but they were jammed.

"Up another level!" Nate shouted, and we all took to the stairs.

Thankfully, the next level was clear and we came

pouring out of the stairwell. The elevator stood there, the up arrow lit in the friendliest shade of white I'd ever seen. We were going to make it.

"At last!" Savannah cried as she jammed her palm against the call button on the elevator.

Nothing happened.

"No!" Nate pounded the metal double doors. "Open, you dumb thing!"

"Nate," said Howard, placing his hand on his brother's arm. "Listen."

I held my breath. I could hear it, the sound of machine parts whirring. The elevator was coming down, floor after floor through the darkness. But I heard something else, too—the sounds of boots on the staircase we'd just left.

"They're coming," I said, in a tone somewhere between a whisper and a cry.

Instantly Nate and Howard threw their weight against the stairwell door, while Eric, Savannah, and I looked for something to block it. The rooms on this hall seemed to be living quarters of some kind. There was a sofa in one of the rooms, but it was too heavy for us to lift. Savannah was dragging out a metal bed frame when the Nolands yelped and the door seemed to jump off its hinges.

"Open up!" yelled Clint, or maybe it was the other guy.

"Or I'll shoot!" No, that one was definitely Clint.

"Step away from the door, Howard," Nate said calmly,

even as he flattened himself against it. "And get your thing ready."

What thing?

"Is that elevator coming anytime soon?" The door jumped again, and Nate braced his feet against the floor.

Just then, Nate went flying across the room and the door burst open. We all screamed and jumped back. The two men stood there, wearing heavy-duty black suits and holsters with all kinds of tools and implements hanging from them: grappling hooks, compasses, walkie-talkies, utility knives, and yes—guns. Their head lamps speared our eyes. Nate pushed himself to his feet and stood in front of us, which was when I realized that we'd all kind of huddled there, across the hall from the elevator. Nate spread out his hands, as if gathering us behind him, and yeah, he was big, compared to us. But he wasn't that big.

"Travis," said Clint. "Contact Fiona. We've got them."

The other guy—Travis—pulled out his walkie-talkie. Just then, the elevator door dinged open.

The two men looked behind them at the sound. For a second, I saw it—lit from within with the same orange-red emergency lights as the rest of this level. There it was, just on the other side of those men. Our ticket out of here.

And then everything went blinding white.

"Run!" Howard shouted. I blinked but only saw a flock of gummy pink flashes that were probably my corneas exploding or something. Still, I turned away from Clint and Travis and started stumbling. Someone grabbed my hand—maybe Savannah?—and pulled me along.

"What was that?" Eric cried. I could barely make out the outline of his body as we careened down the hall.

"Keep running!" said Nate—if the giant silver blob attached to the end of Eric's arm was actually Nate. I blinked furiously and ran to keep up with the giant silver blob I thought was Savannah.

"Stairs," she warned me. Not that it mattered. I could hardly feel them under my feet as we went down one, two . . . three at a time. My eyes started to clear as we passed out of the stairwell and back into the giant main chamber of Omega City. The floodlights still angled against the roof of the cavern, bathing the boxy trailer buildings and the floodwaters in a soft blue twilight. It seemed like ages since we were here last. I rubbed my aching eyes and looked again. We were now on the opposite side of the city from where we'd entered near the turbine.

"Come on," said Nate. "The flare won't keep them for long." We started down the nearest metal walkway.

"Howard had a flare from one of the survival kit things we found in the mess hall," Savannah explained. "We made some plans to defend ourselves while we were waiting for you and Eric in the movie theater."

"Apparently!" I gasped.

As soon as we were off the walkway, Nate and Howard started yanking at levers near the handrails, and with a groan, the whole thing separated from the building and went crashing to the wet stone floor below.

And then we were off again. We were crossing our third walkway when we heard shouts in the cavern and knew Clint and Travis were catching up again.

"I can't run much more," gasped Savannah.

"You eat too much pizza," Nate replied, and kept running.

"Yeah," Eric said, out of breath. "And whose fault is that?"

Next, we went down a flight of stairs. Howard, coming last, pulled a bottle of something out of his pocket and poured it on the steps behind him.

"What's that?" I asked.

"Machine oil," he said. "Found it in the gym by the weights. Maybe they'll slip."

"Are you kidding me?" I asked as we took off again.

"Are you complaining?" Nate replied. "Save your breath and sprint."

But despite the Nolands' best efforts at booby traps, Clint and Travis were gaining on us. We couldn't keep quiet as we pounded over the metal walkways, and neither could they. Their clanging and banging echoed through the cavern, ever louder and ever closer.

"Not to ruin the fun," Eric said, "but we do know where we're going, right?"

"Exit four." Nate's face was grim, his eyes intent on the path in front of him. I imagined he'd spent quite a lot of time studying the map while Eric and I had been underwater. His hair and face were drenched with sweat, but he showed no sign of slowing down. The rest of us didn't dare fall behind now.

I couldn't get the image of that elevator out of my head. Right there, open, and fully operational. We could have rushed inside. We could have pressed the button. What if I'd surrendered to Clint and Travis on the condition that they let my friends go? They could all have been on the surface already.

"There they are!"

A cracking sound echoed loudly off the rock walls.

They'd found us.

THE GLASS GARDEN

NATE SHOUTED A BAD WORD AND CROUCHED ON THE WALKWAY. "DUCK!" he said. "They're shooting! Run!"

How could we do both? We tried the best we could, awkwardly hurrying with our heads down. I could hardly breathe, thinking about that sound. We were being *shot* at. Clint was *shooting* at us. And it hadn't even been an hour.

Then again, we did shove a flare in his face.

As we rounded the walkway around the next building, instead of getting on the metal, elevated path between buildings, Nate jumped down to the rock floor about five feet below. We followed. Down here the ground was slightly uneven, slick with moisture and pockmarked by puddles.

Here and there we saw the silhouettes of stalagmites: giant cone-shaped stone crystals that seemed to grow right out of the earth. Some were nearly as tall as me, and I even risked a few peeks toward the roof to see if there were any matching stalactites hanging from the ceiling.

There may have been. It's hard to look up when you're running for your life.

"Under here," he whispered when we reached the next building. He ducked underneath the platform and we hurried after him. Savannah and I barely had to bend our heads, and Howard and Eric fit just fine.

I'd thought these freestanding buildings were elevated with concrete blocks, like trailers, but that wasn't the case at all. Instead, each stood on four columns made up of giant rings of painted steel. As I got closer, I could see that where the rings touched, chips of paint had flaked off, showing scratches on the metal as if the rings had rubbed against each other.

I touched the rings, feeling the deep grooves and the scratches in the paint. "What are these things?"

"They're springs," Howard whispered. "They help protect the structure by absorbing vibrations from earthquakes or nuclear strikes."

I nodded. That must be what had caused so much damage in other parts of the city. The buildings set into the rocks didn't have that kind of protection. Then again, springs didn't protect the buildings from the floods.

"Guys," Nate hissed at us. "Turn off your lights."

We flipped off the flashlights and head lamps and huddled behind one of the large central springs. It was easily the size of a minivan. The ground was cold and wet and water dripped somewhere close by.

We heard footsteps echoing from somewhere, and then the clang of booted feet on the walkway near our building. I almost expected the springs to bounce like the underside of a couch or a bed, but even though the pounding of Clint's and Travis's combat boots seemed to shudder through my entire body, the springs remained solid. Omega City was built to withstand a nuclear attack. It could handle two bullies with guns.

The question was, could we?

"Check inside." Clint. He must be the leader. A flashlight's beam cast over the chamber floor beyond the edge of the building. We all squeezed tighter together as it occurred to me that silver jumpsuits did not make for decent camouflage. Dr. Underberg should have thought of that. He hadn't properly prepared for the moment the citizens of Omega City may have had to run for their lives from—

Boots stomped right over my head. We wrapped our arms around one another and held our collective breath. Any minute now, Travis would realize we weren't in the building.

Nate began making gestures in the darkness for us to head out in the other direction. I could still see Clint waving his light around on the opposite side of the structure. I shook my head vehemently. We had no plan, we had no escape, and we were wearing shiny silver suits.

And Clint was shooting at us.

Then again, what were our options? Sit around here until they found us?

Again the image of that elevator filled my brain. We'd been so close.

"Now," Nate breathed, and shoved against my back. I ran, and the others ran too, dodging and weaving around the springs until we reached the open air. We were fifty feet from the building when I heard Clint's shout of discovery. I was afraid he'd shoot again—and even if his aim was lousy in the dark, I didn't want to take that chance.

"Don't look back!" Nate called. With his long legs, he could outpace the rest of us easily, but he was sticking close. We followed him over to the right, near the far side of the chamber. Ahead of us was a dark dome tiled in a black honeycomb pattern. There was a metal door in the side, which Nate held open as we all sprinted inside.

He slammed the door, and everything stopped. Light, sound, everything. The air around us felt almost soft, the blackness fluffy, like a pillow, in comparison to the vast, echoing emptiness of the cavern.

One by one, we flipped our flashlights back on, revealing dusty floors strewn with tables and what looked like broken bits of pottery and tile. Nate dragged one of the tables in front of the door, wedging it up under the knob so it wouldn't turn. Howard helped him, collecting shards of broken tile or something on the ground and helping block the table legs from sliding across the floor.

"Where are we?" Eric asked, once we were properly barricaded in.

"It's marked AG on the map," said Howard.

"I don't care. I care about making it to exit four before those guys do. Come on." Nate started marching off into the darkness. I caught flashes of light all around us, quick as shooting stars. What was this place? Our voices were muffled, as if the sound stopped a foot or so from our mouths.

Eric's head lamp beam was tracing the wall, which seemed to be made of a soft, almost fuzzy brown fluff. He found a control panel and turned the lights on.

Instantly the space was filled with an intense yellow light and I squinted, though this wasn't nearly as bad as the flare had been. A steady, humming buzz ran everywhere, and as my eyes adjusted, I could see why. Giant warming grow lights shined down on row after row of tables, each covered with trays of withered brown vines and herbs. Enormous mirrors all over the walls, floors, and ceilings reflected and refracted the light in a thousand different directions. Massive glass bubbles spaced evenly along the outside walls housed gnarled dead trees and tangles of some other dead plant I couldn't recognize. And the interior surface of the dome? Dead moss.

"It's a greenhouse," I said, staring around in wonder.

It made perfect sense. If people were to live in Omega City, they had to get their food from somewhere. Astronaut ice cream and Meals, Ready to Eat were okay for emergencies, but you wouldn't want to live off them long term. I'd bet those were fruit trees in the bubbles, and probably vegetables and herbs all along the tables under the grow lights.

There had to be more, though. This couldn't feed my school, let alone a small city's worth of people. Somewhere there had to be fields of underground grain or—I glanced at the tables of withered plants—pens filled with dead livestock.

I really hoped Dr. Underberg hadn't put animals down here before whatever happened to this place happened.

"The map says there's an exit right here," Nate was saying. He was standing about halfway down the center row, looking puzzled and turning the map around and around in his hands.

We joined him there. He was staring at the ceiling of the dome. "I don't know where it could be."

I looked down. We were standing on another massive

mirror, its surface reflecting the bottom of our shoes. It seemed to be the only mirror set into the floor of the greenhouse, and there were no tables around it. I glanced up, half expecting to see plants hanging from the ceiling. Why was there a mirror on the floor?

Over near the far edge of the mirror sat a small gray control box with a red button in the center.

"What if this mirror moves?" I asked. "What if all the mirrors swivel around, to help direct the lights?" I pointed at the button. "Howard, want to see what that does?"

He brightened as we all stepped off the mirror and onto the concrete.

As soon as he pressed the button, the mirrors in the ceiling and on the wall started to shift, making the light dance and leap across the inside of the greenhouse. The mirror of the floor folded down the center and tilted up into a tent shape, angling light sideways at the growing platforms. All of it was amazingly cool, but Nate and the others only had eyes for the darkness under the mirror, where a metal ramp led down into nothingness. We aimed our flashlights into the hole but could see no farther than a few feet. For the first time since entering the greenhouse, I could hear the drip of water and catch the smell of rot.

I didn't like it one little bit.

"Where does it go?" Savannah asked.

Nate shoved the map under her nose. "Look, we go down through here and through this stairwell and come out over there and go to exit four."

"And what happens if that doesn't work?" I asked. Why hadn't I planned out alternate routes while I'd been waiting for the others back in the Comm room? I don't think I even looked at the AG room—whatever that meant, since this was clearly some sort of garden—when I'd had the chance. I had no idea if it led to operational or offline places on the map. I had no idea if we'd hit more flooding.

"Gills, what's our option?" Eric asked. "This is the only way out."

I heard a pounding on the dome door. "Let us in!" yelled Travis.

"Come on out!" yelled Clint.

And then a rhythmic sound, like they were throwing their weight against the door to try to break it down.

There was another crack of gunfire and then the sound of shattering glass. Giant knife-sharp icicles of mirror and terrarium started raining on us.

What choice did we have? Savannah sprinted down the ramp, with the rest of us hot on her heels. A few yards down was another red button and when Howard pressed it, the door folded shut again. Up close, the underside of the door seemed to be made of metal.

"Look, there's a lock." Howard shoved at a lever but he couldn't make it stick until his brother helped him push it into place.

And just in time, too, as seconds later, we heard boots up top and the sound of the gears grinding again, as if Clint and Travis had pressed the button.

"Open up!" Another shot, but nothing happened.

"You broke it, you idiot." Travis's muffled voice filtered down.

"Nicely done, Howard!" said Savannah. She held out her hand for a high five, and he flinched like she was going to hit him, then lightly tapped his palm to hers.

I shined my lamp around the space. Blackness spread out in every direction, and the narrow, ghostly white ramp continued to descend into the abyss. After a quick consult with the map, we started walking, but if there was another end to the ramp, I couldn't see it. It seemed to be suspended from the ceiling by massive metal poles and we went deeper and deeper into the Earth.

"Um, guys?" Eric said after a minute. "This is the wrong direction. We're trying to get *up*."

At last I could make something out over the side. I saw the dark glimmer of water, and more giant, pale shapes like the backs of whales ballooning up toward the surface. "What are they?" I asked in awe.

"Tanks, maybe," Nate suggested. "Water or oil or something?"

We passed one that was set above the surface of the water. The omega symbol was stenciled on the side in red letters four feet high, and under it the word Grain.

Finally, we saw a rock wall looming in front of us, sheer and massive. We'd reached the end of the chamber. There was a door set in the side and the ramp led right down to it.

Savannah breathed a sigh of relief. "We made it."

"Don't get excited yet," said Eric. "These things don't always open." He reached for the knob.

Just then, a huge explosion rocked the cavern. The ramp shuddered beneath my feet, then gave way. I reached for my brother, Savannah, anything, but my hands clawed nothing but air as we all dropped like stones into the icy water far below.

CREATURES FROM THE REALLY BLACK LAGOON

BACK WHEN WE LIVED IN THE CITY AND DAD WORKED FOR THE UNIVERSITY, we got to have pool memberships at the university gym, which was really fun because it was indoors and warm all winter long. They also had those huge diving platforms like in the Olympics, and every so often they'd open them up for regular people to jump off. Eric really enjoyed it.

I did it exactly once.

Jumping off high places into the water isn't actually very fun. To start with, it hurts—the soles of my feet were red and stinging for a day after my one experience with the diving platform. And you shoot down through the water like a knife, so it was good that the university pool had that diving well right below the platform where the water is like twenty feet deep and you never have to worry about cracking your head open on the bottom. It's also really disorienting: you're up high, then falling, then you're shooting through the water, and even though it's this wide open, well lit, extremely clean swimming pool, it's hard to tell which way is up.

In every way possible, falling off that broken ramp was worse.

I plunged deep into the black water, in a jumble of limbs and metal and more. I hit my arm pretty hard against something, then my butt crashed against something else. My feet kicked instinctively, and it felt like they may have met with someone else's head. The explosion still resounded around the cavern, and even underwater, I heard farther low, giant-sounding booms, like bits of the wall and ceiling were falling all around us. I threw my arms over my head to protect myself from falling objects, then realized there was no guarantee I was even facing up.

I spun in the water, hoping to catch sight of bubbles to follow back to the surface, just like they'd taught us in scuba diving class. It's really easy to get disoriented in the water, especially dark water, and so if you just follow the bubbles you'll aways find up.

A few seconds later, I broke the surface, gasping. My head lamp made out the wrecked remains of the ramp, dangling down into the turbulent water. I tried to tread, but my knee and arm hurt a lot.

"Gillian!" Howard waved to me from the top of the grain tank. "Over here!"

I started swimming when Savannah emerged in front of me, coughing and spluttering. "My arm," she choked out. "Can't move . . ."

I helped her to the tank and let Howard pull her up.

"Where's Nate?" he asked. "Where's Eric?"

"I don't know." Frantic, I looked around. What if they were trapped under some debris? What if they'd hit their heads and gotten knocked out. . . . "Eric!" I screamed. "Eric!"

"He's here!" I heard Nate cry. "He's helping me!"

I paddled over to where Eric was trying to untangle Nate from some cables. I came over to help, which was when I noticed blood streaming down his chin.

"Eric, what happened to you?" I tried to touch his face but he jerked away and yanked the last cable free. We swam back to the tank, Eric keeping one hand cupped protectively around his cheek.

"What happened?" I grilled him the second we were up on the tank.

"Fewmickme," he said without opening his mouth.

"What?"

"You kicked him in the face, Gillian," Nate said. He was digging in his pockets. "Okay, aspirin all around, I think, but mostly for Savvy here and Eric."

Eric looked at the pills in his hand, then gingerly opened his mouth to place them inside. I must have kicked him really hard.

"Did I get you in the teeth?" I asked, grimacing.

He just glared at me and dry swallowed the pills. Yeah, definitely in the teeth.

"Did you get these from the first aid kit back at the mess hall?" Howard asked.

"Yeah," Nate said. "Why?"

"They may be expired."

I didn't care anymore. Expired aspirin was better than none at all. My arm hurt so much, and it was nothing compared to Savannah's and Eric's injuries.

"Let's take a look at your arm, Savvy," Nate said.

Savannah nodded tearfully, and honestly, it wasn't an act. There was a time, I think, when she would have killed for Private Pizza to give her cute nicknames and run his hands along her arm, but that time was long gone.

"There's no bone coming through the skin," he said. "But I don't know if it's broken or just a bad sprain. You'll have to have a doctor look at it when we get out."

When we get out.

"If you haven't set your suits to warming," Howard said, fiddling with his controls, "now is the time to start." It was weird, but ever since we'd entered the dark part of the city, I hadn't noticed his eccentric behavior as much. You don't notice that someone isn't looking you in the eyes when you can't see them. And it was like I could understand him better, too, without seeing his face. I'd have to keep this in mind for when we got back to school.

Except I wasn't sure we'd ever see school again.

I shuddered, looking around at the wreckage where we sat, just a few inches above the rippling waves flooding the chamber. Fiona had done this. There was no doubt in my mind that the explosion we'd just experienced was her fault. She'd sworn she'd seal the entrances if we didn't turn ourselves in, and now she had.

But why would she do it when her men were down here, too? It didn't make sense.

I couldn't see anything but blackness and rock walls. Things had stopped falling into the water now, at least, and sitting here, against the metal, I felt cold in spite of the warm setting of my suit. I'd been wet for too long, tired for too long, without food for too long.

"Hey," Nate said abruptly. "Everyone eat and drink something. Now."

"Again?" Savannah whined. "He made us do this while we were waiting for you, too," she said to me. She was cradling her arm against her chest. "Something about shock or hypothermia or—ow!"

Howard had jostled her while pulling one of the MREs from his pocket.

"Watch it, will you?" she snapped at him.

"You have low blood sugar," he replied calmly. "That's why you're cranky." He opened the package and pulled out a little tin that he filled with water and set flat on the top of the tank before opening an envelope and emptying what looked like a packet of sand into the tin.

"What are you doing?" I asked.

"It's the heating element," he said. "Watch." A minute or so later, I saw the water start to simmer. He placed a foil packet inside and started in on another MRE. I hugged my knees to my chest and watched, fascinated.

"The water and the sand make heat?"

"It's magnesium powder. The water causes rapid oxidation—rust—and that produces heat." He shrugged. "I read the instructions while you and Eric were scuba diving."

"You guys really made good use of your time," I replied, impressed.

"It was listen to Howard read or have an hour-long panic attack," said Savannah. "Turns out, he comes in handy."

In more ways than one, I thought, remembering the

machine oil slick. Sure, Howard had pressed some buttons without thinking things through. He'd also seriously saved our butts more than once. I was really glad he was here. That they were all here.

I looked at my brother, who scooted away, his face stormy. *Come on, Eric. It's not as if I meant to kick your teeth in.*

After another minute or so, Howard handed me one of the packets. "Careful. It's hot."

It was. I almost dropped it, I was so surprised. He hadn't even started a fire. I tore open the packet and the second the scent of meat and spices hit my nose I realized I was starving. I dug in with my bare hands. Teriyaki chicken—the best teriyaki chicken I think anyone had ever eaten.

Howard repeated the process a couple of times. The packet he handed to my brother read Chicken Noodle Soup on the side.

Eric grimaced, but tore off the top and drank the broth.

"Are you okay?" I asked him.

He shrugged. "Yewohme."

"Yeah. I owe you big time." For kicking him in the face, for dragging him down here, for everything.

He hugged one arm around himself and returned to his soup, and when I reached out to him he just shook his head. I didn't blame him. What were a few lost teeth when you were stuck at the bottom of an underground well? I looked over at the dangling ramp, shooting at a steep angle up into the black beyond. Even if we hadn't been injured, I wasn't sure how we could climb up that thing. Savannah definitely wouldn't be able to do it with a broken arm.

Our bizarre picnic continued in silence. I was pretty sure we were all thinking the same thing.

"Everyone warm?" Nate said at last.

"Warm?" I asked. "Or warmer?"

"I'll accept warmer, at this point." Nate looked around. "There's got to be a way out of here."

"Why?" asked Howard.

"What do you mean, why?"

"Why does there have to be a way out?" he said, in the annoyed tone people use when they have to explain their statements often. "Not every room in this city has to have an alternate route. Eventually, we reach the end." He hesitated. "Eventually, there's got to be a dead end."

"Don't say that!" Savannah exclaimed. "Nate's right. They got these tanks in here somehow, and it wasn't through that mirror door thing."

Her words made me think of the parking lot Eric and I had scuba dived through, and how I'd wondered the same thing. But those doors had been bolted shut and deep underwater. I examined the swirling black water underneath us. Maybe there were bolted-shut entrances below the surface here, too. Either way, it wouldn't help us.

"The map is gone," Nate said now. "But back when I had it, I saw all we needed to do was go through that door and down a few halls to reach the fourth exit. It was off a room marked S.L.O."

"No, it was S.I.L.O.," Howard corrected.

Who cared what it was called? We couldn't get there.

"Plus side," Eric said, maneuvering his jaw for the first time since the fall. From what I could tell, he'd only broken three or four of his teeth. I mean, *I'd* only broken them. "I vink I feel a little bedder."

"Really?" asked Howard. "Because you sound like a bad vampire movie."

"Oh, good," said Savannah. "Now we can all die down here to a chorus of Eric's smart remarks."

"Vere are worse ways to go," said Eric. He tried to smile, but just winced instead.

"We're not dying down here." Nate pounded his fist against his knee. "We're not."

But we weren't moving either, just sitting on top of the wet grain tank, our crumpled dinner trash strewn around us, the water lapping insistently at our heels. I was out of ideas. I focused the beam of my head lamp up at the door we were supposed to go through, high, high above us. I didn't see any way for us to get up there. My arm and butt didn't hurt quite so much anymore, but my toes were starting to go numb inside my sneakers. I was glad our lights were still holding strong. I wondered how long they'd keep shining after we froze to death.

I squeezed my eyes shut. That was probably the wrong thing to think about.

I guess Savannah noticed how upset I was, because she put her hand over mine. She was cold, too. Really cold, and her hands were soaking wet, which I thought was a little weird, since I thought she'd been wearing her suit's gloves. I opened my eyes to check it out.

There was a giant white worm in my lap.

I jumped up, screaming and shaking my hand. The worm went flying and landed with a wet plop several yards down the tank. Oh, and it wasn't a worm, either, because it picked itself up on its little white legs and skittered back over the side.

We were all standing up by this time. Eric was basically trying to climb onto Nate's back. "Vere *are* worms!" he yelled through his clenched jaw. "Vere are!"

And he did mean worms, plural. They were all around us now, climbing up the sides of the tank, gliding toward us through the water. Dozens of them. Hundreds, each one several feet long and white and totally wriggly.

"I think they're salamanders," Howard said. "They

have legs . . . and look at their faces."

"No vank you." Eric shuddered and edged farther away from the creatures.

But I looked. Howard was right; they weren't worms. They were more like long, snakelike lizards with milk-white skin. They had eyelids, but I never saw one with its eyes open, which made me wonder if they had eyes at all. They didn't shy away from our lights when we aimed them at them, and they each had huge ears like scaly fans that waved gently as they breathed.

"I think they're blind," Howard went on. "Look, they're obviously listening. They must have been drawn by our noise, and the smell of food."

"Food?" Eric asked in a tone of dread.

I rolled my eyes. "Dinner, Eric. Not us."

"You don't know vat."

"If they lived on people, they would have died out a long time ago," I argued. "Or haven't you noticed that there aren't a lot of people down here?"

"Yeah," Eric shot back. "*Anymore*. Because ve worms ate vem all!"

"They aren't worms," Howard said evenly. "They're salamanders."

"Guys!" That was Savannah. "Who cares? The real question is, where did they come from?"

We all turned to her.

"Maybe they live in this cave," she said. "Or maybe Gillian's right and they swam in here from somewhere else when they smelled the food."

"Which means there's somewhere else to swim to!" Nate grinned. "Stay here. I'm going to go check it out."

"Don't go in vat water!" Eric said, but Nate jumped off the side of the tank anyway. The salamanders scattered in front of him, and he started swimming in the direction they'd come from.

"Why are you so afraid of them?" Howard asked.

"Vey are giant, slimy monsters," Eric replied.

"Salamanders," Howard corrected.

"*Monster* salamanders."

Savannah turned her eyes skyward. "Please don't let me be stuck in here with these two until I die."

After a minute or two, Nate came back, and the gathering salamanders vamoosed again.

"Do you guys want the good news or the bad news first?" He climbed back up on the tank, dripping wet.

"Good news!" Savannah clasped her bad hand with her good one in a pleading gesture.

"The good news is I found a door."

"Ve bad news is it's full of worms?" Eric asked.

"Salamanders," said Howard, on cue.

"Shut up or I'm feeding you to one," Savannah groaned.

Nate cleared his throat. "No. The bad news is it's underwater."

How was that supposed to help us? We didn't have scuba tanks this time.

"But," he added, his tone encouraging, "the passageway is short, and it lets out on a stairwell. You could be out of the water in twenty seconds after going through the door."

Savannah looked doubtful. "You're saying we have to hold our breath for twenty seconds."

"Or thirty. Depends on how fast you can swim."

Savannah cradled her broken arm, looking worried.

"But then we'd be out!" Nate said. "And the staircase—I don't know how far it goes up, but what if it goes all the way? What if that's exit four? We could be *out*."

Even the salamanders seemed to shiver with joy at the thought. I wondered if they spent their whole lives down here, blind in the darkness. I wondered how long it would take us to go blind in this endless black.

"We have to try it," Eric said. "Worms and all. We have to." He gingerly touched his jaw.

Things were going south quick. We were all freezing, Savannah may have had a broken arm, and the only way out of here was a long underwater swim through a river of wormy salamanders. But the only other option seemed to be sitting on top of the water tank until the salamanders decided we were food, after all. Or we froze to death. Or the lights went out.

I don't know why that last option scared me more than all the others, but I felt for my spare flashlight in one of my leg pockets until the blood stopped roaring in my ears and I could speak without choking.

"It's the only way out," I said. "The only one that even has a chance." And we all knew it. We didn't even have to take a vote.

"It's going to be a long swim, so we should rig up the flashlights to keep our hands free," Nate suggested.

Eric and I still had our head lamps from scuba diving, but I traded mine for Savannah's flashlight, figuring she needed all the help she could get. Using stretchy bandages from the first aid kit, Nate tied his flashlight to his head and then repeated the process for Howard and me. We looked ridiculous, but who was going to see us, anyway? Certainly not the blind salamanders.

Then we got in the water. That was the hardest part, because we all had to get in first and shoo away the salamanders before Eric would agree to follow us, and then he insisted on staying surrounded by three other swimmers at all times. I was swimming next to him and he was kicking his legs like a crazy person, as if it would keep the creatures at bay.

"Watch it," I said to him.

"Look whove talking," he replied, his words mangled by his broken mouth.

We swam over to the door Nate had found. The threshold was only a foot underwater, and the sign on the door read **ΩSILO**. We all hugged the wall, reserving our energy.

"So the secret to holding your breath for a long time," Nate coached, "is to take three deep breaths in a row. It's kind of like winding up." He demonstrated. The first breath was sort of short, followed by a long one and then a super long one. "The hallway is short and a straight shot. If you drop your flashlight, don't worry about it, just keep swimming forward. There are enough of us that you should be able to see. When you get to the end, the landing is flooded about halfway up the flight of stairs. I'll be waiting to pull you through. Get out of the way as soon as you clear the hallway so the next person can get up."

We all nodded.

"All right, I want you to buddy up. Eric and Howard. Savvy and Gillian. Do not let your partner get away from you." He looked at me. "Okay with bringing up the rear?"

I nodded. There was no way I was going to let Eric bug out about the worms or Savannah not be able to make it with only one arm. If I had to shove them both the whole way down the hall, I would. I'd brought us all down here. It was only right I be the last one out.

Nate pointed to himself and took three deep breaths, then went under. Howard and Eric followed. I looked at Savannah. It was tough to make out her expression under her head lamp, but her eyes were wide with fear.

"This isn't like the elevator, Sav," I said. "We're not going to get trapped. All we have to do is swim down a hallway, and we're out."

She nodded, but looked no less scared. I couldn't blame her. After all, I wasn't doing this with a broken arm.

"Come on," I coaxed. "Three deep breaths." We did them together. *One, two, three . . .*

Facing each other, we slipped beneath the surface, and I had to steel myself not to gasp as the icy water closed over my head. The underwater world was black and silent, but I was almost used to it by now. I tried to imagine I was one of the salamanders, going about my life in a flooded cavern, swimming, swimming, swimming. I kept my eyes on the hallway's end, past the kicking legs of Eric and Howard several yards ahead of us. I could see the outline of Nate, floating in the water in the landing, holding the door open, waiting. Savannah was at my side, pulling herself awkwardly through the water with her left hand. She was going slow, but I still thought we could make it.

We passed dark doorway after dark doorway and for once, I wasn't even tempted to look inside. *Just get to the end and you can breathe again.* I willed my thoughts into

Savannah's head. *Keep swimming. Keep swimming.*

That familiar burning ache of held breath started filling my chest. *Keep swimming, keep swimming.* Eric and Howard had made it. I watched them pass through the doorway and disappear. *Keep swimming, keep swimming.* I felt Savannah falter to my left and reached for her hand.

And then the world turned upside down.

SILO

END OVER END I TUMBLED IN A RUSH OF WATER AND BUBBLES AND debris. I had no idea which way was down or up. I couldn't find Savannah; it was like being knocked off your feet by an ocean wave. Seconds later I slammed into Nate at the opposite end of the hall and surfaced, sputtering.

"What was that?" I coughed out, as the water frothed around us. We were swimming at the base of another stairwell, though it looked like the sea at high storm.

"Anover explosion!" cried Eric. He was standing halfway up the first flight of stairs, where the water churned around his knees. "Look, ve water levels are rising. We have to get out of here."

"Where's Savannah?" I whirled toward Nate, who was still treading water at the entrance to the landing. His face was grim.

Oh, no. "Savannah!" I screamed, as if she could hear me under the water. "Sav!"

"Get up on the stairs," Nate barked, but I ignored him, breathed deep, and dove back under the water.

It was hard, fighting the current coming down the hallway, but I struggled past two doors until I caught sight of a light in one of the rooms. The explosion must have swept her inside.

I pushed myself in. Savannah was floating near the ceiling. I swam up to grab her and noticed she was treading water. Warm relief shot through me. She was still conscious.

I broke the surface and bumped my head against the ceiling. I couldn't even get my whole head out of the water. I maneuvered until my face was carefully aimed up and surfaced again, into a pocket of air only a few inches high between the water and the ceiling. "Are you all right?" I asked.

That's when I heard it. She was breathing fast, choking, sobbing breaths. "I can't," she whispered. "I can't."

"Yes you can, Sav." I rubbed her shoulder under the water. "You have to. We can't stay here. The water levels are rising. We have to go forward."

"Did you hear me, Gillian?" she snapped. "I can't

anymore. I can't even . . ." She coughed. "I can't even breathe. I can hardly stay up with this arm . . ."

I bit my lip. She wouldn't even be down here if she hadn't wanted to help me. I had to save her. "You don't have to swim, Sav, I promise. There's a current. We'll just get out of this room and let it carry us to the stairwell."

"I can't." She coughed again. Her voice was low.

I stared up at the ceiling. Was it closer than it was a few seconds ago? I wished I could look Savannah in the eyes. "It's only two doors down. Nate is there—"

"I don't care. I'm so tired."

"Sav," I begged her. "Please. This is just like that fast turn in the creek. This is just like the water slide down at the rec center." This was just like all the crazy things we'd done every summer of our lives. Me and Sav, year after year. She'd always stood by me—when Mom left, when I was new at school, when I didn't wear the right clothes or say the right things.

"Just hold your breath and let the current take you. I know you can do it. I've seen you do it a hundred times."

She shook her head and sniffled.

"I *know* you, Sav," I said to her. The real her, not the cool, school Savannah. It was summer Savannah who'd followed me underground. "I know what you can do and I promise you can do this." Under the water, I caught and squeezed her uninjured hand.

She looked at me sideways, since that was all we could manage at this point. There was no mistake. The water level was rising, and fast. In a few seconds, there'd be no air pocket left.

"Three breaths," I said. "Just like before. Ready?"

She breathed in—once, twice, three times. And we went under.

A few seconds later the water spit us out in the stairwell. It was almost all the way up the flight of stairs now. Savannah, coughing, crawled up to the landing, and Eric caught me and dragged me up to him.

"I'm going to kill you," he said to me angrily. "You know you don't actually have gills, right?"

I coughed up some water. "Yeah. I mean, *now*."

There was another rush of water through the hall. Salamanders starting flooding in, turning end over white, slithery end in the turbulent waves.

What in the world did Fiona think she was doing? We all stood and started up the stairs, and the water poured in behind us, bubbling up step after step, careening over handrails and across landings.

Ten flights up. Twelve. Every time we got ahead of the water by a flight or two, we took a rest, but it wasn't for long.

Fifteen flights up. I could hardly breathe. "We have to take a break," I gasped. "A real one." We were still two stories ahead of the water. It looked like it was slowing down.

"Yeah," Howard agreed, panting.

Nate looked up between the bars of the handrails. The stairs went up forever in their awkward, square-shaped spiral. "Can't we rest once we're out? I just want to get out."

"If we don't stop, you'll be carrying us all out of here wiv coronaries," Eric said. I guess his jaw was feeling better. Either that, or the cold water and aspirin had numbed his pain.

Savannah just plopped her butt down on the stair and buried her face in the crook of her good arm.

"No sleeping." Nate went to touch her but she shook him off.

"I don't have hypothermia!" she cried. "I'm just exhausted, okay?"

Howard studied her. "If he tells you you're cute, will you get up?"

She glared at him, then squeezed her eyes shut. "No, Howard. I don't care if he thinks I'm cute right now. I know I'm *not* cute right now."

"That's true," said Howard. "Silver really isn't your color."

Sav groaned and dropped her head back into her hand.

Nate bounced on the balls of his feet with impatience. "We're close, guys. I know it."

Eric looked up between the twisting stairs. "How many more stories?"

"Ten, maybe? Fifteen?"

"Fifteen?" I moaned. "No."

"You know," said Nate, "you should really think about taking a break from those books and joining a sports team or something."

"You sound like my mother."

"I'm just saying, you're out of shape."

I stopped wheezing and glared at him. "I've spent the last six hours running and swimming through an underground city. My shape is fine. I'm just exhausted."

"And lay off the pizza."

"Oh, I see what this is. You just want us to stop ordering pizza from you."

"Yeah." He smirked. "Pretty much."

I peered over the banister. At least the water had stopped rising. "Tell you what. We get out of here, we'll never make you deliver our pizza again."

"Are you kidding?" Nate replied. "I get out of here, I'm never delivering anyone's pizza again. I've decided life's too short to keep that job."

After a minute, we started up again, this time at a much slower pace. This staircase was different—there were no other entrances on any of the landings where the stairs turned, just one unbroken staircase going up and up and up, with numbers written on the wall. We passed twenty and kept going. At twenty-two I wanted another break, but Nate had caught sight of the ceiling, and urged us on. Twenty-three through twenty-five were kind of a blur, and twenty-five through twenty-seven were sheer torture.

When we hit thirty, the top floor, there was no number painted on the wall. Instead there was a giant omega symbol and a single word on a big, reinforced metal door.

Ω

SILO

"Weird," said Nate. "I was hoping for 'exit.'" He reached over and turned the knob. The door opened on a vast round cavern, lit by the same dull blue light we'd seen before. My heart fell. We weren't out. This was just another cave, not exit four at all.

"Oh," said Howard, in his usual flat tone. "Silo. Like a missile silo."

Every muscle in my body seized up. A *missile* silo? In Dr. Underberg's masterpiece? That didn't sound like him at all.

We crowded around the door and peered through. A square metal grate platform about the same size as the landing we were on led to a narrow walkway that jutted out over the space. As my eyes adjusted to the light, I could see that most of the cavern was taken up with a huge rocket ship, as tall and nearly as wide as the silo itself.

"Awesome!" cried Howard, and the sound ricocheted off the silo walls and fell away as the rest of us stared wide-mouthed at the rocket, unable to speak.

There were massive letters painted down the side of the ship but I couldn't quite read them. One by one, we stepped onto the platform and peered out over the narrow metal walkway. It was barely wide enough for a single person, and when Howard went out a few steps, it bounced and waved beneath his feet.

"Howard," Nate said. "Get back here. There's no water down there to land in this time."

But Howard wasn't really listening. He took a few more steps, and the walkway bounced again.

"Howard!" Nate followed him out, making the walkway start jittering around like crazy. I gripped the handrails of the platform in fear.

Behind us, the door shut. Eric tried to yank it back open but there was a strange grinding sound, like something screwing into place. A voice echoed out: that same cheery, disembodied voice we'd first heard in the elevator.

Greetings, space explorers. You have arrived at the doorway to the Rocketship *Knowledge*. Please come prepared with your blood type,

life support gear, and thirst for adventure. All entrants must have passed a NASA Class A physical and either hold a commercial jet pilot license or have completed U.S. Air Force or Euro-NATO jet pilot training programs.

"Howard!" Savannah called, cradling her broken arm against her chest as if to protect it. "Did you hear that? You're not a pilot. Remember the Russians!"

Savannah was right. The last time the recording thought we were impostors, it had almost killed us.

But somehow, I knew this was different. After all, there was no way for the walkway sensors or whatever it was that had triggered the recording to know that Howard wasn't an Air Force pilot. Plus, the voice of Dr. Underberg didn't scare me anymore. He was the voice in the Comm room, speaking about the wonders of Earth while Fiona threatened me. He was the mind who had built this whole city for no more glorious purpose than to try to help normal people in times of trouble. People like me and my brother and my "impractical" father. All the scary stuff that had happened to us here in Omega City hadn't been his fault. It was because the city had been abandoned, because it was broken and lost and dying, due to people like Fiona.

Dr. Underberg was on our side.

I stepped out on the walkway, too.

"Gillian!" Savannah squealed. "What are you doing?"

I looked back at her. "There are no more stairs, Savannah. No more exits. Twelve stories of water back the way we came. If there's something in the rocket ship that can help us, I say we check it out."

"Easy for you to say," Savannah said. "You can hold on with both hands."

"I'll help you," I replied. "You aren't going to fall."

"Watch out!" Nate called back. "There are some missing rungs on this thing."

Savannah fixed me with a look. "You were saying?"

With Eric taking up the rear—for once—we edged farther and farther out, wincing in fear every time someone else's steps made the walkway bounce and shake. A few times I had to leap across places where the metal plates had fallen through or rusted away, and every time I landed, the whole thing juttered so wildly I thought it might throw me off the side. Savannah tucked her entire good arm around the railing, holding on with an elbow.

"This," she declared, "is worse than the swimming."

"Move," Eric slurred from behind her, nudging her back.

At last I reached the far end, where a big, curving door was cut into the side of the rocket ship, right above the final E in *Knowledge*.

"How do you open it?" Nate asked as we met the

Nolands at the end of the walkway. It dipped now, in a slow, bounding bounce, at our combined weight. We felt around the seam to see if there was a lever or a button or something, but nothing happened. Howard pushed on one side of the door and then the other, as if that would make it release. Nothing worked, and Eric had already turned around to head back to the platform when there was another rushing, whirring sound and the door popped out automatically.

Just like the silo door had. I narrowed my eyes. Nothing in this city worked, until it did. The turbine, the elevator shaft doors, and now the rocket ship.

"Can I open it?" Howard asked.

Nate shrugged. "I don't think it'll be the stupidest move we make today."

Howard pulled the door open. A ladder led down from the door and we climbed in, single file. Savannah had some trouble navigating the rungs with her bad arm so I helped her, spotting her from below as she slowly came down. The inside was well lit, and it looked like those pictures of spaceships you see from NASA. Every available space on the wall had a purpose: screens, control panels, cabinets, and holders and fasteners of all varieties. A porthole in the side of the floor led down to another layer, and another and another below that. Nate and Eric went down to check them out, and Howard just stood in the middle of the first compartment, basically shaking with excitement.

He started naming every item and contraption and control on the wall. After the fifteenth entry on his list, I sort of tuned him out and wandered off on my own. There was a panel much like the one in the Comm room on one wall, and an orange light was blinking next to a label that had the Ω symbol on it. I flipped the switch.

". . . please respond at once. All Channels. Repeat. Gillian Seagret. Eric Seagret. Friends of the Seagrets. If you can hear this message, please respond at once."

Fiona again. I clenched my jaw and pressed the button marked Speak. "Killing us didn't work."

"Gillian?" There was a rustling on Fiona's end. "Are you okay? Is everyone all right?"

"No thanks to you!" Savannah hissed at the speaker. She shouldered me aside. "Listen, lady, how would you like being almost drowned three times? How would you like—"

"I didn't authorize any of that!" Fiona cried. "That was my men who set off the explosions, trying to get the door open in the agro-dome. Trust me, they did not run their sorry excuse for 'strategy' past me. They will be properly dealt with. I have spent the last hour sick with worry that something happened to you children."

Oh yeah? Well, we spent the last hour almost dying. "Nothing's ever your fault, is it, Fiona?" I stepped back in front of the microphone. "When you broke into my dad's house, you were just following orders. When we almost died because you started dynamiting the city, it was people not following *your* orders. Isn't that convenient? You'd be more than happy to take the credit for Dr. Underberg's inventions, but there's no way you'll ever accept responsibility for the horrible things you've done."

I heard more rustling and then a muffled voice. "*They're in the silo.*"

"Don't you dare come after us again, Fiona," I warned her. "We're done here."

"We're coming to help you get out!" she insisted.

I believed that like I could believe those salamanders in the granary could sight read.

"I can't wait to tell my father what a liar you are." I turned the switch off. I didn't want to listen to her anymore.

What I wanted was to explore the spaceship. And when I turned around, it was to discover the others looking at me in shock. My face flushed and I bit my lip, even as Eric shot me two enthusiastic thumbs up. Everyone else gave me a wide berth—or at least as wide a berth as they could in the cramped confines of the rocket. And after the way I'd yelled at Fiona, I wasn't surprised.

"Hey, Gills," said Eric, "have I ever told you that when you're right, you're very, very right?"

I smiled weakly. "I'm never going to let you live it

down. Now, let's check this place out."

If you followed the ladder up past the door to the rocket, it went through another porthole. I decided to explore that area. I climbed up the ladder and eased myself through the port. This section of the interior was smaller in diameter than the others, with a domed ceiling that made me think I'd reached the top level. The light here was a deep marine blue, shining out from the giant screen that took up half the wall. The rest of the space was all control panels and two giant command chairs, both facing away from me and toward the giant, pulsing blue screen. I supposed this would be where pilots sat. The ones with the certification the recording wanted to make sure we had.

It was odd that Dr. Underberg had included a spaceship in his city, especially after all that talk about not abandoning Mother Earth and the other things he'd said on the video back in the Comm room. Maybe there was information here about what the ship's purpose was. I walked over to the command seats to see what was written on the controls but stopped short. My breath caught, my bones froze, and my stomach dropped down to my feet.

Dr. Underberg was sitting in one of the chairs. And he was dead.

THE MAN IN THE CHAIR

HIS SKIN WAS GRAY AND PAPERY, HIS HEAD BALD WHERE THE PICTURES I'd seen of him had once shown hair. Age spots speckled his skin, and there were all kinds of tubes running in and out of his body—in his nose, and up under the loose-fitting shirt and pants he wore. I tried not to look too closely at those. He was so, so still.

"Guys?" I tried, but it came out like a squeak. I swallowed and tried again. "Um, guys? Come quick."

They climbed up the ladder. Savannah was first. "What is it, Gill—eww, gross!"

"Whoa," Nate added as he arrived and caught sight of the man in the chair.

"Is that . . . Dr. Underberg?" Howard asked.

Eric came up last, his bruised, swollen face somber as he heard the others. Only Eric would really understand what this meant. All this time, Dad would have done anything for a chance to meet with Dr. Underberg. We thought he'd died years ago. But here he was, wasting away alone in a spaceship.

"How long do you think he's been gone?" I asked the others.

Nate blinked at me. "Gillian, have you ever seen a dead body before?"

I was confused. "No. Why? Have you?"

He chuckled. "Trust me, they don't look like this." He leaned over and touched Dr. Underberg's shoulder. "Sir? Sir, can you hear me?"

The body jerked in its seat. I stifled a scream. He was alive!

Dr. Underberg blinked his eyes open and took a deep breath. "You've come at last," he croaked. "Is there anything at all left above?"

"Excuse me?" Nate's brow furrowed.

I came forward, my hands clasped in front of me to keep me from tossing them in the air or throwing them around Dr. Underberg's neck or anything else crazy. I couldn't believe it. This was way better than any battery.

"Yes, sir. Everything's fine up there. I mean—well, not

fine." There were wars and famines and natural disasters and everything else there'd ever been. But the world was still spinning merrily along. "I mean, we're not here seeking refuge."

He looked at me, his dark eyes wide and watery with age. "Then why have you come?"

"We've come . . . seeking you," I said. "The truth about you."

"We found a page from your diary," Eric explained, "and we followed your clues about Pluto—"

"I did that," Howard volunteered.

"And then we found the elevator," I said, "and came down and . . ." And what? What would be a sufficient description of everything that had happened to us in the past day? All the frights and the discoveries, the adventure and the near-death experiences? "Here we are," I finished lamely.

Underberg pressed his head back against the seat cushion. "All these years I've waited. I've waited for you to come. Y2K, I was sure, would send you scurrying down here, terrified that a bunch of ones and zeroes had the power to bring the whole world to its knees."

"What's Y2K?" Savannah cocked her head to the side.

Eric waved his hand dismissively. "When people invented computers, vey only programmed in two spaces for the year, instead of four. So when it turned from nineteen ninety-nine to two vousand, it was going to go from ninety-nine to zero zero."

"That's dumb," she said.

"Yeah, it was. But it wasn't as big a deal as everyone said it was going to be. People were afraid all computers would shut down—banks, airliners, missile defense systems—at midnight on New Year's Eve. But it didn't happen."

"No," said Underberg. "It did not. And then came the secret war."

"The secret war?" The very named thrilled me. I imagined my father would go nuts for this information.

"The one that started with the plane crashes."

"9/11?" Howard asked incredulously. He turned to me. "No wonder you like this guy so much."

Nate gave his brother a dirty look. "I think maybe he's been down here a while."

"Yes, sir," I said. "There was a war after 9/11, but it wasn't a secret. There have been lots of wars."

But he didn't seem to be listening. "And then, when the calendar of the Mayans reached its end . . ."

The Mayan apocalypse? Okay, that was a stretch, even for me. Here's what that whole thing was: Once, thousands and thousands of years ago, the Mayans made these huge stone calendars, like giant wheels, that supposedly counted out the entirety of time, but the calendar ran out in December of 2012. And because the Mayans were amazing ancient astronomers, a lot of people—not Dad, but friends of Dad's—believed they knew when the end of the world was about to happen.

But Dad said that was silly. What happened when the free wall calendar you got from the auto mechanic or the dentist ran out? You just go get one for another year, another calendar of race cars, cartoons, or puppies in teacups. There's no evidence that the end of a piece of carved stone indicates the end of time. People were just being crazy.

I wondered if Dr. Underberg was crazy. Staying underground, alone in this city all these years, just waiting for the world to end—it had to make you a little weird, right?

"Sir," I said softly. I went to touch his arm, but it was papery and cold. "All of those things happened, but none of them destroyed the Earth. We're not in any danger."

"Yes, you are!" he exclaimed. "You are in the greatest danger the world has ever known. Worse than the Cold War . . ." He trailed off.

I looked to the others for help. Savannah twirled her finger around her temple in the universal sign for *crazy*. Nate looked like he wanted to head back down the ladder and make a run for it. Eric wore an expression I knew well and dreaded most: disgusted pity. He pitied Dr. Underberg's crazy theories the same way I'd seen him pity Dad's. This whole time in Omega City, he'd had to drop the skeptic act. After all, the proof was right in front of his face. But now it was back, full force. I hadn't realized how much fun it was hanging out with the old Eric until I had to see the doubtful, angry one again.

Only Howard was still invested. "What is it?" he asked. "What's the danger?"

"The Shepherds," he intoned solemnly. "They have gone too far. Their goal was always to guide humanity, not destroy it. But they value our species above all others, our survival over that of our home planet. They've become warped."

"Like . . . German shepherds?" Eric asked. Savannah snickered.

"Don't," said Nate. "It's not nice. He's senile."

Howard pressed on. "Who are the Shepherds?"

"You know them. You speak to them." He turned to me and suddenly, my hand was captured in his terrifying, oddly strong grip. I felt his bones through his too-soft skin. I started to pull away, but he stopped me with a single sentence. "I know who you are, Gillian Seagret. I've been watching you."

My eyes widened. "You have?"

"From the moment you arrived in my city. You'd never have made it this far without my help."

"You . . . helped?" Eric asked. "Explain how."

"Shh." I waved at Eric. "That was you?" I said to Dr.

Underberg. "That was you who turned on the turbine?"

"And the water cannon?" Nate added.

Dr. Underberg's eyes hadn't left mine. And as I stared into his face, I thought about all the other times things randomly started to work in the city. The elevator shaft doors that mysteriously came unstuck. The Comm room lights that didn't work, although the diagram and the speakers did. The Russian elevator that didn't end up gassing us after all.

"That was you helping?" Savannah asked, incredulous. "We nearly got ourselves killed. Wait, did you try to drown me in that turbine control booth?"

Dr. Underberg lifted one bony shoulder. "Some things, alas, are in slight need of repair."

"Slight," echoed Howard.

"And I find, these days, I . . . sleep a lot. There is not much to stimulate me down here, and you were not always in a section of the city where my monitors still worked."

"So when we were trapped below the dome," Savannah suggested, "you what? Got bored and took a nap?"

Dr. Underberg made no reply, just stared at me for several long seconds. "I have watched you in my city. You love it, don't you?"

I blinked and met his clear, penetrating gaze. "Yes."

Yes, I loved it—every broken, flooded inch. I loved that this man loved the world so much that he created a sanctuary for the human race. I loved his old-fashioned gym and his freeze-dried ice-cream bars. His Russian booby traps and his luxurious movie theaters. I loved that he didn't want guns in his world; he wanted space suits. I loved Omega City, and as much as I hated to see it in ruins, I was thankful that no one had ever had to live here.

And if he'd been watching me, he knew exactly how I'd felt. Every room where I'd lingered, every videotape I'd stuffed in my pockets.

"You know what this place has been to me, don't you? I was driven here, so long ago, by the Shepherds. I waited for the others, but they never came."

"The other . . . people?"

"I thought it wouldn't be long until the Shepherds released their scourge upon the world. Do you remember Earth Day?"

"Earth Day?" I asked. "Like the holiday where we all remember to recycle and stuff?" He wasn't making any sense. Maybe he *was* senile, like Nate had said. "Sir, how long have you been down here?" According to Dad's book, Dr. Underberg had disappeared soon after the fall of the Berlin Wall, way back in 1989.

"Just a year or two."

"Where have you been ve rest of ve time? It's been twenty-five years!" Eric asked. I looked at my brother in surprise. Well, wouldn't you know it. Little Mr.

I-Don't-Believe-Any-of-This-Stuff had actually been paying attention.

"I told you—the Shepherds drove me down here."

"Well, vat's what vey do," said Eric. "Herd, I mean."

"Eric!" I looked at Dr. Underberg. "What he means is, where have you been since the fall of the Berlin Wall?"

"Here." The man lifted his shoulders in a pitiful shrug. "I await the disaster that is to come. Maybe I'll wait into the new century."

"That's a pretty long wait," Savannah said. "I'm not sure you're going to make it that long. I'm not sure any of us are."

"Speak for yourself," said Howard. "I intend to live to be a hundred and twenty. Ray Kurzweil says it can be done—"

"Kurzweil!" Underberg snapped. "That child! I mean the century to come in a few years."

This was starting to make a little more sense, in a twisted way. "I think," I said slowly, "that Dr. Underberg may have forgotten what year it is." That could happen too, stuck down here, where you didn't even notice the passage of a day, let alone a season.

"He remembered it five minutes ago," Savannah pointed out. "He remembered 9/11."

"Savvy, give him a break," said Nate. "He's an old man. He gets confused."

Dr. Underberg fixed me with a look. "If at all possible, can you get the tall one to stop calling me senile? I know precisely what I am about."

With great effort, he leaned forward and started tapping buttons on the control panel. The screen came to life, showing multiple views of Omega City. It was even more damaged than it had been before. The main chamber was completely flooded now, as was the greenhouse. Water poured through the blades of the turbine.

"My beautiful city," he said sadly. "What has the Shepherd done to you?" He sat back in his chair. "She didn't start it, of course. The destruction has been going on for years. There was an earthquake, then a flood. I could not manage the pumps on my own. As more and more sections of the city became uninhabitable, I was forced to retreat to smaller and higher ground. So much of my work has been lost. I feared that the city would not be able to support inhabitants, should the need actually arise."

Something dark moved across one of the images, a kind of inflatable speedboat, zipping across the dark water in the main cabin. I saw three blurry figures onboard.

"Look! Fiona."

Dr. Underberg nodded. "The Shepherd. Still she comes. They never stop, do they?"

"So Fiona is one of these Shepherd people," Howard prompted.

I looked down at my suit. "Arkadia Group," I said softly. "Fiona worked for Arkadia Group. Are they the same as the Shepherds?"

"Yes. Once, I thought we worked together to build a better world, but they have given up on our home, and now seek to drive us from it. As this Shepherd is driving me from my precious city." Dr. Underberg sighed and looked around the cockpit. "This ship is my masterpiece. When I first built the city, I programmed it to send survivors into space should Omega City fail. I knew *Knowledge* would be able to support me, even if the rest of the city could not."

"Fiona—" I began. "I mean, the Shepherd? She wants to take the inventions you've hidden here and claim them as her own, out in the world." You know, that world that isn't actually destroyed? "That's what's she's doing here. She told us that unless we help her she's not going to let us get out."

"That is a foolish claim," he replied. "For you are in a rocket ship and she is not."

"Good point," said Howard.

"Good point?" Eric echoed in disbelief. "Yeah, if you want to go into space."

"I do want to go into space." Howard didn't hesitate for a moment. "Can we? Can we go into space?"

Nate didn't hesitate either. "No."

Howard looked down at the ground.

"Sir," I said, in as convincing a tone as I could manage, "you have to come with us, to show us the way out. I want you to meet my father. He's your biggest fan. He even wrote a book about you. And they—I mean, the Shepherds or whatever—they destroyed him for it. You have to come with us and prove them wrong."

"Show myself to the world? Not a chance. The Shepherds would be on to me in a second. Look, they're coming for me now." He pointed at the screen, then went back to his buttons and levers and dials.

"But my dad . . ." I trailed off. Dr. Underberg didn't care about Dad or his academic reputation. And it wasn't like I could promise him that we'd keep him safe. What, was Dad going to take some old NASA scientist off grid?

Still, Fiona had said Dad wasn't her target anymore. I'd bet she didn't know Dr. Underberg was alive. All she wanted was the tech. Like me, she'd come looking for the Underberg battery, but unlike me, she wouldn't be happy until she found it.

"However," Dr. Underberg continued, "you're right. We all must leave. The city will soon be destroyed. We will not let this Shepherd woman get her hands on our treasures."

"Finally!" Nate let out a sigh of relief. He rubbed his hands together in anticipation. "Let's get a move on."

Dr. Underberg reached out, caressing the screen as the

city filled with water. "My beautiful, broken city. How I loved you." He sat back in his seat. "Are you ready to go?"

"Up?" Savannah asked.

"Of course, my girl. Like the boy said, we're going into space."

LIFT-OFF

HOWARD LET OUT A WHOOP, JUST AS HIS BROTHER YELLED "NO, WE ARE NOT!" and Savannah's and Eric's mouths dropped open.

"Dr. Underberg!" I exclaimed. "We can't go into space."

"Nonsense. Rest assured, there are plenty of berths aboard *Knowledge*. And plenty of supplies, too. Now, go strap yourselves in."

Howard was jumping up and down with excitement. "Yes, sir!"

"No, sir," Nate said, putting his hands on his brother's shoulders until Howard stopped leaping. "I'm declining for you. There's no way Mom and Dad would sign the permission slip for this."

I had to agree. Plus, the rest of Omega City was broken. What made Dr. Underberg think his rocket wouldn't just explode right here on the launch pad?

Now, there was a scary thought.

"If you could just direct us to the exit, that would be great," I said. "And maybe, really, think about coming along? A man your age in space? That can't be good for your . . . heart." Or anything else. Besides, what was he going to do up there? Rockets had to *go* someplace, right? Space stations, or the moon, or into orbit for a few days, then back down. You didn't just get to go into space in a rocket ship and live there. If Omega City was ruined, where was Dr. Underberg going to go once his little space flight was over? "This is really dangerous. Think about the future—"

"Young lady," he growled, giving me the side eye, "all I do is think about the future. My whole life. I think about my future, which is almost over, and I think about your future, which is yet before you. The planet is doomed. Humankind is bent on its destruction, both inadvertently and very much on purpose. If you choose to remain here, I cannot guarantee that another rocket will be available to you when it comes time for you to flee."

"Flee . . . Earth?" Savannah shook her head in disbelief.

He sighed. "I know. I thought I'd never have to do so

either, but clearly, in my heart, I knew what lay in store. I have loved this planet, but maybe the Shepherds are right—it's time to let go."

"No," Nate stated. "No, it's not. No one here is letting go of anything. Open the door, sir, and tell us how to get out." He whirled on me. "Not a word from you, Gillian."

I raised my hands in defeat. "I'm with you this time." I didn't want to go into space on a crazy old man's rocket ship. And sure, Dad would be disappointed that we didn't convince Dr. Underberg to come with us, but how much more disappointed would he be if we left the planet?

Which was when we all noticed that Howard had buckled himself into the other command chair.

"Get up," Nate said.

Howard crossed his arms.

"I said, *get up*."

"I don't *fit* here, Nate," he replied, and there was a note of pleading in his voice. "You know that. I want to go to space. NASA shut down manned missions. This is my only chance."

"There are still private missions," Eric suggested.

"Shepherds," Dr. Underberg muttered, almost to himself. "All Shepherds."

Howard looked defiantly at his brother. "I'm going."

"If you don't get up, I'm telling Dad," said Nate.

"See if I care."

Nate worried his bottom lip as Dr. Underberg kept turning knobs and pressing buttons and flipping switches.

"I do recommend you all either exit or find a safe place to sit soon," he announced.

Nate swallowed. "Howard," he said, in a very different tone than the one he'd just used. A tone that sounded less like bossing, and more like begging. "If you don't come with us, I won't be able to see you anymore. I'm not going to lose my brother."

Howard turned toward him.

"Please?" Nate added.

After what seemed like an endless moment, Howard reached down and started undoing the fastenings on his harness.

I turned back to Dr. Underberg. "Please, sir. Don't shoot into space. We need you here. Your inventions, your stories, the truths you can bring to light. . . ."

"I told you I've been watching you." He patted me on the knee pocket of my suit, the one stuffed with flashlights and ice cream and videotapes. "I think you have many of these things already. You don't need me. And I need the stars."

"But, Dr. Under—"

"Please, Gillian," he said. "Call me Aloysius. We're good friends now. We almost went exploring the solar system together."

"Yeah, well, I'm not sure Dad would condone that."

He laughed. "You give your father my best." He turned another dial and his voice—his other one, the big, booming recorded one—said:

Lift-off minus fifteen minutes.

"The easiest way to leave," he explained, as if we'd asked directions to the nearest park, "is to go up the set of emergency stairs on the inside of the silo to the launch control center. There you can access the minimum safe distance tunnel."

"What's the minimum safe distance?" Nate asked.

"Oh . . . I'd say three miles." Dr. Underberg turned back to the control panel.

"*Three miles?*" Savannah exclaimed. "You gave us fifteen minutes!"

"True." Underberg tapped his chin. "Better skip the stairs. I think I keep a couple of grappling guns in one of the cabinets below. For space walks."

"Oh, for Pete's sake." Nate vanished down the hole.

"You should be fine," Dr. Underberg said. "Provided the tram is in place."

"We're going to die," Savannah moaned. "This time, we're really going to die."

"We could always just go to space with him," Howard suggested.

"No, Howard," said Dr. Underberg. All this time, he hadn't stopped moving—checking levels, readouts, going down checklists, pressing buttons, and typing commands. The spacey, senile old man seemed gone completely. "Your friends are right. You still have work to do here. Don't worry, I have no doubt you'll make it to space. And to a hundred and twenty. But you'll definitely need to wear your hood."

"Hood?"

Underberg gestured to Howard's neck. "In the suit, boy. In the suit."

Howard pulled on the zipper at the collar of his suit. Just as with the gloves hidden in the wrists of the suits, a silver hood came tumbling out. The hoods attached at the back of the suits and came down in front of our faces, where we could see out through clear visors.

"It's not airtight, but it'll do," Underberg said. "Alas, I was never able to complete my final prototype of the utility suits."

"So these *are* yours?" I looked at the gloves on my hands. "But the packaging said Arkadia Group."

"I know." Underberg shook his head sadly. "It is the biggest regret of my life that I ever called myself a Shepherd."

Nate poked his head through the porthole. "Got 'em. Time to go, guys." He looked at us. "You look like Daft Punk."

I turned toward Dr. Underberg one last time. "Please, sir. Please shut this down and come with us."

But he didn't even look in my direction. Maybe I should have called him Aloysius. Maybe he would have looked then.

Eric grabbed me by the arm. "Let's go!"

That was the last I saw of the scientist, bent over the controls of his rocket ship, one hundred percent focused on reaching the stars.

We came out through the air-lock door onto the rickety metal platform behind us. As the whirring sounds of the locking mechanism started up, I looked down over the chasm and saw the golden glare of fire, thirty stories below.

"Look, the engines are already heating."

L minus nine minutes.

Nate had pulled out a bunch of harnesses and clipped them onto the grappling guns. "These things are rated for two hundred and fifty pounds, and I could only find two. So we're going to have to do our best here. What do you weigh, Gillian?"

"Ninety-two."

"Savvy?"

"Ninety-eight." She turned to me. "Really, Gillian?"

I shrugged. She had at least an inch on me, and other stuff, too. The orange glow from the base of the rocket was growing brighter by the second. I decided to turn the warming function off on my suit. The boys didn't know their exact weight but Howard said the last time he'd had a checkup, he'd been ninety-three pounds. I knew Eric was lighter than me. He always had been, so maybe ninety at the most?

Nate rubbed his forehead. "Okay, I'm a hundred and sixty-five, so that means . . ."

"We're not all going to fit," Sav said. "Even with the best way to divide us, the one with the three light ones is going to be around two hundred and seventy-five pounds, and the one with you and me will be two sixty-three."

He stared at her, incredulous. "That's the best way to divide us? And you did that in your head?"

"Um . . ." I couldn't see her well through the visor, but I could tell what she was thinking. *Busted!*

L minus eight minutes.

"And wifout all the stuff we're carrying," Eric added. We all froze for a second as we realized what it meant.

I clutched at my pockets. "No!" I cried. "I need these

videotapes for proof to show my dad."

"Don't you think your dad cares about you more than the videotapes?" Nate asked. He was emptying flashlights and MREs out of his pockets. "Come on, guys."

Eric and Savannah dropped their heavy head lamps. I watched them tumble off the side of the platform and plummet into the depths. Howard jettisoned a few more flares and the rest of the motor oil, then weighed a couple of packages of astronaut ice cream in his hands.

"These are really light," he argued.

"So are the videotapes," I added, desperate. I couldn't come so far for nothing.

"Gills," Eric pleaded. "We gotta go."

I swallowed thickly. But I needed these videotapes. Omega City was about to be totally flooded. Dad would never be able to come back here and see for himself. The tapes were the only proof I had that any of it was real.

Nate was attaching Savannah to his harness, while Howard and Eric were hooking up to the other. I looked at the tapes in my hands. One would be okay, right? One tape wouldn't make a difference. I shoved the Founder's Message back in my pocket and threw the others over the side. Howard hooked me onto his harness.

Nate took aim with the grappling gun at some distant point in the ceiling. "Bet you're glad I know how to shoot a gun now, right, Gills?"

I didn't even mind that he'd called me that when I saw the rope tug tight. He shot our gun next, then hooked the contraption back onto Howard's portion of the harness.

"Count to three, then press the retract button," he said. He put his arm around Savannah. Once upon a time, she might have been in heaven at the idea, but what little I could see of her face through the visor was terrified, not thrilled.

He pressed a button and they flew up into the sky.

"Wait," said Eric. "I don't know . . ."

Howard grabbed the cable. "One, two—"

"I said waaaaaaaaaait—" Eric's words were lost to screams as Howard pressed the button and we were jerked off our feet.

You know those rides where they strap you into little seats that face outward around a pole, then catapult you up really fast? That's what this felt like, except the grappling gun pulled us up by the waist. It cut into our bodies and swung us sideways so Eric and I shrieked and clutched each other for dear life. I imagined we looked kind of ridiculous, flying up sideways in our hooded silver suits. Like someone's lame idea for a superhero movie. But then we reached a platform just below the smooth walls and wide windows of launch control.

Or at least, there used to be windows. Something, sometime, must have broken them. No wonder Dr. Underberg had spoken to us about minimum safe distances.

Eric peered over the ledge at the tip of the rocket. "I can't believe vat worked."

"I can't believe you still have a voice left to scream with," Savannah said. "Did you know you're literally louder than a rocket engine?"

I stared down into the abyss. We'd come up with no problem. We probably could have kept those videos.

L minus six minutes.

Then again, if we didn't get out of here, soon, we'd never see Dad again.

There was no mistaking the heat in the silo now. The air shimmered before my eyes. Nate was pulling up his hood and detaching the grappling hooks from the wall.

"I should keep these, right?" Nate said.

"Sure," I replied, my attention on the rising red glow from below. "It's not like they'll survive the blastoff if you leave them here."

"Score."

I glowered at him. Sure, Nate. Keep whatever *you* want. As soon as he had the guns secured, we all climbed up the last set of stairs and into the launch control center.

Like everything else in Omega City, launch control was a ruin. Wires hung from the wall and there seemed to be birds' nests in what should have been the window seats. At least none of them were there now, or they might have been roasted alive. Still, the thought of birds made me feel good. We were getting closer and closer to the surface. If they could make their way down here, we could make our way out.

As if to drive this point home, there was a giant rumbling from above, and dirt and debris started falling down around the rocket. The silo was opening up. I leaned over to look out of the launch control windows and try to catch a glimpse of the sky, but Eric and Savannah pulled me back.

"Gills, *not* a way out."

Savannah nodded vigorously. "Come on. I didn't make it this far just to get liquefied by rocket fuel."

"I don't think you'd be liquefied," said Howard.

"Tram!" Nate called, pointing at a sign. "This way!"

L minus five minutes.

We sprinted out the door of launch control, down a short hallway and out onto what looked like some kind of underground parking garage. The paved floor was painted with yellow stripes and there was an odd-looking tram car backed up against the far wall. I stared down the dark tunnel ahead of us. Three miles. Five minutes. Yeah, that was possible. Barely. If the tram worked.

"How does it go?" Nate asked. "Is there a key?"

I pointed at the round metal rings where the tram met the wall. "I think these are springs, just like on the buildings underground."

"So it's spring-loaded?" Eric asked.

L minus four minutes.

"No time to waste," said Nate, all bossy again. "Everyone in." We piled into the cab, which was when we saw it again. A big red button, just like the one inside the boulder. We all looked at Howard.

"Hold on tight," he said. He pressed it and we were all instantly thrown back against the seat.

"Steer!" Nate screamed as the walls of the tunnel rushed past us at enormous speed. Howard panicked and grabbed the wheel, steering us up an unsteady path in the gently sloping tunnel.

L minus three minutes.

"Hurry!" Savannah said. "Hurry!"

But if anything, the tram was slowing down.

L minus two minutes.

"Let's take a vote," Eric said, to break the silence that had descended in the cab as it sped forward. No one was talking or even moving, just sitting there, feeling the tram getting slightly but steadily slower, staring at the blackness ahead of us as if we could beam ourselves away by will alone. "Who prefers burning over drowning?"

No one laughed. Or voted, for that matter.

L minus one minute.

Fifty-nine.

Fifty-eight.

Fifty-seven.

Fifty-six.

"That voice needs to shut up," said Savannah. "It needs to shut up right now."

But it didn't. Recordings didn't stop because Savannah Fairchild ordered them to, just like spring-loaded tram cars traveling on an upward slant didn't speed up on their own.

Thirty-five.

Thirty-four.

Thirty-three.

Thirty-two.

Thirty-one.

"I see it!" Howard cried. "The exit."

Nate leaned forward. "Really? All I see are rocks."

Seconds later, those rocks went flying as we burst through the pile marking the end of the tunnel and the tram car bumped along for a moment, then came to a stop in the sweet, fresh, outdoor air.

Fifteen.

Fourteen.

Thirteen.

Twelve.

Eleven.

Ten.

"We made it." Savannah slumped in her seat. I turned around to face her, and caught sight of the fireball erupting in the tunnel behind us. We weren't out of the danger zone yet.

"Run!"

We scrambled out of the tram and started sprinting. I don't think I'd ever moved so fast in my life. We were in a field of some kind, covered with tall yellow grasses, each and every one of them a firestarter. Everything was ablaze as far as I could see. If the rocket was lifting off, I couldn't tell through the blinding light.

"Don't look!" Eric shouted over the roar of the flames and the jets. "Just run!"

Columns of fire erupted all over the place, and everyone was running as fast as they could, but through the visor of my helmet I could see the blades of grass all around us turning black and singeing from the heat before a single flame touched them. My feet felt hot, like the rubber was melting on my soles, but I kept running.

Behind me, I heard a massive groan, as the very earth opened up and a wall of flame shot skyward. The rocket was lifting off.

A split second later, something blew me off my feet and across the boiling grass. For a moment there was nothing but the roar of flames, and then I felt a hand clutch mine. I don't know whose it was, but I held on for dear life as a tsunami of fire drowned the world.

THE FORGOTTEN FORTRESS

IT ENDED WITH A FIRE. A BLAZING HOT FIRE THAT DEVOURED EVERYTHING it touched, and left five kids in silver suits lying in an empty black field. A bright, gleaming fire that turned into a comet and arced through the night sky, containing all the dreams and secrets of a man the world thought it had lost long ago. A shining, beautiful fire that brought cops, paramedics, and firemen down the lonely dirt road where so many hours earlier, Nate had parked his truck.

At least, I think it used to be his truck. Right now, it looked a little bit like one of Dad's failed pot roasts: charred and smoldering.

The fire faded as quickly as it started, and after a

minute, we all sat up in the grass, unharmed except for some seriously ruined sneakers. Far above our heads, the rocket glowed orange, then yellow, and finally white as it ascended.

"Everyone okay?" Nate asked in a shaky voice.

"Yeah," I said.

Eric nodded.

"My arm is killing me," said Savannah.

Howard just stared up at the rocket heading for the stars.

When the cops first arrived, they weren't all that happy to see five people in silver suits standing around as the heat evaporated into the cold fall night. But once we took off our hoods and they realized we were a bunch of kids, the accusations went from "crazy space aliens" to "delinquent arsonists." That didn't last for too long, though, since even the most resourceful delinquent arsonist couldn't launch a four-hundred-foot rocket into space. So while the paramedics were treating the minor burns on all of our feet, and Eric's jaw (just bruised, but the broken teeth are going to have to get fixed), and Savannah's arm (actually broken), we did our best to explain where we'd come from and how we'd found ourselves in the middle of an unauthorized rocket launch.

Obviously, they didn't believe us.

While the paramedics were stabilizing Savannah's arm, the police search parties turned up three very disoriented would-be thieves. Fiona, Clint, and Travis were found wandering what was left of the woods, a little singed and stone-cold deaf. Under all the soot, their descriptions matched the ones we'd already given of the three "stalkers" who'd chased us through the woods, threatened us with guns, then set off explosions in the underground bunker we'd found in order to smoke us out.

I guess, in the end, they were the ones smoking. I wish I could take credit for that line, but you know where it's from, right? Eric, of course.

After a while, someone got the brilliant idea to call our parents and have them come get us, so they took the Nolands, Eric, and me to the police station and Savannah to the hospital to set her arm. I guess her mother went there to get her. The police station was basically a two-room office building and so we had to sit next to the cell where they were holding Fiona and her men. She kept yelling at me—"Gillian! Gillian!"—in an earsplitting tone until the police officer threatened to tase her unless she stopped bothering us. It was extremely awkward, and that was before Eric started trying to get her to start up again.

"I've never seen anyone get tased," he explained.

The whole time, they kept playing the TV, where the television news anchors were having a ball with the story of the rocket.

Local officials say the flight is an unmanned, amateur suborbital rocket of modest size, and that any videos you may have seen indicating otherwise are certainly faked.

Eric rolled his eyes and smirked at me from the side of his face that wasn't buried under a cold pack. I couldn't help but smile back. This was one story he couldn't be skeptical about. It was safe to say his mainstream phase was officially over.

The police officer in charge kept grilling us for details about what we'd been doing, but I kept my mouth shut. I wanted to talk to Dad about it first. I kept thinking about what Dr. Underberg said, about how there was no way to be free of the Shepherds. He obviously wanted them to think he was dead.

And maybe he was. The rocket had gone up all right, but I had no idea what had happened afterward, and I could already see that any news I'd hear about it would be nothing but spin.

On the plus side, Dad still had a chance to break the story himself. That was, he would have, if I could have provided him with all our proof.

At last Dad showed up, along with Nate and Howard's parents. The Nolands went to hug their boys, and Dad beelined toward us and gathered us close.

"What have you been doing?" he whispered against my hair. "And where did you get this suit?"

"It's Dr. Underberg's," I said softly.

Dad gave me a sad smile. "Sweetie, he never even got to the prototype stage of his survival suit. You know that." He went to examine Eric's injuries, leaving me alone on the chair.

But there'd been a whole stack of them in the city. The city that Dad hadn't exactly known about, either. And the suit was absolutely functional, as the scuba diving and rocket launch and everything else had proved. The world might not know it, but Dr. Underberg had gone far beyond the prototype.

Well, later I could show him the video I'd kept. I patted my pocket, and beneath the bulky rectangle of the tape, I could feel something cylindrical. I reached into my pocket and pulled out one of our flashlights. That's right. I still had my flashlight. I'd traded Savannah my head lamp back when we were in the water. The flashlight I'd tossed back in the silo was hers.

Wait a second. My fingers clenched around the flashlight in my hands. Funny—we'd used them for hours in Omega City and not a single one had dimmed or gone out or gotten ruined in the water. That was nothing like the flashlights Dad took with us when we were camping. They were total battery hogs. You could barely use them for a few hours before they went dead.

Far beyond the prototype.

I looked up at Dad but he was still with Eric, tilting his head into the light to examine his broken teeth.

I was wrong anyway. I had to be.

I held my breath and opened the case of the flashlight, shaking the batteries out. Instead of the D battery I'd been expecting, a trio of silver spheres the size of ping-pong balls fell into my hands. Each was marked with polarity points and the Ω symbol.

Stupid Gillian. I'd been looking for the prototype. But we'd had the Underberg battery all along.

I looked up to see Fiona staring at me from behind the bars of her jail cell. Her manicure was utterly destroyed and her hair was a burnt mess. They hadn't even given her towels to wash the soot off her face. But her eyes were like missiles that had locked on to their target.

"You found them," she rasped. "Give them to me!"

I shoved the batteries back inside the case and jammed the flashlight into my pocket.

"She has them!" Fiona banged her fists against the bars. "She has them!"

Dad looked up from Eric's mouth. He glanced at me for a moment, and then at Fiona. Then he walked over to her cell and stood between us. Fiona's face went from excited to coy to scared in a matter of seconds.

"You stay away from us," Dad growled at her, in a deep and ringing tone I'd never heard before. A voice she could probably feel in her bones. "You stay away from me, and you stay away from my kids. If you ever come near anything that is mine again, I'll make you sorry, I swear. This is over, do you hear?"

"Well, no," Eric pointed out. "Actually, she doesn't."

But she seemed to get the picture anyway, as she lowered her gaze to the floor and dropped her hands to her sides.

After that, there was a lot of paperwork to fill out, but I guess we got off easy. No lectures, no interrogation. Nate didn't even get a ticket for illegally parking his truck all day, which was kind of sweet, considering he now had to buy a new truck.

We got in Dad's car to drive home, and we weren't two minutes on the road before he started in on us. "Okay, you two. What really happened back there? And what's up with the rocket?"

"I told you," I said. "It's Dr. Underberg. We found him for you, Dad. And we found these." I pulled the batteries out of my pocket.

He almost drove the car into a ditch.

WE GOT A chance to tell him the whole story over the next few days. It helped that we had the proof—not just the batteries, but the suits and the grappling guns and the one remaining videotape filled with Underberg's lecture and images from the building and development of Omega City. Dad even drove us out to find the bunker again, but overnight, the whole field and forest had been surrounded with a massive fence topped with tangles of barbed wire and a sign reading:

NO TRESPASSING.
VIOLATORS WILL BE SHOT.

There was a symbol on the sign, too: a pair of crossed, upside-down Js over the shape of the Earth, just like the Arkadia Group symbol that had appeared on the packaging of the silver jumpsuits.

"What is this, Dad?" I asked him, pointing at the sign. "We've seen it before."

"I have too," Dad said. "On stuff from Underberg's early life."

"Fiona told me she once worked for the Arkadia Group, whoever they are." And so, apparently, had Dr. Underberg. So if she knew about the city from her old job, was that because Dr. Underberg had been building it when he worked for Arkadia—or when he was, as he put it, a Shepherd?

With the barbed wire and everything, we couldn't get back into the city, but that was okay. I'm not sure how much would be left, between the flood and the fire. Dad believed us and everything—he just wanted to see it himself. Something about primary sources being important for the writing of history.

I said I thought I was a primary source now. After all, I'd been there. I'd witnessed the destruction myself.

Going back to school on Monday was kind of a letdown. Sure, first everyone oohed and aahed over the bandages on our feet and asked to sign Savannah's cast. There was a little bit of a scandal when she let Howard sign it first and he decided to draw a big omega symbol in red Sharpie. And he was wearing his silver jumpsuit to school. It might not have been so bad if he hadn't also insisted on wearing the hood up. They made quite a picture, there in the crowded lunch room. The old Savannah would have been mortified, but the new one just shrugged off the stares.

"I love it," she said to Howard when he finished. "It's like a designer logo."

That's when I realized that all the popularity Savannah always harped on was actually good for something, because no one said a single word when he put his lunch tray next to ours every day that week.

We didn't hear much more about the rocket. The newspapers treated it like a matter of local interest—just an amateur rocket enthusiast who got a little too big for his britches. But in Dad's circle of friends we heard other stories. Stories about how the US government tried to shoot it down and failed, about how it was hiding out even now on the dark side of the moon, and about how it wasn't a rocket at all, but the disc-shaped spacecraft of a subterranean alien species.

Eric may have a point that Dad needs to find some new friends.

But he didn't have a whole lot of time to spare. After all, he's busy working on a new book. This one is about Underberg's later years—his lost years, when he worked for the Arkadia Group and built an underground city. Though it was really hard to find any information about the Arkadia Group, which, as far as Dad could tell from the papers they filed to enclose the Omega site, was nothing more than a real estate development firm that bought the property to build townhouses.

If they thought we'd buy that story, they hadn't met Dad.

THURSDAY NIGHT WAS still pizza night at the cottage, but now Dad stayed home, too, to write down all our stories about Omega City.

"He's here!" Savannah cried when the doorbell rang. "Good, I'm starving."

Eric answered the door to see Nate and Howard on the steps, balancing pizza boxes. Their mom's car was parked in the driveway. Nate did in fact quit his delivery job, but it's not like he had a truck anymore, anyway.

"Are those two golden disks of the seven heavens?" Eric asked.

Nate rolled his eyes. "Don't start with me."

"Plus egg-roll calzones," Howard added. He was still wearing his jumpsuit. He always wore it now.

"Nate, Howard!" Dad called out. "Come in! I had a few questions about where you went on the Training Level while my kids were diving . . ."

Nate let out a pained sigh. "Can we eat anything other than pizza next week?" he begged.

"Trust me," said Eric. "If you've tried my dad's cooking, you'd know Chinese pizza is a step up."

Howard leaned over to set the pizza on the table, and we all drew back a foot as a wave of stink hit us.

Dad waved a hand in front of his face, eyes watering. "Wow, son. You . . . did you, uh, did you step in something?"

"Good luck with that, doc," Nate said. "I've been trying to convince him for a month that 'waterproof' is not the same as 'unwashable.'"

"There are no washing instructions on the suit," Howard said, crossing his arms over his chest. "And I'm not going to risk destroying it until I know how it can be properly cleaned."

"Lunch *and* dinner with Howard," Savannah whispered to me. "Aren't we lucky?"

I was very careful to breathe through my mouth. "Dry-cleaning?"

Howard looked offended. "Gillian, you of all people know the danger of letting a piece of technology like this out of your sight. You guys can do what you want with your suits. I'm keeping mine on my person. It's the safest way."

"Sure," said Eric. "Until you get the plague."

Dad considered this for a moment. Over the past few weeks, he'd gotten to be almost as good at talking to Howard as Nate was. I'm sure their shared love of the space race helped.

"You know, Howard, there's a guy in one of my classes down at the VA who owns a dry-cleaning store. I know I can trust him."

Howard brightened. "Really? Well, if you're sure he isn't one of *them*, Dr. S . . ."

We all breathed a sigh of relief, then immediately regretted it. Because, you know, breathing.

But, yeah, things are good. Even Eric is excited about Dad's book, though he's wondering if maybe Dad should look into a publishing contract for it sooner rather than later, because Dad promised when he sold the book, he'd buy Eric's dinghy back. But of course, Dad is keeping the manuscript a secret for the time being, just in case.

I mean, except from me. I get to read every single page of *The Forgotten Fortress* just as soon as he's done typing it up. I'm getting a real research assistant credit on this one. He says it's going to blow the doors right open for us again, in terms of opportunity. And if it doesn't, well, we still haven't told anyone about the batteries. Dad isn't sure who we can trust, but once we figure it out, I'm sure they're worth a fortune.

So things are pretty good. Mom even called to see how we were all doing, and Eric said she sounded like she missed us. I didn't hear that in her voice, but who wants to disappoint him?

Unlike Howard, the rest of us don't wear our Omega City utility suits around very often, though Nate took his gloves rock-climbing the other week and said they were the best he's ever used. Mine's hanging in my closet, back behind the fancy Easter dresses I never wear anymore. I can see it from my bed sometimes in the night, glinting silver in the starlight. I like it; it makes me think that, just like in the city, Dr. Underberg is still out there, watching over me.

Turns out, he is. But that history's still being written.

AUTHOR'S NOTE

You may have noticed during reading that Gillian and her father have a lot of strange ideas about the "real" stories behind the history we all know. These alternative explanations are sometimes called "conspiracy theories" and some people out there really believe them. Gillian's statements about the Apollo 11 moon landing; the mystery of Area 51 in New Mexico; and the Tunguska Event are all based on well-known "conspiracy theories" about those moments in history. Are they true? Well, that's up to investigators better than I am to decide. Maybe you'd like to take a crack at it?

Speaking of fun projects, if you are interested in making your own model of the solar system, you can find a downloadable worksheet and the formulas Savannah and Howard used on my website: www.dianapeterfreund.com.

And finally, dear reader, I must inform you that I have lied. Astronaut ice cream was not invented by Dr. Aloysius Underberg. It was invented by the Whirlpool Corporation—yes, the same one that probably made your dishwasher—for the Apollo missions.

At least, that's what *they* want you to think.

ACKNOWLEDGMENTS

Books, like buried cities, can never be the work of a single person. And so I am grateful for Kristin Rens, who planted the clue; Dan Peterson, who uncovered the city; and Michael Bourret, who made me explore it all. Along the way, I got help and support from Carrie Ryan, Mari Mancusi, Julie Leto, Lavinia Kent, Joy Daniels, Sean Williams, Starla Huchton, and the DC YA crowd. For research tips and advice, superhero props to the patient and always-understanding Jon Skovron. All fumbles are my own. Thank you to my parents and my in-laws for letting me crash with them while in crazy drafting mode, and to my daughter and dog for understanding when "Mommy's working."

I'd also like to thank not-at-all-bad astronomer Phil Plait for being so remarkably approachable on Twitter, and for answering my questions about the measurements of celestial bodies. (I apologize for calling Pluto a planet.) I am also deeply indebted to the assistance of NORAD expert Brian "Bear" Lihani, who helped me envision what giant underground cities would actually look like, and how much cooler I could make Omega City even than I'd imagined. And finally, thanks to the editorial, marketing, and design team at Balzer+Bray, who always show so much care in shepherding a project from dream to reality, and a huge round of applause to Vivienne To for her remarkable visual.

And of course the Goonies. Never say die.

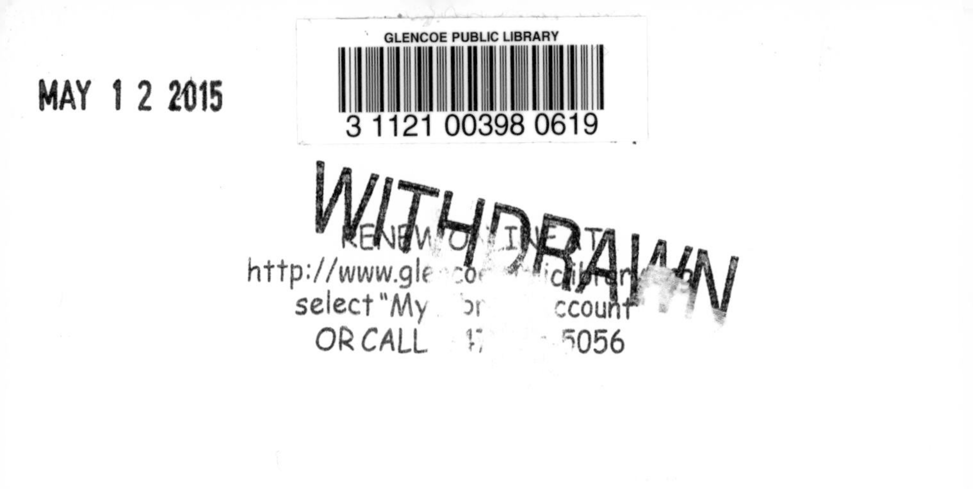
MAY 12 2015
GLENCOE PUBLIC LIBRARY
3 1121 00398 0619
WITHDRAWN